A car rumbl‌... an impatient purr and Sam's hope faded. She'd worked on enough engines to know a sports car when she heard it, and in her experience, sports car drivers usually weren't big nature lovers. She wondered idly whether this one would be annoying or just plain bored by their little junket.

Pasting a professional smile on her face, Sam turned toward the parking area and stopped short as the driver unfolded his length from the low-slung car and then scanned the area with one all-encompassing glance.

Sam's eyebrows shot up in surprise. Weekday cruises tended to attract retirees in polyester and plaid. This guy was a whole different animal. Though he was dressed in tan chinos and a light blue polo shirt, his California tan, sun-bleached hair and dark glasses made him look like he should have a surfboard tucked under his arm. Add a scruffy beard and he could be Matthew McConnaughey, one of People magazine's sexiest men alive.

Sam stepped onto the dock to greet him, but when he turned in her direction and flashed that lopsided, boyish grin, all white teeth and relaxed confidence, Sam's world shuddered to a frantic, screeching halt.

Her breath backed up in her lungs and her heart thundered louder than a summer squall. With shaking hands, she adjusted her sunglasses, pulled down the visor on her ball cap, and tried to wrap her mind around what she was seeing. *Stay calm, girl. Breathe.*

It couldn't be, but it was.

Danny Hastings.

The one man she never, ever expected to see again. What was he doing here?

Trapped!

by

Connie Mann

To Fred + Pat –
Enjoy!
Connie Mann

This is a work of fiction. Names, characters, places, and incidents are either the product of the author's imagination or are used fictitiously, and any resemblance to actual persons living or dead, business establishments, events, or locales, is entirely coincidental.

Trapped!

COPYRIGHT © 2008 by Connie E. Neumann

All rights reserved. No part of this book may be used or reproduced in any manner whatsoever without written permission of the author or The Wild Rose Press except in the case of brief quotations embodied in critical articles or reviews.

Contact Information: info@thewildrosepress.com

Cover Art by *Kim Mendoza*

The Wild Rose Press
PO Box 708
Adams Basin, NY 14410-0706
Visit us at www.thewildrosepress.com

Publishing History
First Crimson Rose Edition, 2009
Print ISBN: 1-60154-455-3

Published in the United States of America

Dedication

For Ben and Michele -- The two most amazing kids a mother could want. I'm so proud of you both.

Prologue

In a nondescript brick house in the little town of Riverlake, Florida, The Exterminator sat down at his kitchen table. He poured his second cup of morning coffee, black, and placed the cup precisely three inches to the right of his plate. His English muffin was split with surgical precision, one pat of butter per side.

He sipped his coffee and frowned as he reviewed the previous evening. Lindsey Collins had seen him. What was an eleven-year-old doing outside so late? Had she been alone? He was pretty sure of the last part. No way would Samantha have taken her daughter out that late.

But had Lindsey known it was him? It had been so dark, the only reason he'd recognized the little girl was the flash of blonde hair. He was dressed completely in black, so chances were good that while she might have seen something, she probably wasn't sure what it was.

He hoped that was the case. Because if she had seen too much, then he had a completely new infestation to eliminate. And since Sam clearly doted on her daughter, he'd hate offering condolences to a grieving mother.

But he would if he had to. He had to protect Sam—he had to protect their future.

Whatever it took.

He took a bite of his muffin and chewed exactly ten times. A careful search of Jeremy Castle's car last night had not turned up the man's cell phone.

He calculated the odds and finally decided it didn't matter. Nothing could be traced back to him.

Over the years, he'd learned murder done right required careful planning, meticulous attention to detail and a large dose of cunning and imagination. Murder done wrong led to mistakes, which inevitably resulted in lifetime imprisonment and death by state decree. That's where so many other dealers of death went wrong; they just didn't plan every detail, or they let emotion cloud their judgment. If you let either one happen, failure was inevitable.

Actually, a murderer was a lot like a bug exterminator. Both rid the world of unwanted pests with a minimum of fuss and inconvenience for all involved. Those nondescript white trucks had innocuous little slogans on the side, but everyone knew their deadly-purpose killing bugs.

A murderer had his own little white truck, his bland personality which allowed him to blend in perfectly, to carry out his mission without anyone suspecting what he was really doing. Like an exterminator, his job was to determine the source of the problem, find the point of entry, then zap the unsuspecting pest when it least expected it. Problem solved. Everyone's happy. Except the bug, of course. But the bug didn't matter; it was immaterial and had usually bothered an innocent before the exterminator was called in to begin with.

Insects and exterminators. Human bugs and murderers. Not so very different. Both provided an important societal function, but neither got any recognition for it. It was really a shame.

Of course, in his case, nobody knew he'd been called in, which was just the way he wanted it. Samantha Collins had no idea she'd put her very own exterminator on the case. But he'd taken care of her problem. Like any good exterminator, he'd gotten the job done quickly, efficiently and with no one the wiser.

Sometimes he wished he didn't have to do things like this. But somebody had to and no one else would. He pushed away his momentary irritation with Samantha for putting him in this position. Never mind. She was safe. It was all that mattered.

All he had to do now was figure out how much Lindsey had seen.

Connie Mann

Chapter One

Samantha Collins stepped out onto the back porch and paused to lean against the railing, watching the sky begin to lighten. She should head straight to the bait shop, but if she didn't take a moment to settle her jumbled thoughts, she'd snap and snarl all day.

The memory of her daughter's blood-curdling scream in the middle of the night still raised goose bumps on Sam's skin. Something had seriously upset her daughter, and unfortunately, Sam knew exactly what it was. She'd never yelled at her daughter the way she had last night. Sam plopped down in one of the wicker rockers, tossed her braid over her shoulder, and sighed, heart-sick. She'd apologize to Lindsey as soon as she woke up.

The old wind-up alarm clock on her nightstand had read five-thirty a.m. when Sam woke up, so the regulars should be arriving in search of live bait and fresh coffee any minute now. Sam upended her work boots and gave them a good shake. She'd been four-years-old the day she stuck her bare foot into a tennis shoe and got bit by a scorpion. She'd limped for a week. Since then, she checked for scorpions or other critters before she stuck her feet inside.

Sam tucked her tank top into her cargo shorts, clipped her utility belt around her waist and was walking down the dock towards the bait shop when the first tires crunched on the gravel driveway. No matter how bad things were, simply stepping

4

through the shop door always lifted Sam's spirits. Every time she looked up at the weathered sign above the door, "Collins Marina & Fish Camp — A little bit of Heaven," she smiled. To her way of thinking, it was exactly that, and had been for four generations. A place to fish, to relax, to get out and enjoy nature.

Unless this Castle guy with his big fancy development company somehow succeeded in forcing them out. Her smile faded and the ever-growing ball of fear settled in her stomach like a lead weight. She couldn't let it happen. Wouldn't. This was their home and nobody was going to force them out. She'd just have to make sure everyone understood how important the marina was, what an asset to the community it had always been.

Ideas and plans whirled in her head as Sam automatically turned on the overhead lights, started both pots of coffee brewing and coaxed the ancient ceiling fans into a listless rhythm. She opened the windows, straightened the red vinyl stools at the lunch counter and was just unlocking the cash register when the screen door slammed. She jumped and spun around, locking eyes with Marco Juarez.

Dark eyes steady on hers, he touched a finger to the brim of his ball cap, a small smile playing around his lips, as though he knew he made her uncomfortable—and liked it that way. "Morning, Miss Collins."

Sam willed her voice to sound steady, but the man threw her off balance. "Morning, Marco." Tall, well-muscled and tattooed, his haunted gaze and fierce expression yanked her close and shoved her away at the same time. It had been this way since third grade, when he rescued Sam from a couple of bullies who had stomped her sandwich into the mud.

Hands propped on her hips, she met him stare for stare. "When are you going to start calling me

Sam?"

He shrugged as he always did and headed towards the fridge in the back, a beat-up cooler tucked under one arm, his loose-hipped stride eating up the distance. Every morning, he brought her newly-caught shiners and night crawlers before he headed for the Lady Bug Diner in town, where he bused tables and washed dishes.

He opened the fridge and unloaded the bait. "Got a mess of 'em for you today," he said, looking over his shoulder.

Feeling as tongue-tied and awkward as she had in middle school, Sam thanked him politely and aimed what she hoped was a friendly smile his way. If only she could jettison the frisson of unwelcome awareness that sizzled down her spine every time their gazes met.

According to the rumor mill, Marco had returned to Riverlake about six months ago after a stint in the penitentiary. Local speculation had the crime ranging anywhere from robbery to murder. Besides his questionable reputation, his dark eyes and mixed-race heritage kept him on the fringes of the community. Since Sam never quite fit in either—not many proper southern girls owned a marina or trapped gators for a living—she and Marco had always shared an unspoken connection. Without meaning to, she looked his way again, irresistibly drawn by the pain she sometimes glimpsed in his dark eyes. When he winked, Sam spun towards the coffee pot, mortified.

"Would you like some coffee?" she blurted.

"No, thanks. I'll grab a cup at work." He headed for the door and paused, as though waiting for her to say something.

Unable to meet his gaze, she focused on the bruised and scabbed hand he had wrapped around the doorframe. Had he been in a fight? Before she could ask what happened, he murmured, "Thanks for the offer. See you tomorrow," and disappeared.

The next few hours passed in a blur. The sun shone brightly, the ancient thermometer recorded a balmy 84 degrees, and a brisk breeze coaxed the humidity down from insane to bearable. The change brought a gratifying number of fishermen who launched boats, bought bait, drank coffee and traded fish tales. By the usual mid-morning lull, Sam was ready for a break.

She pulled the old-fashioned ledger out from under the counter and perched her wire-rimmed reading glasses on her nose. Paperwork wasn't exactly her idea of a break, but it was a change and needed doing. Stalling, she tapped the pencil on the ledger, grateful when her mother came sailing through the screen door, a tray of sticky buns in her hands.

"Morning, Mama," Sam said, pulling two "Collins Marina & Fish Camp" mugs from the glass-fronted cabinet. "Smells good."

"Good morning, honey." Before Sam could duck, Katherine yanked her into a too-tight, too-long hug. Sam's instinct was to wrench free, but instead, she slowly eased from her mother's grip, ignoring her hurt look. Something about the desperation with which Mama clutched her always made Sam equally desperate to escape. During the awkward silence afterward, Katherine tied a white apron around her ample figure and Sam pulled a bun from the tray. Fresh from the oven, it was a warm, gooey mix of cinnamon and icing that melted on her tongue. "Mmmm," Sam murmured, licking her fingers.

When Katharine slid the ledger from her grip, Sam smiled, grateful for the reprieve. She licked the last bit of sugar from her fingers. "Thanks, Mama. For breakfast and for taking over the books." She set a mug of coffee beside Katharine and frowned at how much gray threaded the tight bun Mama wore at her nape.

"I smell sticky buns," a sleepy voice mumbled a little while later. Sam grinned. Lindsey had never been a morning person, but she was usually cuddly when she was half asleep, so Sam wrapped her arms around her and nuzzled Lindsey's neck.

Lindsey rubbed her eyes and started squirming. "Let go, Mom. You're all sweaty."

Sam laughed at the indignant tone, but sadness pricked her heart. When had Mommy become Mom, and hugs become something Lindsey avoided, the way Sam avoided her own mother's? Her daughter was growing up and away from her with every passing day. "Yeah, well, it's warm this morning, Princess. What can I say?"

Lindsey peered at her from bleary eyes. "We must be the only people in Florida who don't have air conditioning."

Sam gave one of her daughter's curls a playful yank as she passed by on her way to the cooler. "Oh, I bet there are one or two others out there. Besides, the bait shop and the house were built before AC. They're designed to stay cool without it."

"Uh, huh," Lindsey snorted. "We can't afford it, right?"

Sam opened a bottle of water and grimaced. "Right. But I'm working on it, okay?"

Still groggy, Lindsey plopped down on a stool, chin propped on her hands, polished orange fingernails on display.

Sam took a deep breath and set a sticky bun in front of Lindsey. She brushed the hair from her daughter's face, but Lindsey wouldn't meet her eyes. "Princess, I'm so, so sorry I yelled at you last night. Asking why we couldn't just move to town was a reasonable question. I totally overreacted and went ballistic. I'm worried and scared of losing our home and somehow, I took it out on you and I shouldn't have."

"It's okay, Mommy," Lindsey mumbled, keeping her head down.

"I'm sorry you had a nightmare about it, too."

Lindsey froze and all the color drained from her face. She leaped off the stool and bolted for the door.

"Lindsey, wait," Sam rounded the counter.

"I don't want to talk about it," Lindsey shouted over her shoulder, crashing into Emma Jean Tucker as the other woman stepped through the doorway carting a tower of sandwiches.

"Why's Miss Lindsey runnin' like her tail's on fire?" Emma Jean asked, dropping the basket on the counter with a thud. When no one answered, she said, "The girls and I figured, what with the nice weather and all, ya'll would have lots of hungry customers today."

Sam grinned. Emma Jean was nothing if not an optimist. The squat, no-nonsense, fifty-something African American widow ran Haven House with the same mixture of compassion and high expectations she'd used when she taught fourth grade. Only now, instead of corralling ten-year-olds, Emma Jean helped set unwed mothers on the right path.

As she did every time she stopped in, Emma Jean paused in front of a framed photo of Sam, Annie and then-seven-year-old Lindsey standing on the dock, three largemouth bass proudly displayed in front of them. Emma Jean kissed her index finger and pressed it to Annie's face. Three years after Annie's death, the action still brought a hitch to Sam's throat.

"Listen, girlfriend, I read that piece in the paper and I want you to know we're going to do everything we can to help you—"

"Wait. What piece? What are you talking about?"

"The one about our bubble-headed commissioners trying to steal your property. Eminent domain, child, please. We won't let them get away with this. We'll fight them."

Sam's heart sped up until she thought it would pound its way out of her chest. It hadn't just been a bluff, then. The commissioners were really going to try to take her property away. She could barely get the words out. "When, Emma Jean? When was it in the paper?"

"Today, front page. But don't you worry, girlfriend, we'll fight them and we'll win."

But Sam wasn't listening. Fear and fury boiled and churned in her heart, searching for an outlet. She marched into the house, grabbed the sheaf of papers Jeremy Castle had tried to foist off on her last night and snatched his business card from the top of the pile.

Her hand shook so badly, she had to dial the number three times; but when the answering machine picked up at the other end, Sam's voice was steady. She was fighting for her family and her heritage.

"Mr. Castle, this is Samantha Collins. I must not have made myself clear last night. So I'll say it again. Our property is not for sale. At any price. And if you don't stop harassing my family, you will regret it."

Sam tossed the phone back into its cradle and pounded down the porch steps, blood rushing through her veins. She deliberately slowed her steps, took a few deep breaths and willed her frustration and fear to the background. She had to get a grip. She had a business to run.

She looked up and swallowed hard. She would do what she had to do and be polite, even if it killed her, which, given that the three city commissioners had just pulled up, it might.

Chapter Two

Danny Hastings arrived at the downtown Los Angeles office of Castle Development early Sunday afternoon. He took the elevator to the penthouse suite and walked down the marbled hallway, flipping on light switches as he went. The place was eerily quiet on a Sunday afternoon, the windowless hallways lit only by the exit signs. He'd have preferred less flashy office space, but Jeremy staunchly maintained if you wanted money from investors, you had to look like you didn't need it. Which Danny supposed was true.

After Jeremy's odd phone call the night before, Danny had cut short his Hawaiian vacation and caught the red-eye back to L.A. After a few hours of sleep, a shave, shower and enough coffee to float the Titanic, he wanted answers. What was Jeremy doing in Florida? And why the sudden urgency? They had more projects in the works than they could handle. Besides, scouting property and sweet-talking the owners out of it had always been Danny's job. Jeremy tended to be too pushy and arrogant, while Danny had learned the fine art of sweet-talking from a master: his father. He didn't have much use for the old man's cold heart and controlling nature, but the man knew how to finesse a deal. So Jeremy hot-footing it to Florida out of the blue made no sense. Unless...

Danny checked his answering machine. His line always had lots of messages. Leads on properties, commissioners with questions. A thousand and one details.

But nothing from his business partner.

Danny sipped more coffee and drummed his fingers on the desk. When the phone rang, he snatched it up on the first ring. "This better be good, Jer."

"Where have you been?" a female voice demanded. "I've been calling you for hours. Oh, Danny, something's wrong, something's really wrong," Laurie Castle's voice dissolved into slurpy sobs.

A call like this from anyone else would have put him on high alert, but Danny had known Laurie a long time. To say she was a tad dramatic would be a decided understatement. He leaned back in his chair, sipping his coffee. "Deep breath, Laurie. Okay, now, tell me what's wrong."

"Jeremy's missing. He's gone. He...He..."

Danny gave her a moment to sniffle into a tissue. "Take it slow. That's a girl. He—what?"

"He didn't call me last night, so I left a message on his cell phone, but he didn't call back either. Then—" Her voice disappeared under the crackle of a PA system.

"Laurie, where are you?"

"I'm at the airport. That's what I'm trying to tell you. I came to pick him up and he's not here and I can't reach him on his cell."

He chose his words with care. "Is it possible you may have mixed up the flight or gate information?" It wouldn't be the first time.

"No. I know you think I'm an airhead, but no. I'm not wrong."

"Okay. I had to ask." He pulled out his cell phone and checked for missed calls. Nothing. "Let me check with Olivia. Maybe she knows something." Their office manager-cum-travel agent and good friend always had things well in hand.

"I already did. She said I had the right flight."
Laurie paused for another loud nose blowing. "So
what are we going to do?"

"Did you check if he took an earlier flight?"

A pause. "No. I never thought of that."

"Where are the girls?"

"They're here with me."

"Tell you what. Take them home and I'll do a bit
of checking and get back to you. I'm sure it's just a
simple mix-up, a bit of miscommunication." L.A.
traffic was always a nightmare, even on a Sunday.
And if it turned out the miscommunication involved
another woman, he was going to take it out of
Jeremy's hide. In triplicate.

"Something's wrong, I know it. Jeremy isn't like
you. He's not impulsive; he doesn't do spur-of-the-
moment things."

That much was true. Unpredictable was usually
his domain, not Jeremy's, except when it came to
women. "Think positive, Laurie. Don't scare the
girls, okay? I'm sure he's fine."

After a quick conversation with Olivia to make
sure Laurie did, in fact, have the right flight
information, Danny checked his home phone again,
just in case. Several frantic messages from Laurie,
but no word from his partner.

He walked across the hall to Jeremy's shrine to
modern furnishings and sank into the ankle-deep
steel-gray carpet, finally perching on the edge of a
chair that was a chiropractor's dream. Five minutes
in this contraption and you'd need a month of
adjustments.

He checked Jeremy's incoming messages. Banks.
Investors. Yada, yada, yada. When he reached the
last of fifteen messages, he froze. The voice was
female—and cold as ice.

"Mr. Castle, this is Samantha Collins. I must
not have made myself clear last night. So I'll say it

again. Our property is not for sale. At any price. And if you don't stop harassing my family, you will regret it."

Danny's first instinct was to shrug it off, but couldn't quite manage it. He scrubbed a hand through his hair as he listened to the time stamp. This morning at 5:00 a.m. About 8:00 a.m., Florida time. The caller had to be the local holdout Jeremy wanted him to sweet-talk.

It certainly wasn't the first time they'd been threatened. But generally, calls like this were all bluster and helpless frustration, which Danny would personally go in to diffuse. This sounded different, like the caller meant every word and things could get ugly.

Danny dialed Jeremy's cell phone again, just in case. When voice mail picked up, he said, "Where are you, Jer? I'm at the office, and Laurie is frantic. Call me."

He hung up, then dialed Olivia again. "Hey, Olivia. Can you check to be sure Jeremy got on the plane?"

"I told Laurie she had the right flight."

"I know. But before I hop a plane South, I want to be sure I've covered the basics here."

There was a pause. "You know that's not public information, right?"

"I know. And I wouldn't ask if it wasn't important."

"I'll call you back."

While he waited, he poked around Jeremy's office, but didn't find anything about the Florida deal. Jeremy must have it on his laptop.

He drummed his fingers on the glass-topped desk. Florida. Samantha Collins. Samantha.

Recognition hit him like a slap to the forehead. He replayed the voice mail again just to be sure. No, he wasn't going crazy. It was the voice he still heard in his dreams. Samantha. His cousin Annie's best friend.

He reached for his wallet and pulled out a tattered photo he kept way in the back. He tilted it to the light so he could see better. It had been taken almost twelve years ago at Annie and Jimmy Wayne's wedding with one of those disposable cameras. Danny stood in the center in his black tux, his right arm around a beaming Annie, with a smiling Samantha tucked under his left. Chin-length red hair, killer legs in a form-fitting green dress, and the biggest, saddest, most beautiful green eyes he'd ever seen. He'd taken one look and been hooked.

The weekend they spent together had been amazing. She was everything he'd ever wanted in a woman: beautiful, fun-loving, spontaneous. But he also recognized she wasn't the kind of girl you dated; she was the kind you married. After all the affairs his father flaunted under his mother's nose, Danny had always said he'd never marry. Casual dating, a little fun, nothing serious and no hard feelings when it was over.

Samantha, though, made him think about things like forever and mortgages and kids and minivans. The whole idea had scared him spitless, so he'd snuck out on Monday morning, leaving nothing but a rose, a note, and a lifetime of might-have-beens behind.

When he'd called Annie later and asked for Sam's number, she said Sam was seriously involved with a new man and to leave her alone. Since he wasn't sure what he'd do once he called, he'd done as Annie asked. But he'd never forgotten Samantha. At odd times, he still heard her husky voice, still found himself searching stranger's faces for those sad green eyes, still missed her touch. There had been something about her, stirring needs in him he'd never acknowledged, a desire for connection, companionship, maybe even love.

Now Jeremy was trying to buy her property?

An online search turned up several dozen Sam's and a couple of Samantha's listed in Central Florida, but it didn't take long to discover none of them operated a river cruise service and marina.

He finally got to the last Samantha Collins on his list. Would she remember him? As he listened to the phone ring, he mentally kicked himself. *Yeah, right.* From what Annie had said, Samantha had gotten married and probably had three kids, a dog and a minivan.

"Collins Marina and River Cruises. May I help you?"

Danny sat up in the chair. The voice was older, friendly, but with a hint of reserve. Not Samantha, but he'd found the right number.

"Good morning, this is Danny Hastings. I'm with Castle Development and I believe my partner Jeremy Castle took a river cruise with Ms. Collins several days ago. May I speak with her?"

"She's unavailable." *Click.*

Danny drummed his fingers on the desk. He dialed again.

"Collins Marina and River Cruises. May I help you?" This time the voice was a shade less welcoming.

"Hi, again. I think we were cut off. I was asking for Sam Collins?"

"And I already answered your question. She's not available. And our property is not for sale. Good day."

Click.

Obviously, Jeremy had understated how deeply Sam opposed selling. They'd deal with that, but something else was going on.

First, Jeremy was predictable as the sunrise. If he booked a certain flight, he'd be on it. On that,

Danny agreed with Laurie.

Second, if he'd missed his plane, he would have found a way to get in touch. Cell phone, pay phone, smoke signal. Even if he was holed up somewhere with a little cutie, he would have called. He and Laurie's relationship had almost shipwrecked on her assumptions several years ago. Since then, nothing short of death would keep him from checking in with his wife. Death? Danny shivered and shoved the thought away.

He turned back to his computer, typed in Riverlake and pulled up a list of local accommodations. Two motels and three bed-and-breakfasts. He started with the B&Bs and got lucky on his second call.

"Mr. Castle is registered here, sure enough, but he didn't come down to breakfast this morning, and now that I think on it, I haven't seen him all day," an older man said, papers rustling in the background. "Would you all like to leave a message for him?"

"Please ask him to call Danny. He has all my numbers."

Danny locked the office and headed for Laurie's where he spent the next few hours playing cards with the twins and talking Laurie off the edge of panic.

"I'm sure we'll hear from him before long. But if we don't, I'm catching an early flight to Florida. There must be a logical explanation, some kind of mix-up." He didn't mention the threatening voice mail.

Laurie turned wide, pleading eyes his way. "Do you really think so, or are you just trying to keep me from hyperventilating?"

"I really think so. And keeping you from hyperventilating is more for the girls' sake. They need you calm, Laurie."

Her big blue eyes filled with tears, but she blinked them away and squared her shoulders. Danny wasn't sure exactly what had drawn Jeremy to her, but he'd do all he could to help. And when he got his hands on his partner, he'd beat the crap out of him for worrying everyone.

Chapter Three

Sam stood on the weathered dock behind the bait shop and inspected the aging canvas sunshade atop their twenty-five foot pontoon boat. She preferred to get out on the water with the sun on her head, but knew city folks wilted fast in the Florida heat. And it just didn't do to antagonize paying customers.

Get a grip, Mary Sunshine, she scolded herself. Her grumpy attitude had nothing to do with the heat or the tourists. It was aimed at the city commission and their crazy scheme. She'd stopped at Haven House last night and done some internet research on Emma Jean's computer. Buying her own was still on Sam's "someday" wish list.

What she learned had made her blood run cold. Not only were more and more cities trying to take private property through eminent domain, but judges were ruling in favor of big developers. She had printed out some helpful info from a site dedicated to helping people like her fight back. Of course fighting involved money, which she didn't have...

Sam pulled her thoughts up short. She had to stay positive.

In the meantime, she had another river cruise scheduled. Over the years, Sam had learned there were generally two kinds of visitors to the marina. The first were the fishermen, families and tourists who were thrilled to discover the native plants, birds and wildlife that lived in the area. They asked questions, chatted, took pictures and generally made Sam's day. Then there were the other kind, the ones who acted as though this little backwater town was beneath them and they couldn't wait to get back to civilization. They turned up their noses at fried chicken and spent the whole trip scanning the Withlacoochee for gators and questioning her about the cost of waterfront property. Though both kinds paid the bills, Sam hoped today's guests were of the first variety.

A car rumbled into the gravel parking lot with an impatient purr and Sam's hope faded. She'd worked on enough engines to know a sports car when she heard it, and in her experience, sports car drivers usually weren't big nature lovers. She wondered idly whether this one would be annoying or just plain bored by their little junket.

Pasting a professional smile on her face, Sam turned toward the parking area and stopped short as the driver unfolded his length from the low-slung car and then scanned the area with one all-encompassing glance.

Sam's eyebrows shot up in surprise. Weekday cruises tended to attract retirees in polyester and plaid. This guy was a whole different animal. Though he was dressed in tan chinos and a light blue polo shirt, his California tan, sun-bleached hair and dark glasses made him look like he should have a surfboard tucked under his arm. Add a scruffy beard and he could be one of the sexiest men alive.

Sam stepped onto the dock to greet him, but when he turned in her direction and flashed that lopsided, boyish grin, all white teeth and relaxed confidence, Sam's world shuddered to a frantic, screeching halt.

Her breath backed up in her lungs and her heart thundered louder than a summer squall. With shaking hands, she adjusted her sunglasses, pulled down the visor on her ball cap, and tried to wrap her mind around what she was seeing. *Stay calm, girl. Breathe.*

It couldn't be, but it was.

Danny Hastings.

The one man she never, ever expected to see again. What was he doing here?

Before she could form a coherent thought or force her muscles into action, he stepped towards her, hand extended. "Hi, I'm looking for Samantha Collins."

Relief almost knocked her to her knees and she managed to return his firm shake, praying he wouldn't notice her clammy palms. When he didn't react to her in anything but the most perfunctory fashion, Sam managed a shaky smile hoping she looked more friendly than frantic. Was it possible he didn't recognize her?

Sam tucked her hands in the pockets of her cargo shorts lest he see them shaking. "Hi, ah, may can I help you?"

"Are you Samantha?"

"Mom!"

Before Sam could spring into action and stop her, Lindsey raced through the marina's office door and almost plowed into Sam full tilt. Sam steadied her with hands that badly wanted to shake. *Oh, not now. Not now.*

"What, Princess?" It took everything Sam had to keep her voice calm and unruffled.

"Memaw said to tell you the other man, Mr. um, Somebody, said he couldn't come." She flicked a glance at Danny. "Something came up."

"Thank you, Linds. Now go help Memaw with lunch." She turned her daughter by the shoulders and pointed her back towards the safety of the office. And safely out of Danny Hastings' line of sight.

"Okay." Lindsey turned towards the door, then

stopped and looked over her shoulder at Danny, scanning him from head to toe with a suspicious, fearful scrutiny Sam had never seen in her daughter before. "Are you going on a river cruise with my mom?" she demanded.

Danny's eyes flicked from Lindsey to her and back again. "It depends. Does your mom give river cruises?"

Lindsey nodded. "She's the captain." She folded her arms and narrowed her eyes at Danny. "She's also really strong and carries a gun."

Sam felt her cheeks burn as Danny's eyes slid over her, from her sleeveless button-down shirt over her worn cargo shorts with the wide utility belt and down to her dirt-streaked boots. "I'll make sure I don't make her mad, then," he said gallantly.

Sam couldn't see his eyes, but from the way his lips were twitching, she knew he was holding back a smile, the same smile she hadn't been able to resist all those years ago. But there was nothing calculating or speculative in his laughter. Her secret was safe. For now.

She wouldn't let herself think about what would happen if he found out about Lindsey. Annie had said he'd married some socialite several months after their weekend together, but still, he came from money. It wouldn't take much for him to use his wealth to take Lindsey from her if he decided he wanted to. Panic clenched Sam's stomach, but she ignored it.

Sam turned Lindsey firmly towards the bait shop once more. "Enough, Linds. Go help Memaw. I've got work to do."

Then she took a deep breath and faced her customer. If she could just remember to think of him that way, and only that way, she could—probably—get through the next few hours without making a complete babbling fool of herself. Or worse, throwing up in the river.

****

Danny settled back on one of the comfortable seats under the canopy and watched Samantha expertly steer the pontoon boat down the river. What an intriguing woman. Where she was all warmth and friendliness with her daughter, she tiptoed around him as though he had live ammo strapped to his back and one wrong move would explode them both.

As they putted along the river, he studied her as she robotically spouted facts on the flora and fauna, each word precise and clear, but without an ounce of warmth or a glance in his direction. Her husky voice was the one that haunted his dreams, so he knew this was his Samantha. Did she know it too, and that's what was making her so nervous? Or was it something more basic, like it wasn't worth her time and gas to take the boat out with just one passenger on board?

"Is there a problem with me being your only customer?" he finally asked. The tired look of the marina and outbuildings suggested she was barely keeping things afloat. Which made her refusal to sell and threat to Jeremy even more puzzling.

Her head snapped in his direction so fast, he feared she'd give herself whiplash. "No problem. Everything's fine." Her words shot out like gunfire.

Interesting. "You can check my credentials if it would make you feel better, make sure I'm not a serial killer or anything." He'd intended to make her smile, but the look of trepidation she'd been wearing since they met only intensified.

He held his hands up, palms out. "I come in peace. Really." He waved his digital camera. "I'm just here to sightsee, snap a few photos."

She snorted and mumbled something that sounded like, "Yeah, right," before she resumed her tour guide spiel.

Danny shrugged and decided to let the matter of their history ride for the time being. Though her hair was pulled up into a ratty-looking ball cap and dark glasses hid her eyes, Danny knew this was his Samantha. She had to have recognized him, too.

Danny froze. Could she be the reason Jeremy hadn't come home? No, the threat did not come from a happy woman. Then was it possible she had something to do with Jeremy's disappearance? He immediately dismissed that idea, too. The Samantha he'd known wouldn't have hurt a fly.

Maybe if he looked busy, she'd let down her guard. He pointed his camera skyward. Huge live oak trees formed a canopy over this section of the river, and he could imagine how the first explorers must have felt when they arrived in this unknown land. Excitement sizzled in his bones and he grinned. Jeremy was right on target about this area. This stretch of river was a developer's dream; it was endless possibilities just waiting to happen. And he and Jeremy were just the people to turn the dream into reality.

****

Sam watched Danny's excitement build as he snapped photo after photo of the land on either side of the river. They passed several alligators sunning themselves at the water's edge, but he paid them no mind. Why was he here? There was no way she would believe his showing up so unexpectedly was a coincidence. He had to know who she was. So what was he after? Was he looking for property?

"Who owns the big old house over there?"

Sam swallowed hard. "That big old house is a beautiful example of Queen Anne architecture, built in the late 1800s, with original hardwood floors and stained glass."

He squinted at the partially repainted structure.

24

"Is it a bed and breakfast?"

"No. It's a home for unwed mothers." And Sam's pet project. Since Haven House opened four years ago, Sam had been one of its regular supporters, both in time and money. But judging by Danny Hastings' face, the home's history and mission didn't interest him. He was looking at the house the same way every developer did.

Her heart sank as the truth dawned: he *was* here to buy property. He had to be. *Oh, dear God, please no. Don't let him come here.*

Her heart started pounding and panic threatened to shut down her lungs. But before she completely freaked out, her walkie-talkie chirped. She wiped her clammy palms on her shorts and unclipped it from her belt. "Sam Collins."

"Sam honey, I just got a call from Fish and Wildlife. There's a gator in a pool; they want you to go get him," Mama said.

"Where? Did they say how big?"

"Out by the new development, just upriver. Mike Sanchez says it's a good-sized one; he'll fill you in when you get there. I told them you'd be right over."

"I'm on my way. I'll call you about getting my passenger back to his car."

Sam stuck the phone back into the clip and turned towards Danny. Not Danny, her customer, she reminded herself. Whatever he was—or wasn't— in Florida to do, would have to wait. "I'm sorry, but I have to go out on a nuisance gator call. I'll drop you off at the marina and someone will drive you back to your car." She didn't need any distractions.

"What do you mean, nuisance gator call?"

"An alligator wandered into someone's brand new pool, which sits in a brand new neighborhood, which is built on what was once the gator's turf. So now I have to go get him."

His eyes widened, the way everyone's did when

they learned this about her. "You catch alligators? But how?"

"Very carefully, Mr. Hastings, very carefully."

He studied her for a moment and Sam fought the urge to squirm.

"So I guess you don't like the idea of development."

Her jaw clenched. "You could say that. Do you have any idea how many Florida black bears get run over by cars every year?"

"No idea. I didn't even know Florida still had bears."

"If they keep paving over everything, pretty soon we won't."

"What will you do with the alligator once you catch him?"

"Depends on several factors."

They watched each other in silence for several seconds, then he asked, "Can I come along?"

Yeah, right. That was all she needed. She opened her mouth to tell him no in no uncertain terms, but what came out instead was, "Only if you stay out of my way."

He flashed his lopsided grin again, all boyish and engaging. "Yes, ma'am. No problem. I don't have a death wish."

She looked down her nose at him. "Neither do I."

****

Transfixed, Danny watched her focus turn from whatever it was that had made her so stiff and starchy, to what lay ahead. She checked the various gadgets on her belt, one of which was a wicked-looking hunting knife. Amazing, his Samantha trapped alligators for a living.

"Would you come hold the wheel for a minute?" she asked.

Suddenly fascinated, he was only too happy to oblige. His captain was one big mass of contradictions. From loving and gentle with her daughter to downright frosty to him. And now? All intense focus and concentration.

Right now, she was rooting around under one of the seat cushions and he couldn't help but admire her shape. She was a tall woman, but sleek and toned, not an ounce of flab anywhere. She wrestled a long pole on deck and he watched, curiously drawn. This was no hot house violet, that was for sure.

She turned suddenly and when she caught him staring, her face flamed. Strong, yet shy. A one-two punch straight to the gut. With this woman, Danny got the impression what you saw was what you got. No pretense or coy posturing. And he'd bet she was one heck of an arm wrestler. He smiled, trying to picture it.

"I'm glad you find me so amusing," she snapped.

Steam practically rose from her skin, and not due to the humidity, either. Had a temper, did she?

"Actually, I was just thinking how you'd be quite a challenge to take in arm wrestling."

"There'd be no taking in that contest, Mr. Hastings." She eyed him haughtily. "You'd have to work hard to even be a real challenge."

Danny laughed. He hadn't had this much fun talking with a woman in years. Actually, not since their weekend together. Most flirted and batted their lashes to attract his attention. This one had no compunction about setting him straight. He wished she'd take those sunglasses off. And the hat. He wanted to see if her eyes were as green as he remembered, see if her hair was still the same deep red it had been years ago.

When she stepped over, he got a faint whiff of some clean, citrusy scent before she nudged him aside and took over the wheel. Memories of absorbing the same scent as he nuzzled her neck surfaced, but he pushed them aside. Now was not

27

the time.

They rounded a bend in the river and pulled up to one of those docks made from recycled tires. Danny looked around at the boats lying at anchor, the fenced swimming pool overlooking the water, the clubhouse with condos on one side and a rolling golf course on the other. Very nice. Too bad Castle Development hadn't gotten here first. Though if they had, they would have done things differently. The houses were too modern, too glossy and boxy to fit in with the surroundings. This area cried for Cracker style architecture, an old-fashioned-looking marina, and a casual, laid-back ambiance.

As they stepped onto the dock, the knot of white-haired onlookers suddenly parted and a tiny bird-like woman rushed towards them, her cheeks stained with tears.

"Are you the trapper?" she cried, grabbing him by the arms.

"Not me, ma'am." Danny nodded in Samantha's direction. "She is."

"What happened?" Samantha stepped up beside him, a pair of leather gloves in one hand. In the other she held her pole, which now had a wire noose at its end.

"He stole my baby," the woman cried. "Maybe he's still alive. Please, you have to hurry."

Chapter Four

The word "baby" turned Sam's insides to liquid. *Not a child, oh God, please not a child.* They didn't have a second to waste. But she needed more information. "Ma'am. Please take a deep breath and tell me what happened."

While the woman tried to catch her breath, Sam looked up as Sheriff's Deputy Mike Sanchez stepped up behind the woman. He mouthed the word "poodle" and Sam released her breath. *Thank you, God.*

"My baby was on the patio by the pool when that monster snatched him right off his little pillow. Before I could get outside, he was gone." She turned to the woman behind her and burst into sobs. Her friend murmured soothing words and glared accusingly at Sam, as though this was somehow her fault.

"Ma'am, I'm so sorry for your loss. If you could step over with Deputy Sanchez, I'll get this sorted out."

"You have to kill him. Now! He took my baby. Cut him open; my baby could still be alive."

Sam sighed and met Sanchez's eyes. He led the woman over to a group of friends, who surged forward and formed a protective barrier around her. Then Sanchez fell into step with her. "What's the story, Mike?"

"I just got here. Woman said she looked out the window and saw the gator in the pool. Her dog is missing."

"Gator still there?"

"Yep. No sign of the dog. No sign of a struggle though, either."

"So maybe Fifi is hiding."

"Possible, but not likely."

Sam nodded. "How big's the gator?"

"He's a big one. Easily ten feet."

Sam checked the gun in her holster; then calculated how much income the meat would bring. She hated to destroy a gator, but the additional money was always welcome. "You feeling strong today, Mikey?"

He raised a brow at her teasing. "You bag it, I'll carry it, Sammy. Don't I always?"

Sam sent him a brief smile and then cleared her mind of everything but the task at hand. If the gator had been a little thing, less than three feet long, she'd have moved him and set him free. If he'd merely scared people by making an appearance; same thing. But a ten-footer who'd taken a dog AND wandered away from the water and into a pool...unfortunately, she'd have to destroy him. She called Fish and Wildlife to let them know.

As they walked up the street and over one block, the crowd of onlookers trailed behind, the poodle's mama sobbing loudly. Mike pointed to a house sporting pink stucco and matching pink flamingoes in the flower bed. Sam shuddered.

She turned and faced the crowd. "Any of you folks been feeding the alligators?"

There was a general shifting of feet, several murmured no's, but no one met her eyes.

She looked them over more carefully. "Maybe tossing a few hot dogs off the dock when the grandkids come to visit?"

More shuffling, throat clearing. Finally, a balding gent in the back said what everyone was thinking. "So what if we did? What's the harm?

Doesn't make it okay to take Minnie's dog." Nods of agreement all around.

Sam took a deep breath to keep her temper under control. "What's the harm, you ask? Alligators have been living in this area for thousands of years. When developments come in, they are suddenly in close proximity with humans. Now, alligators are naturally afraid of people, but if we feed them, however innocently or unintentionally, they lose their fear and begin to view us as a food source. Then they're much more likely to wander on shore and see if there's anything else to eat."

This brought on deep, sucking sobs from the devastated Minnie.

"So get rid of it," Baldy shouted. "Get rid of all of them. We don't want them here."

Sam smiled to take the sting out of her words. "I think they might say the same about humans."

A heavyset man in the back called out, "What are you going to do with this one?"

"Because of his size and the fact he's lost his fear of humans—with a little help from you folks—he'll have to be destroyed."

"Well, good riddance, I say," Baldy responded.

The vigorous head nodding that followed made Sam see red, but she bit back any further words. It wouldn't do any good anyway. They didn't understand—didn't want to understand—the gator's part in nature. All they wanted was to get rid of them, now that they'd built their new houses.

Mike motioned everyone back. "You'll have to stay out here, folks, and let the trapper do her job."

"But we wanna watch," Baldy complained.

Mike stood firm, one hand casually dropping to his weapon as a silent reminder of who was in charge. "Wild animals can be unpredictable. For your safety, as well as the trapper's, I have to insist you all stay out here."

Baldy jutted his chin in Danny's direction. "Why is he staying?"

"He's with Ms. Collins," Mike said. "Now move along, folks, and let the trapper do her job."

Minnie broke free of her group and marched up to him. "This is my house and I'm going inside. I want to see that animal killed." The venom spewing from such a friendly face was shocking.

"Sorry, ma'am. We'll let you know as soon as it's safe." He sent her a hard look, then slowly scanned the crowd. "Stay out here. I won't repeat myself." Then he turned and followed Sam around the side of the house to the tiny backyard.

"Think they'll stay put?" Sam asked.

Mike sent her a hard look. "They'd better."

"Ten to one Minnie's in her living room peeking through the curtains already."

He sighed and opened the screen door for her. "You're probably right, but I can't be in two places at once and you're going to need a hand with this one."

The pool was kidney-shaped, with a waterfall at one end. The gator was at that end of the pool, head up behind the waterfall, keeping a wary eye on the proceedings. One section of the pool-enclosure flapped in the breeze where the reptile had gone through the screen on his way to nab the dog.

Sam dropped her bag on the tiles surrounding the pool and fished out a roll of heavy-duty duct tape. She took her pole and attached the snare with duct tape, then scanned the area for a good spot to attach the end of the Nylon rope. The pillars supporting the porch roof weren't sturdy enough, since she knew the gator would roll once she got the snare over his head. Ultimately, she wrapped the rope around a big decorative rock and hoped between it and she and Mike's strength, they could keep the gator under control until he tired. It would be more work to trap him this way, but she couldn't just shoot him in Minnie's pool. Even if it wasn't procedure, old baldy had looked just a shade too bloodthirsty.

Sam fished in her bag again and came up with a vial and a syringe. Once she had the gator tired out, she'd tranquilize him, so she and Mike could get him wrapped and transported back to her pontoon.

But first, they had to trap him. She stood and pulled on her leather gloves, then reached for her snare. "Ready?"

Mike eyed the end of the rope she'd wrapped around the rock. "You really did think I was feeling strong," he said, getting a solid grip on the rope.

She gave an exaggerated bat of her eyelashes. "My hero."

He laughed, the sound rich and deep. His laughter echoed in her lonely heart and momentarily stopped Sam in her tracks. Not for the first time, Sam caught a look in his eyes that made her wish they were more than friends, made her think he sometimes thought the same. She immediately dismissed it. Mike and Lynn had been married a long time, had two adorable boys, and from all appearances, a marriage many envied. She smiled. "Let's do it. Snag, tranq, and wrap."

Mike nodded and tightened his hold on the rope. Sam glanced back and saw Danny standing back, expression intent, looking like he was ready to dive into action. Which could be dangerous for all of them. "The best way you can help is to stay out of the way. We know what we're doing."

He nodded and Sam blocked him and everything but the gator from her mind. She approached the waterfall, then leaned over and turned off the water. The gator went very still, waiting. From above and behind him, she moved her snare into position. With her feet braced, she flipped her wrist and looped the snare over his snout.

He responded just as they'd known he would. He tried to dislodge the rope around his neck by diving, turning as he went. The rope broke away from the pole and it fell to the side. Sam let a few feet of rope zing through her gloved hands, lest he pull her right into the pool with him. Dive, roll. Dive, roll. Dive, roll, thrash tail.

Sam jumped out of the way, anticipating his every move. She ran up and down the side of the pool, keeping the line tight, thankful for Mike's support behind her. Back, forth, up, down. Splash, roll, splash, roll.

Her shoulders ached and her jaw hurt from gritting her teeth. Gradually, after what seemed like hours, the gator tired. The rolls became less frantic, the tail splashes less forceful. Only a few more minutes.

Sam kept her grip tight, waiting for the last hurrah. She wasn't disappointed. Sure enough, one more deep dive, powerful double roll and huge tail splash.

Then he stopped, exhausted. In case he had one more in him, Sam kept the rope tight in one hand, and used her other arm to wipe sweat out of her eyes. She risked a quick glance at Mike, who was sweating as hard as she was. "Okay back there?"

"Whew. Those big ones pack a whallop, don't they?"

"They do. Can you hold him while I get the tranquilizer?"

"Be careful, right?"

"Always." Sam pulled off her gloves with her teeth, picked up the syringe and crept up behind the alligator. With its thick hide, the needle had to be extra thick and strong and she'd only have one chance to do this right. One hard jab, take off running, and then wait a safe distance away until it kicked in.

She took a deep breath, plunged the syringe deep into the gator's hide, depressed the plunger and then leapt backwards. She wasn't quite quick enough, though, for his tail whipped her legs out from under her and tossed her into the pool.

As she went under, she heard Mike's frantic shout, felt the water rushing past her. But only one thought materialized: Get out. Fast. He's coming for you.

Her head broke the surface and she lunged for the edge. She had one leg up when hands grabbed her and hauled her to safety. She plopped onto the tiles a few feet away and looked up to see Danny Hastings beating the gator's snout with her snare pole. Not swinging it like a baseball bat, but pounding it straight up and down like a piston in an engine. Wham. Wham. Wham.

Sam struggled to her feet. She didn't want him getting blood in the woman's pool. Then she'd really make a stink. Sam grabbed his arm and tried to pull him away. "Danny. Stop," she said, gasping for breath. "He's already sl-slowing. Let the drug do its job."

He shrugged her off like a pesky insect. His rhythm didn't slow, didn't falter. He just kept going, up down, up down.

Sam's gasping breaths had finally slowed to pants when the gator stopped thrashing and Danny stopped pounding. One more swish of his huge tail and his eyes slid shut and he started to sink.

"Grab him," she shouted, knocking Danny aside. She reached over the gator's back and grabbed hold of the line. A quick nod in Mike's direction and he began pulling the beast over the edge of the pool, working the line hand over hand. She didn't remember Danny until she felt him step in behind her, pulling on the rope.

All three of them were soaking wet and shaky

from exertion when they finally heaved the beast up and over the rim of the pool, snare still tight around his neck. Sam dove for her duct tape. She straddled the alligator and began taping his jaws shut. She'd barely started when hands grabbed her from behind and hauled her off the animal's back.

"Give me that," Danny snarled, yanking the tape from her hands.

"What?" For a second Sam was too stunned to react. She shook her head to clear it and focused on Danny, sitting astride the gator, wrapping its snout as though it was something he did every day. She stepped in his direction, ready to take a strip off his hide, when something caught her eye. The entire crowd from the street watched from behind Minnie's lace sheers. She shook off her anger, tucking it away where it could simmer. She'd let loose on Mr. Hastings later.

As soon as he finished with the tape, Sam snatched the roll from his hands, then grabbed more line from her bag. Like a rodeo cowboy with a steer, she tied the critter's arms and legs together, then Mike threaded her pole through them. She eyed Danny.

"You ready to make yourself useful?"

"As opposed to what I've been doing?"

"That wasn't useful, it was getting in the way. Grab an end." She nodded towards the pole. Mike unfastened the end of the line and took hold of the other end. While the men hoisted the gator between them, she stuffed the rest of her supplies into her bag and lifted the tail section, part of which wasn't fastened to the pole as tightly as she'd liked.

"Look, I was only trying to help," Danny panted as they slowly, awkwardly trudged around the side of the house.

Sam glanced at the wide-eyed crowd peering through the patio doors again. "I'll deal with you when we don't have an audience."

In silence, broken only by the sounds of exertion, they marched down the street and back to the marina. It took all three of them to wrestle the large reptile onto the pontoon boat, where he landed with a thud that shook the craft.

Sam looked up and met Mike's eyes.

"We can do paperwork later," he offered easily. He cut his eyes to Danny and back to her, a half-smile lurking. "Go easy on him. He's not from around here."

Sam bared her teeth at him and he laughed and backed away. "Hey, it was just a suggestion."

Once the alligator was secured, she shot Danny a look. "Get on if you're coming. Otherwise, I'll get Mama to pick you up here."

He eyed the prone gator, then threw back his shoulders and climbed aboard. She'd give him points for courage, if not brains.

As soon as she pulled away from the dock, Minnie and company materialized around Mike. She saw him grab his clipboard and form the crowd into a ragged line so he could get his report started. She didn't envy him. She'd have her own to do, but later. Right now, she had other fish to fry, so to speak.

Sam waited until they rounded a bend in the river before she grilled her erstwhile companion with a look hot enough to sear meat. "Since you're merely a passenger on my boat, you want to tell me exactly what you thought you were doing back there?"

He'd been slouched on one of the bench seats. At her opening volley, he stood and crossed his arms over his chest. Good, at least he'd take his punishment like a man.

"I thought I was helping."

"Really," she drawled. "Just how many alligators have you subdued in your lifetime, Mr. Hastings?"

He scanned the cypress trees along the far bank. "None, actually. But I'm strong, stronger than you are."

"Maybe, but it isn't strictly a matter of strength with a gator. It's experience."

"Which you have lots of."

"I bagged my first gator when I was eight."

His eyes widened. "Eight? Who lets a kid near an alligator?"

This time, she was the one avoiding eye contact. "I went with my father."

He muttered something she couldn't catch, then heaved out a breath. "Look. You're right. I had no business getting involved. You obviously knew what you were doing." He rammed a hand through his hair. "I reacted on instinct."

"What instinct?"

He looked shocked, as though it was an insane question. "The instinct to help a lady." He eyed her speculatively for a moment. "I'm sure you've got guys falling all over themselves to help you. Even Mike almost tripped over his tongue, watching you work."

Sam snorted. "Mike and I have been friends for years. His wife and I went to school together. We're pals, nothing more."

They drifted into silence, while Sam maneuvered them around sunken trees and fallen logs, until they finally pulled up at a ramshackle tin-roofed shack perched at the water's edge. "Ahoy, Rupert," she called, then killed the engine, hopped off the pontoon, and tied it up to a badly listing piling.

A grizzled old man scurried down the overgrown path from the shack, his wicked-looking knife glinting in the sun. "What you bring me, Sam-Sam?"

"Got a big one, Rupert. Should be plenty of meat and hide to go around this time."

Rupert hopped onto the pontoon, surprisingly

agile for a man of his years, and inspected the gator. "Ah, I know this one. Been around a long time. You get him from the new development?"

"Woman claims he ate her poodle. We dragged him out of her pool."

He shook his head, resigned. "Them developers. They just don't learn." He checked his knife, then eyed Danny Hastings, judging his ability to help. "Well, then, let's get him to my "office," then we send him to the big gator den in the sky, find out if dat old woman be telling the truth."

Getting the gator off the boat proved even more difficult than getting it on, but they eventually managed it, then loaded the still-snoozing reptile onto a flat cart Rupert kept by the dock. Together they trundled it up behind the shack to a clearing in the woods. It had the cutting table, sink, bait buckets and other supplies typical of a fish camp, only with bigger knives and longer tables.

Rupert pulled on a big rubber apron. "Better get it over with, Sam-Sam."

Sam pulled out her gun, checked it. This was the part she hated. The alligator's only crime was not knowing his habitat didn't belong to him anymore. He'd wandered where he'd wandered for decades, found a food source, and would pay for it with his life. Still, if he came all the way into Minnie's yard, which was a good block and a half from the dock, he'd lost his fear of people. It could be deadly for everyone, because his next food source could be a person.

"Wait."

Sam looked over her shoulder and saw Danny standing there, suddenly uncertain.

"I can do it, if you want."

Rupert let out a big, booming laugh, then hitched a thumb in her direction. "Son, Sam-Sam here has been catching and killing gators all her life.

But it's right gallant of you to offer to help. Sam-Sam here don't need no help, ain't that right, girl?"

Sam tried to smile. Rupert was right, of course, she had been doing this almost all her life. Didn't make it easier, though. "Thanks. I can handle it."

Danny reached a hand out, laid it on her arm. "I don't doubt you can, only that you want to."

Sam looked at the hand on her arm, then up at his serious face, and something warm expanded inside her. When was the last time anyone tried to make her life easier? She honestly couldn't remember. Then she brought herself up short. This was Danny Hastings, the guy who could ruin her life. He probably said this sort of thing all the time, whatever it took to get into a woman's good graces. She didn't need anybody. She and Lindsey were fine on their own.

"Step back and let me do my job."

He raised his hands in the air, palms up, and stood beside Rupert. Sam raised her weapon, took careful aim, and fired, putting the bullet into the gator's skull, right where she wanted it. In moments, they had him turned over, and Sam neatly sliced his gullet open. Sure enough, there was enough left of Minnie's poodle to confirm they'd killed the right alligator. Sam sighed, backed away, and turned to wash her hands while Rupert went to work. He'd process the meat, and pay her a fair price for the sale of the meat and hide. It usually wasn't much, but every penny helped.

****

Samantha was a mystery, Danny decided as they putt-putted back up the river to the marina, and he was in danger of getting seriously sidetracked. What kind of woman trapped and gutted alligators for a living? He studied her, strong hands loosely gripping the wheel, back ramrod straight, hair bunched up under her cap. Even dirty and sweaty, she had an intriguing air of quiet confidence about her. But it didn't matter. He was here to find out about Jeremy, buy her marina. He couldn't afford to get involved.

He stood and walked over to where she stood, so he could see her expression. "You took my business partner out on a cruise the other day. Jeremy Castle."

He needn't have moved. Anger rolled over her features like a thundercloud, easily visible from either shore. Her hands tightened on the wheel and her pretty mouth pinched together. "What, so he didn't get what he wanted from me, now he sent you? I don't think so, Mr. Hastings."

"He tried to buy your property." It wasn't a question. He simply wanted confirmation.

"He did. I declined. He didn't take no for an answer."

Everything in him stilled. "So what did you do?" he asked slowly, carefully.

Blonde brows rose above dark glasses. "I chased him off my property."

"Was that before or after you left him a threatening message?"

She huffed out an annoyed breath. "Before. I wanted to make it clear we're not selling. The message was simply to reiterate my point."

"Jeremy was due back in California yesterday. He didn't show up."

"I see." Every single muscle in her body tightened. She drew herself up even straighter, words coming from between clenched jaws. "And you're assuming I had something to do with it?"

A change of tactic was in order. "I'm not assuming anything. I'm trying to retrace his steps on the last day anyone heard from him—the day he spent with you."

"If he didn't show up on schedule, he probably

missed his flight or something."

"I already checked." His eyes bore steadily into hers, looking for answers.

"Where did he stay in town?"

"At The Azalea House Bed & Breakfast. I'm headed there next."

Sam pulled up to the marina, cut the engine and hopped off to secure the pontoon. "He probably got held up somewhere. There are still pockets out here between cell towers where you can't get service."

Maybe she was trying to offer encouragement, but it seemed to him she was brushing him off. He didn't like it. He stepped up next to her, put his hands on her shoulders, and turned her to face him. "I'm here to find out what happened to Jeremy. If I find out you had something to do with him being missing..." he let his meaning sink in.

Sam tried to shake off his grip. "Take your hands off me."

He stared into her face, eyes hidden behind the dark shades and brim of her cap, and decided her disguise wasn't working for him anymore. Still holding her with one hand, he reached out and snatched off her ball cap and glasses.

Her eyes widened at the suddenness of the movement. "What are you doing?" The words came out soft, pleading.

Everything inside Danny stilled as he stood and looked his fill. She was even more beautiful now than she'd been then. And those clear green eyes still beckoned, still made him want to lose himself in their depths. "Your hair was shorter," he murmured before he could censor the words. He reached out and ran his palm over the thick braid. "And it was dark red."

Sam hadn't moved, not even the flicker of an eyelash. "Let me go," she whispered.

He looked back into those deep green pools and

saw fear there, real fear. Of him? He released her and stepped back.

"You knew who I was," he said, arms crossed over his chest.

"Of course," she snapped, grabbing her hat and glasses from him. She slammed her shades back on, hiding her eyes once more.

His eyes caught the glint of sunlight on her plain gold wedding ring. He felt a momentary pang knowing she belonged to someone else, and caught himself. She had a husband and daughter. She didn't need him causing trouble now. She'd obviously moved on. Still...

"I'm sorry about that weekend," he said quietly, seeing his own face reflected back in her dark glasses. "I had too much to drink, and let things get way out of hand." He winced at the understatement. "I always meant to call you and apologize..." he let the words trail off.

"Yeah, well, it was a long time ago," she repeated, stuffing her hair back under her ball cap.

"I'm glad you have a family. Your daughter's a real cutie."

Her eyes darted to his left hand. He added, "I never found anyone like you."

For a minute, Sam didn't move a muscle, just stared at him. Then she turned and walked towards the marina store. "I hope you find your friend," she tossed over her shoulder.

"I'm not leaving until I do."

Chapter Five

Sam closed the door to the bait shop behind her and leaned against it while she caught her breath. Her heart pounded like a runaway train and sweat beaded her forehead. He knew who she was. *Oh dear God, don't let him find out about Lindsey.*

"Sam, are you okay, honey?" Katharine Collins came around the counter, concern darkening her green eyes.

Sam waved her away. "I'm fine, Mama. It's just been a long morning."

"You get the gator over to Rupert's?"

Sam nodded and reached behind the counter for a bottle of water. "All taken care of." She unscrewed the cap and drank as she gathered her wits about her. The morning had stretched her nerves to the breaking point. "The man I took out this morning, Danny Hastings, is Jeremy Castle's business partner. He said Mr. Castle is missing. He never showed up back in California."

Katharine propped her fists on her ample hips. "And this Mr. Hastings thinks you had something to do with it?" She snorted.

"Something like that, I suppose." Sam worked the kinks out of her shoulders. "I guess he heard the message I left for Mr. Castle."

"What message?" Penciled eyebrows rose.

Sam sighed. "The one telling him to leave our family alone or he'd be sorry."

"Oh, Sam, you didn't," her mother admonished, sinking into the rocker she kept beside the cash register.

"I did. I was furious at the man's nerve, coming in here, wanting our property. As though I'd just hand it over."

Mama picked up her knitting, wouldn't meet Sam's eyes. "Maybe we should consider it. He's offering a good deal, Sam, you know he is."

"Tell me you're not serious," Sam demanded. "This is our home."

"And you're working yourself to death trying to keep it afloat."

"So are you. It's what families do, they work together to protect what's theirs. This marina and fish camp has been in the Collins family for a hundred years."

Sam's mother looked up then, sadness in her eyes. "I know you've done everything in your power to save this place, to bring it back out of the red. But why, Sam? You couldn't wait to leave this place once, and with good reason."

How could she explain what she didn't understand herself? "I want Lindsey to grow up here, free to be a child, to run around in the woods and play, not be stuck in some concrete jungle."

"Lindsey would be happy wherever you are, you know that, Samantha." Katharine paused. "Make sure you're fighting so hard for the right reasons."

Sam eyed her mother for a moment, then went in search of her daughter. When everything in her life was in chaos, Lindsey was the anchor, the one who reminded Sam why she did what she did. All for Lindsey. She was the reason for everything.

****

Danny Hastings pulled onto the main street in the little town of Riverlake and slowed down, searching for a parking space. Like many small towns, this one had a courthouse in the middle of the square, surrounded by small shops and restaurants on all four sides. He parked in front of the Lady Bug Diner and was just about to cross to the courthouse when a Sheriff's SUV pulled in beside him.

Danny waited while a tall, fifty-ish man unfolded his length from the front seat and jammed a cowboy hat on his head. "Excuse me, could you tell me where I can find the sheriff?"

The man pushed back his hat brim and twitched his thick mustache. "You found him." He extended a hand, his grip firm. "Luke Porter. How can I help you?"

They were almost equal in height, but Danny fought a wince at the man's grip. There was a message here, and Danny wasn't dumb enough to misinterpret it. "Danny Hastings. A friend of mine, Jeremy Castle, was here a few days ago and he didn't come back home."

Luke Porter's eyes narrowed as he looked him up and down; then he jerked a thumb over his shoulder. "I'm heading over to the Lady Bug. Why don't you give me the particulars over a side of grease."

Danny followed him into the diner, where a bell tinkled when they walked through the door. Two old-timers at the counter tipped their hats, several other patrons called out greetings. Luke Porter smiled easily as he led them to a booth in the far corner, shaking hands and slapping backs as he went like a politician on the campaign trail.

As soon as they were seated, a young girl wandered over, her face hidden behind a hank of hair. "Afternoon, Sheriff, sir. What can I get you?"

Luke leaned over and brushed her hair back. Danny's breath hissed out at the ugly bruise covering her cheek. She'd tried hiding it with a thick layer of cheap make-up, but it didn't work. "When are you finally going to leave that pile of horse hockey and file charges, Annabelle?"

Annabelle busied herself with her order pad. "I just ran into a door, Sheriff, is all."

Luke sighed deeply and ordered coffee and a burger and fries. Danny did the same. After Annabelle scurried away, he met Danny's eyes, his own still burning with anger. "Start at the beginning and give me the whole story."

"My partner came here earlier this week to check out some property—" he began.

"What kind of partner?"

"I beg your pardon," he asked.

"What kind of partner?" Luke repeated. "Business? Domestic?"

When his meaning sunk in, Danny felt his face flush. "Not that kind. Business partner. He's happily married, two stepdaughters. Twins. They're adorable."

"Go on."

"There's not much else. He stayed here at The Azalea House B&B, took a river cruise with Sam Collins. He called me all excited about some property. Told me all the owners but one had agreed to sell and we agreed to meet at our offices in California yesterday afternoon. He didn't show up and the B&B owners haven't seen him either. After I found a threatening message on his answering machine, I caught the red eye out here last night."

The Sheriff's brows beetled. "Who threatened him?"

"Sam Collins."

The man threw his head back and laughed. "If he tried to buy Sam's property, I'll bet she was madder than a wet hen."

Danny cocked his head. "As a matter of fact. Why is that funny?"

"Because I've known Sam all her life and she wouldn't hurt a fly. But she's real particular about developers trying to buy her family's property."

"What does her husband say about it?"

The Sheriff gave him a blank look. "She's not married."

"She wears a wedding ring."

"Widowed. Years ago." He looked like he wanted to say more, but stopped when Annabelle delivered their food.

For a few minutes, they ate in silence. Finally, the Sheriff said, "Look, I'll be happy to file a missing person's report, retrace your friend's steps, that sort of thing. But are you sure he didn't just take a detour to check some other places? Cell phones still aren't real reliable out here."

"Why aren't you more concerned about this?"

"Because nine times out of ten, when an adult goes missing around here it's because they were fishing and lost track of time."

"Jeremy hates to fish."

The Sheriff nodded and picked up his hat, slid out of the booth. "Then let's get the paperwork started and we'll track your friend down."

****

He looked up and saw a man talking to Luke Porter. Another stranger. That meant two in one week, although this one looked vaguely familiar. His hands clenched at his sides. If this was another outsider, come to hassle his Sam, he would have to go, too. He didn't want to have to exterminate another bug right now, though. It was too soon, much too soon.

Frustration rippled through him and his jaw hardened. If he didn't wait and let the dust settle, Porter would get suspicious for sure. He couldn't risk it. The sheriff was slow and methodical, but he wasn't stupid. He didn't need any kind of official attention. Besides, he still hadn't been able to figure out how much Lindsey had seen the other night.

He released the breath he'd been holding. First

things first. If he rushed things and made a mistake, who would take care of Sam? Protect her? Make sure nobody took their fish camp away? He'd have to find out who this man was and what he wanted in their town. Then he could decide what to do.

Sam was his first priority. Always.

****

In their usual booth on the far side of the Lady Bug, city commissioners Tommy Sooner, Rudy Emerson and Bill Farley held a whispered conference. They were too far away to hear the conversation at Sheriff Porter's table, so Tommy did the next best thing: he questioned Annabelle.

"Annabelle, honey, do you know who that is, over yonder with Sheriff Porter?" Tommy asked, his voice calm, soothing. Everybody knew Annabelle's no-account husband beat her on a regular basis so the young woman was afraid of her own shadow.

Annabelle poured them each more coffee, but kept her eyes on her pot. "Don't rightly know, Mr. Sooner. Just heard him ask about Jeremy Castle."

"So he knows Castle?" Rudy demanded.

Annabelle jumped at his booming voice. "I, um, I'm not sure. I got the impression they were friends or something. I think they know each other."

"It's okay, honey," Tommy soothed. "We were just curious is all."

"I'll get your orders right out," she whispered, then scurried off.

"Something ain't right," Bill Farley pronounced, his scowl even deeper than usual.

Tommy sipped his coffee, studied the other patrons, and casually wiped the ring from the table with his napkin. "Why do you say that?"

"It's just peculiar, is all," Bill said. "Castle meets with us, we set things in motion, then he takes off and we don't hear from him."

"Bill's right," Rudy added. When Tommy

scowled at him, he made an attempt to lower the volume. "Why hasn't the man called us back? He was supposed to go back to California to talk to his partner..." his voice trailed off.

They all looked across the room, where the Sheriff and another man were just leaving their booth.

Tommy stood and tossed his napkin on the table. "I'll go find out what's going on."

He intercepted the men at the cashier. "Hello, Sheriff." He shook Luke's hand, waited for an introduction to the other man.

Porter looked from Tommy to where Bill and Rudy watched from across the room and sighed. "Danny, this is Tommy Sooner, one of our commissioners. Tommy, Danny Hastings."

They shook. "What brings you to our fair town, Mr. Hastings?" Tommy asked, when it became obvious the Sheriff wasn't going to provide any more information.

"I'm looking for my business partner, Jeremy Castle." Danny Hastings' piercing look made Tommy want to check if he had sausage stuck between his teeth. "Did you meet with him while he was here?"

"Yes, I did. Along with two other commissioners, Rudy Emerson and Bill Farley." He pointed towards their booth and both men raised their coffee mugs in salute.

"What did you talk about?"

Sheriff Porter held open the door and said, "Let's finish this outside."

Tommy scowled at Luke, but relented when he saw the avid glances aimed their way. Once on the sidewalk, he turned to Hastings. "Your partner asked us to help him put in a new development on the Withlacoochee."

"Was Sam Collins' property part of the discussion?"

"Actually, her property was the main focus, as it will be the centerpiece of the development." Tommy studied the other man and chose his words with care. "How is it you don't know the details, Mr. Hastings?"

"I was vacationing and Jeremy said he would do the initial legwork on this one. Then I'd come in and close the deal."

"Usually, that's your job?" the Sheriff asked.

"Right. I scout real estate and handle acquiring the property. Jeremy usually handles the actual developing of the land."

The Sheriff crossed his arms over his chest. "Where were you vacationing?"

"Hawaii. Doing some surfing."

"Anyone able to verify your whereabouts?"

Danny Hastings affable demeanor slid away and his eyes hardened. "If you're accusing me of something, Sheriff, you'd better spell it out."

"Just doing my job, son, just doing my job."

"Yes, there are plenty of people who can verify my stay in Hawaii." Tommy watched as Hastings looked from him to the Sheriff, seemingly debating with himself. Finally, Hastings asked, "You discussed eminent domain in relation to the Collins property?"

Luke Porter straightened, eyes narrowed.

Tommy swallowed, cleared his throat. "Yes, actually, the possibility was discussed. We decided we'd try to convince Sam to sell, first. Eminent domain can be a nasty business and we don't want our community divided."

"I can't believe this," the Sheriff exclaimed, shaking his head. "You know Sam won't sell."

Tommy slanted him a look, delighted to have something on the Sheriff for a change. "She might not, but Katharine might."

"Katharine doesn't own the property, Sam does."

"Actually, they both do. And since the deed is listed with an 'or' not an 'and' between their names, either one could sell the property at will."

The Sheriff muttered something under his breath before asking Tommy, "When was the last time you heard from Castle?"

"Not since our meeting with him. He said he was going to try talking to Sam again, maybe her mother, and he'd let us know. But we haven't heard from him."

"Thanks, Tommy. Let's get the paperwork started, Hastings."

Tommy waited until the two men left before he went back inside to Bill and Rudy.

"Well," Rudy demanded.

Tommy leaned closer. "Castle is missing. This guy is his partner, Danny Hastings, trying to find out where Castle went."

Bill stared into his coffee mug. "Kinda creepy, what with the same thing happening to that other guy last year."

Tommy swallowed hard. He had forgotten about that. He sipped his coffee and tried to ignore the chill racing down his back.

****

"Afternoon, ladies," Sheriff Porter said as he walked through the door into the bait shop. He nodded towards the counter. "Jimmy Wayne."

"Sheriff," Sam nodded, her back stiffening instinctively at his presence. "What can we do for you?"

Sam watched the Sheriff smile at Mama and saw her mother blush and duck her head. Anger welled up again, buoyed by frustration. She wanted her mother to be happy, to have a real marriage, be loved by a good man. But in her mind, Porter wasn't the man. He was a coward. Back when they'd really needed him, he'd turned a blind eye, just like everyone else in town. Mama might be ready to declare bygones, bygones, but Sam wasn't. Not even close.

The Sheriff removed his cowboy hat and ran a hand through his thick hair, his expression troubled. "Need to ask you ladies a couple of questions. Just talked with a fella named Hastings. Says he's business partners with that developer, Castle. He's legit. I checked."

At the mention of Danny's name, Sam's anger spiked. Had he run to the Sheriff and accused her of something? She folded her arms over her chest. "So, what's your question?"

Porter made a calming motion with his hands and Sam noticed Jimmy Wayne rise from his usual spot at the counter and take a protective step in her direction. He stopped by for a cup of coffee every morning; it hadn't bothered Sam until lately. But his proprietary attitude was wearing on her last nerve.

"Now Sam," Porter said, "don't go getting your feathers all ruffled. I just need some information. Castle offered to buy your property and you turned him down, right?"

Her chin jerked up. "Of course."

Porter nodded. "Right. That the last time you saw him?"

Sam hesitated, exchanging glances with Mama. "He stopped by the house later that night."

"And?" Porter prompted.

"And I let him know we weren't interested in selling."

Porter looked from her to Katharine and back again. He sighed. "Let me guess. You were holding your twelve-gauge during this so-called discussion."

Sam nodded. "Didn't shoot him though."

"According to Hastings, you also left a threatening voice mail on the man's phone."

Sam huffed out an irritated breath. "I wouldn't

call it a threat. More like a reiteration of my position."

"Not smart, Sam, and you know it."

"I have a right to protect what's mine."

"But you can't go around threatening people. Not with your shotgun, either."

"You know I didn't shoot him, Porter," she shot back before what he hadn't said registered. "So the guy hasn't turned up yet, huh?"

"Apparently not. His wife is frantic. I figure I'll—"

The phone rang and Sam missed the rest of what he said.

"Collins Marina and River Cruises. May I help you?"

"Sam, this is Elsbeth Dower, from over to the elementary school. We seem to have a little problem here."

"What kind of problem?" When she realized Mama, Jimmy Wayne and Porter were openly listening in, she turned her back and lowered her voice.

"You know we have a policy against cell phones at school. Well, it seems Lindsey brought hers today and its buzzing disrupted her class. I'm afraid you're going to have to come get her and the phone. And we trust you'll make sure this never happens again."

"Mrs. Dower, Lindsey doesn't have a cell phone."

"Ah. Well, then, I guess you and your daughter will have an even longer conversation, then, won't you?"

Sam thanked the woman and hung up, rubbing her forehead. A cell phone? Where would Lindsey get a cell phone? Borrowed a friend's? Surely she hadn't stolen it from someone?

"Is everything all right?" Katharine asked.

Sam started and looked up, surprised to find Jimmy Wayne right behind her. She fixed a smile on her face. "It will be. Little problem at school. I have to go get Linds. Can you cover for me?"

****

Katharine watched her daughter hurry out to her rusty Jeep, Jimmy Wayne right behind her before he headed to his own vehicle. Sam was too young to be so burdened. Her childhood had been a nightmare, for which Katharine would never be able to forgive herself. And now? Sam worked herself to the bone trying to keep a roof over their heads.

"She's a strong woman, Katharine. She'll be all right," Luke murmured.

Katharine jumped, surprised to find him standing beside her. For such a big man, he moved like a cat. She turned to look at him, her heart fluttering, and tucked her restless hands into the pockets of her apron. He'd never called her Katharine before. Well, not since the day she got married, anyway.

"Sam's always been strong," Katharine murmured. "She had no choice."

"Neither did you," he said quietly.

Despite her efforts to hold them back, her eyes filled with tears. "Oh, I had choices, if only I hadn't been such a coward. If I hadn't been so scared, I would've stood up to him, taken Sam and run."

One work-hardened hand gently cupped her chin. "You know it was never that simple, Katharine. We both know he would never have let you leave alive. Or taken Sam with you."

She flinched at his harsh words, but recognized the truth in them. Her husband would have killed both of them before he let them leave.

"I was so relieved when he died," she whispered, then clapped a hand over her mouth, appalled she'd said such a thing aloud. But his death had been such a welcome, unexpected blessing, as though the sun had come out after a lifetime of swirling clouds and terrifying darkness.

"There's no need to feel guilty. The man was a monster. Besides, don't think I didn't consider taking him out myself a time or two."

Her eyes flew to the gun at his hip.

His mouth pulled up at one corner. "I said I considered it; not that I did it. Besides, looks like he managed it all on his own."

Katharine searched for a way to change the subject. She didn't want to talk about her dead husband anymore. "Sheriff—" she began.

At the same instant, he said, "Katharine—"

He cleared his throat. "Go ahead."

Katharine studied her clasped hands, swallowed hard, but the invitation to supper just wouldn't come. "I—"

The phone rang and she leaped on it like a starving cat. "Collins Marina and River Cruises. May I help you?"

As she jotted down a cruise reservation, the Sheriff's cell phone rang. Before she could get rid of the long-winded tourist, Luke turned to her with a smile, tipped his hat, and disappeared out the door.

****

The elaborate Queen Anne Victorian, with its turrets, stained glass and wraparound porch had been built in 1888, according to Mrs. Dorothy Mertz, proprietor of The Azalea House Bed and Breakfast.

"Though azalea bushes come in every shade from palest pink to almost red," Mrs. Mertz said as they climbed the stairs to the second floor, "Mr. Mertz and I decided to paint The Azalea House a dusky rose, in honor of the most common variety."

Danny tried to sound sufficiently interested in all this trivia, as well as the cost of the property's upkeep and history of its ownership, but his sleepless night and increasing worry were catching up with him. "Ma'am, if you could just show me

Jeremy's room?" he prompted when the tiny woman stopped long enough to draw breath.

"Of course. Right this way," she chirped. She led him up the sweeping staircase with its mahogany newel posts and down a long hallway lined with the photos of aforementioned previous owners. By the time she stopped at the third painting to begin another lecture, Danny blurted, "Were you a schoolteacher, Mrs. Mertz?"

She fingered the cameo at her neck and peered through her lashes at him. "Why, yes...yes I was."

Danny gave her his best grin. "I could tell. I'm sure your students loved you." He walked around Mrs. Mertz and headed down the hall. "So which of these lovely rooms did you rent to Jeremy?"

"I know what you're trying to do," she said, wagging a bony finger at him. She marched over and stuck the old-fashioned key into the lock. "You young people are all so impatient." She huffed out a breath, then stuck her arm out to block Danny's way when he would have pushed the door open. She eyed him up and down like a student who claimed the dog ate his homework and then she knocked once on the heavy wooden door. "Mr. Castle? Are you in there?" She knocked twice more before she deemed the room empty and turned the key.

Danny curbed his impatience and allowed Mrs. Mertz to precede him. He stopped and stared, stunned to see so much purple in one room. Purple flowers all over the wallpaper, purple flowers on the bedspread, in pots and vases along the windowsill. Everything that wasn't white wicker was covered in purple. He tried to picture Jeremy in this room and couldn't, yet his friend's clothing hung in the closet, his empty suitcase rested in the corner and his laptop sat on the small writing desk.

Danny swallowed hard. Here was proof Jeremy hadn't simply headed to some other town to scout more property. Or worse, holed up somewhere with a cute young thing. He pulled his thoughts up short. As the sheriff said, he might have gotten lost in the forest. It was completely possible, since Jeremy had no sense of direction.

He pulled out his cell phone and dialed Porter. "I'm in Jeremy's room at The Azalea House. All his clothes are still here, so he didn't leave the area."

"I'll put a search effort in motion. Are his car keys there?"

Danny scanned the room again. "Not that I can tell."

"Just wondered. Meet me at my office in twenty minutes."

As soon as the other man disconnected, Danny turned to Mrs. Mertz. "Thank you so much." He scooped up Jeremy's laptop and turned to leave.

Mrs. Mertz eyed the laptop, then pinned him with her stare. "The computer stays here. It belongs to Mr. Castle."

"Look Mrs. Mertz, I understand your position and ordinarily, I'd agree with you. However, this is not an ordinary situation. My friend is missing and I'm hoping this will help me find him."

The woman hissed out a breath and her eyes widened. "Missing?" She swallowed hard. "Oh, dear, just like that other man," she murmured as she turned away.

"Wait," Danny said, and grabbed her arm. Loosening his grip when she winced, he gently turned the tiny woman to face him. "What other man?"

"Another developer. A year or so ago. Just up and left and was never heard from again."

Danny studied the woman a moment more, then turned and raced down the stairs.

****

Sam walked into the elementary school and

58

fought a wave of déjà vu as the smell of floor wax, chalk and crayons assaulted her. When she arrived at the principal's office and saw Lindsey perched in one of three chairs against the wall, the picture of dejection, Sam's heart melted, despite her frustration. She remembered her friends in the same situation, more than once. But not Sam. She knew if she got in trouble at school, things would be even worse for her and mama when she got home. But that was the past. Sam vowed she'd get the facts before she passed judgment.

She stopped in front of her daughter, keeping her voice neutral. "Hey, Linds. What's up?"

Before Lindsey could respond, the principal stepped out of her office, hand extended. Elsbeth Dower had been a teacher for fifteen years before she became principal and despite her laid-back demeanor, she was tough but fair. "Thank you for coming, Ms. Collins. I trust you'll take care of this."

Sam nodded, then the principal handed her a cell phone she'd never seen before. Sam studied the phone, then met Mrs. Dower's eyes. "I'll get to the bottom of this." She turned to Lindsey. "Let's get you signed out, then we're going to have a little chat."

Sam ignored the way Lindsey shrank further into herself as she stepped to the receptionist's desk. Gina Northrup, round and jolly, pointed toward the sign-out list and sent a sympathetic smile in Sam's direction.

"She'll be okay," Gina said.

Sam didn't know the woman well, but she knew she had several kids of her own, saw them all in church most Sundays, though Gina had never spoken to her before. Sam was so surprised by the show of support, she blurted out, "thanks," signed the form, and left.

She and Lindsey walked to the car in silence, passed through town without saying a word and were almost home before Sam spoke. "So tell me where you got this cell phone, Linds. I don't know what you told Mrs. Dower, but we both know you don't have one."

Lindsey continued to stare out the window in silence until Sam said, "Answer the question, young lady."

Lindsey still wouldn't meet her eyes. "I found it," she finally whispered.

"Where?"

Sam watched her daughter's throat work, watched tears spill from her eyes, which she quickly swiped away. "Out in the woods, okay?"

"Not okay. Where in the woods? When did you find it and why didn't you tell me about it?"

Lindsey shrugged.

"Not good enough, Linds. Where and when?"

The silence stretched. Finally, Lindsey blurted, "The other night, okay?"

A thought occurred to Sam and she stiffened. "What night?"

Lindsey studied her fingernails, bright orange this time. "The night the developer man came to the house." Her voice came out small and scared.

Sam pulled into the marina's gravel lot and cut the engine before she turned to her daughter. "Are you telling me you snuck out of the house?"

Lindsey nodded, her expression a study in misery.

"Why? The woods can be dangerous at night."

"You do it," she said, chin tilted defiantly.

"I'm a grown-up; you're a kid. Totally different story." She studied her daughter, the sunlight glinting off her blonde curls and stubborn chin. Sam's heart swelled with love and fear of what could have happened out there. "So you went out walking and you found this cell phone just lying there?"

Lindsey nodded.

"How did you see it in the dark?"

Lindsey shrugged. "It rang."

Sam sighed. "So why didn't you tell me?"

"You'd want to know where I got it and I'd get in trouble. It doesn't matter, 'cause I'm in trouble anyway."

"Yeah, you are, because sneaking out at night is just plain dangerous and I know you're smarter than that. Then you tried covering your tracks." Sam sighed. "I'll let you know the consequences for this incident later. Right now, head to your room and spend the rest of the day there, thinking about better ways to spend your time."

Lindsey stepped out of the Jeep, then turned back, eyes still averted. "I'm sorry, Mom. It was dumb. It won't happen again."

Sam waited until Lindsey went into the house before she pulled the cell phone from her pocket. Sam knew enough to know this one was state of the art, with all the bells and whistles. She checked the contact list under "home." When she hit autodial, a number flashed on the screen that had the breath backing up in her lungs. A California area code. Just like the one for Jeremy Castle's office.

"Jeremy?" a female voice shrieked. "Is that you?"

Flustered, Sam hung up. The phone immediately rang again, but she didn't answer it. Heart pounding, she grabbed her own, much less fancy cell phone and dialed Luke Porter. He picked up on the first ring.

"Sheriff, Sam Collins. I think you'd better get out here." She swallowed hard. "Maybe bring search and rescue." She told him about the phone, then added, "I just called the home number programmed into it to see if I could find the owner, and a woman thought I was Jeremy."

She heard the Sheriff huff out a breath. "Did you talk to her?"

Sam swallowed. "No. I-I just hung up; she caught me off guard."

"Stay put. I'm on my way."

****

Danny watched the Sheriff's face as he listened to the person on the other end of his cell phone. As soon as he disconnected, he scrubbed a hand over his face, then placed another call. "Hey, Hal. This is Sheriff Porter. Can you meet me out at the Collins place, on the double? Yeah, I think we may have a lead on the missing developer."

Danny was out of his chair before the Sheriff grabbed his hat. "What's going on? Did you find Jeremy?"

"Looks like Sam's daughter found Jeremy's cell phone out in the woods. I'm going to check it out. Why don't you head back to The Azalea House? I'll call you with any news."

Danny was already halfway out the door. "Not on your life, Sheriff."

Luke Porter stopped and eyed him sternly for a moment. "You don't get in my way, understand?"

"Of course," Danny answered as they strode quickly down the hall, their strides evenly matched. "You think he's dead, don't you?"

The Sheriff didn't answer the question. "We'll swing by the B&B, get a piece of his clothing for the dogs to sniff. With the underbrush out there, if he's lost, the dogs can find him a lot quicker than we could."

"You think we're looking for a body."

At the door to his official SUV, the Sheriff met his eyes over the hood. "I hope we find your friend safe and sound. But I can't discount any possibility."

Danny nodded and climbed in, steeling himself against a truth he wanted to deny. One thing at a time. But if there was a chance Jeremy was alive, he'd do everything humanly possible to find him.

Chapter Six

Porter's jaw worked as he drove back to the Collins' place, but otherwise, he offered no clue as to what he was thinking. Danny looked out the passenger window, wrestling his own thoughts. Part of him wanted to hop the next plane to some sunny locale, do a bit of hang gliding or rock climbing—anything but this.

A fine sheen of sweat coated his skin and a sick mixture of dread, worry and uncertainty churned deep in his belly. It was the same stew of helpless rage he'd felt when his brother was kidnapped when they were kids. Back then, Danny was too young to act, couldn't do anything but wait for his father to make decisions. Only his father had hesitated; he'd waffled and waited and debated until it was too late. Brian had paid with his life. This time, Danny was in charge, and he'd take action, do whatever it took.

Please, God. Let him be alive. Laurie and the girls needed him. Jeremy and Laurie had even been talking about having a child of their own.

Danny clenched his jaw and stared out the window. The rolling pastures suddenly reminded him of the cemetery and the nagging question inspired by Annie's tombstone. He turned to watch Porter's face, still unsure whether he could trust this man. "Did Annie and Jimmy Wayne Drake have any children?"

Porter's eyebrows shot up past his sunglasses and he glanced Danny's way. "You know the Drakes?"

"Annie was my cousin. We grew up together." Danny folded his arms. "I stopped by the cemetery on the way into town. Her tombstone said, 'Beloved wife and mother.'"

Porter nodded. "It was Jimmy Wayne's idea. Annie was pregnant when she died. He wanted that included on the stone."

"Was she happy about the baby?"

Porter chewed the inside of his cheek while he pondered the question. "I can't say. She looked...unsettled. But she had morning sickness real bad, so that may have been part of it."

"How far along was she when she died?"

"About five months."

Oh, Annie. I'm so sorry you didn't get to be a mother. You'd have been a terrific one. He took a deep breath and asked the question he'd been avoiding. "How did she die?"

Porter turned his way, his surprise evident. "You don't know?"

"I only know she drowned," Danny said as he squirmed in his seat. He'd been out of the country at the time, and after getting Jimmy Wayne's terse message, he'd never been able to make himself call for the details. "But it never made any sense. She was a great swimmer."

Porter nodded. "Came as a shock to everyone in town, for the same reason. All we know is she went out on the river in her canoe and never came back."

He straightened. "Wait. You didn't find her body?"

"No. Though we sent divers and dredged extensively. But it's not unusual out here."

An ugly suspicion slithered at the back of Danny's mind. "You know, Porter, you sure do have a lot of unexplained deaths for such a little town."

Porter stiffened. "What are you talking about?"

"Annie dies and no body is ever found, and now

Jeremy is missing. And Mrs. Mertz told me another developer disappeared last year."

Porter's grip tightened on the steering wheel. "What are you getting at, Hastings? I don't care for your line of questioning. Nor do I have to explain myself to you."

"I think you know exactly what I'm getting at." He wanted to say more, but caught himself in time. He needed this man's help.

Neither man said another word until they pulled up at the marina, where a white-faced Sam Collins paced in front of her ancient Jeep. The minute the Sheriff stepped out of his SUV, she thrust a cell phone wrapped in a plastic bag at him.

"I'm sorry, Sheriff. Right after the other woman picked up the phone, I realized this could be evidence, so I wrapped it in plastic."

Porter frowned at her as he accepted the package, turned it over in his hands before he looked at Danny. "I'll have my men see if they can get anything off the phone. Wait on calling Castle's wife until we know more. This may not mean a thing. "

"Jeremy was never without his cell phone. Ever," Danny said, absolutely certain.

"Understood," Porter said. "But let's wait a bit, just the same, see what's going on." He handed the plastic-encased phone to Danny. "This is his phone?"

Danny flipped it open, checked the photo of Laurie and the girls inside and nodded, his chest tight. "Yes. No question."

Porter turned back to Sam and crossed his arms over his rock-hard chest, staring down at her. "So give me details, Sam."

Sam, Danny noticed, didn't cow to the sheriff's stance. She folded her arms, thrust her chin in the air and matched him stare for stare. "I got a call from Lindsey's school, as you know. Principal said she'd brought a cell phone to school. Since Lindsey doesn't have a cell phone, I questioned her about where she got it. She claims she found it in the woods near the river and took it to school to show off for her friends."

Porter examined the phone again, turning it around in his hands. "That's when you placed a call."

"No, I sent Lindsey inside first. I didn't want to scare her if there's more to this."

"I'm hoping this is a simple case of your friend getting lost; maybe hitting his head and getting disoriented," Porter said to Danny.

Danny nodded, but given the grim expressions on his and Sam's faces, he knew Porter didn't hold out much hope. "So what do we do now?"

As if on cue, they heard baying in the distance and an ancient pickup rattled into the lot, three hunting dog cages strapped to the bed.

An old man who looked like he was about ninety eased out of the cab, bringing his shotgun with him. He hitched up his overalls and spit a stream of tobacco before he issued one sharp command to his dogs: "Quiet." The dogs abruptly stopped yapping and plopped down on their rumps.

Porter stepped over and extended his hand. "Thanks for coming so quickly, Hal. I appreciate it."

The other man's eyes were wide with curiosity as he looked from Danny to the sheriff and back again. "So what's happening, Sheriff. Another hiker wander off?"

"We surely do hope that's all it is, Hal. But we could use your help tracking down a Mr. Jeremy Castle from California."

"Another one of them developers, I reckon. Don't have the sense God gave a chicken." Hal shook his head and spit again. Danny jumped out of the way just in the nick of time. The old man cackled, then sobered and turned to his truck. "You bring me the scent?"

Porter held out one of Jeremy's shirts. Hal nodded and unlatched the cages. The dogs scrambled out, heading straight towards Danny. Danny backed up a step. He didn't mind dogs, he just wasn't used to being surrounded. He held out both hands, palms down, for the dogs to sniff. Satisfied, they quickly moved on to the sheriff and Sam, before returning to the truck and sitting on their haunches, waiting for instructions.

Hal clipped a lead onto the collar of each dog, then held the shirt out for them to sniff. As soon as he did, they sprang up, tails wagging excitedly, straining at their leads.

"Easy now, boys, just hold up a minute." Hal wrapped the leads around his hand and then said, "Okay." The dogs raced away with Hal merely a step behind. Porter and Sam instantly followed. Danny was so shocked by the old man's speed, it took him a minute to catch up.

The dogs barked furiously and Hal shouted encouragement as the three of them crashed along through the brush behind them, going deeper and deeper into the woods. Danny guessed they'd gone about half a mile when the dogs suddenly started jumping in circles, whining.

When they arrived at the spot by the river, Hal quieted the dogs and said, "This is where they lost the scent, Sheriff."

Porter braced his hands on his thighs while he drew several deep breaths. Then he straightened, wiped the sweat from beneath his Stetson and studied the riverbank. Beside him, Sam was also breathing hard. Danny pulled his soaked shirt away from his chest and wiped at the sweat dripping into his eyes.

Porter stepped to the edge of the water and muttered under his breath. "Get the dogs back from here, Hal." He carefully stepped back, whipped out his cell phone, then muttered some more before slapping it shut. "No service."

"What is it, Sheriff?" Danny asked, though he was afraid he knew.

There was sympathy, and something else, in the Sheriff's eyes when he said, "I don't think your friend is lost, Mr. Hastings."

"What did you find?" Danny stepped closer, but the big man blocked his view.

The sheriff studied him a moment, then stepped aside.

As first, Danny didn't see anything but the ledge hanging over the slow-moving water. He leaned further out, gasped and squeezed his eyes shut. He waited a moment, then opened them again, tried to absorb what he was seeing.

There was an arm lying on the bank below, with a wedding band on the left hand. Nothing else.

He swallowed the bile in his throat and looked a third time, just to be sure.

Porter placed a hand on his arm, turned him away from the sight. "Do you know if that's your friend's ring?"

Danny rubbed a hand over the back of his neck, cleared his throat twice before he could get any words out. "It might be. But I know his had an inscription in it."

Porter sighed, turned to Hal. "Thanks for coming. And I'd appreciate it if you could keep this quiet until we know more."

Hal nodded gravely, and turned to Danny. "I'm sorry." Then he and the dogs vanished.

"We need to head back and call this in. Sam, I'm going to have to talk to you and Lindsey some more."

"Of course."

Danny followed them back to the marina, his mind a blur. Jeremy wasn't dead. He couldn't be. The arm had to belong to some other poor guy.

Reality made his stomach churn. The dogs had followed Jeremy's scent.

He sat in the sheriff's SUV, dimly aware of the other man talking on his radio, of other vehicles pulling in, of Sam's mother offering him a cup of coffee.

"Laurie, we have to call Laurie," he finally realized. He got out of the vehicle and walked to the sheriff, who was now surrounded by several more people in uniform.

"We have to tell Laurie," he blurted.

Everyone stopped and looked at him. Porter separated himself from the group and turned him back towards the SUV. "Let me get the crime scene people out there first, get the coroner here, and make sure it's him before we call. We don't want to be wrong."

Danny nodded and plopped back into the truck and waited. And waited. Voices rose and fell around him, but they didn't register until someone said, "gator." He shook his head to clear it and then strained to listen.

"Looks consistent with a gator attack," Porter said. "Get the divers out here to see if the rest of the body is submerged in the vicinity."

"You going to question Sam?" another voice asked.

Danny's head snapped up.

Porter's voice was rock hard. "I'm going to question everybody."

****

After the various law enforcement agencies had converged on the marina, they'd all traipsed back to the crime scene, where Sam leaned against a Cypress tree and tried to force her stomach back down where it belonged. Her hands had started tingling, so she knew she was in danger of hyperventilating. She had to stay focused.

Leaning forward, she braced her hands on her knees, trying to slow her heartbeat and avoid throwing up at the same time. She'd seen the aftermath of many a gator attack. Hadn't she dealt with Minnie's poodle just this morning?

But never a person. She swallowed convulsively and squeezed her eyes shut, but the sight wouldn't go away. She knew she'd never forget it. At least Lindsey was safely in the house with Mama. No way did she want her daughter anywhere near this.

Sam wiped her face with the hem of her tank top. If a gator had killed Castle, then it would be her job to trap and destroy it. She would need her equipment.

She took a slow, deep breath. She could do this. She straightened and flexed her fingers, relieved to find the tingling was subsiding. She had a plan. All she had to do was follow it. She'd deal with the emotional element later.

She turned in the direction of the house.

"No one leaves until I say so," Porter said from behind her. He didn't sound angry, just implacable.

Sam turned, surprised. "Sorry, Sheriff. I figured I'd grab my gear and get started trying to find that gator." She glanced up at the sky beyond the dense canopy of trees. "There's not much daylight left."

"Where's the next closest state-licensed trapper live?"

Sam bristled. "I can do my job, Sheriff, contrary to what you might have seen a minute ago." She hitched her thumb towards the tree where she'd just thrown up. "I'm good at what I do."

"No argument, Sam. But there's a problem."

"How so?"

"Until we find a body and can get a fix on cause of death, I have to treat this as a suspicious death. It might have been an accident, or it might not." His eyes bored into hers. "By all accounts, you had

70

reason to want the man dead, had threatened him, and were quite possibly the last person to see him alive."

"He was very much alive when I chased him off my property!" Sam rubbed her arms against a sudden chill. "I was angry. But it doesn't mean I killed him."

"I have to consider every possibility. You know I do."

Sam sighed. She did. But she didn't like it. "So what will you do now? Do you want me to call another trapper? He probably can't get here until morning." Sam looked past the sheriff into the river, where a large reptile had been watching the proceedings from behind a submerged tree root. "Though if it were me, I'd say the gator that got Mr. Castle is right over there." She nodded towards the Cypress tree along the bank. "That'd be where I'd send the divers, too. But it's your call."

Porter followed her gaze, then turned and called over his shoulder. "Sanchez. Over here."

Mike, who'd just arrived, trotted over. "Accompany Ms. Collins while she fetches her trapping gear, and then stay with her while she apprehends the gator." He pointed into the water.

Sam watched the two exchange looks and heard what they weren't saying. *Watch her like a hawk and make sure she doesn't do anything to cover her tracks, in case she's a killer.*

Sam turned back towards the marina and Mike fell into step beside her. "Sorry about this, Sam. But we gotta do it by the book."

"I know. But it doesn't mean I like it."

He reached out and gave her a one-armed hug, sympathy—and something else Sam couldn't identify—in his eyes.

Confused, Sam dismissed it as an unexpected gesture of comfort. They walked the rest of the way back in silence, while Sam tried to figure out what to say to Lindsey. How would it affect her daughter when she heard the cell phone she found belonged to a dead man? Sam shuddered and wished she had someone to talk this over with, someone to share the burden. She studied Mike a moment, then shook her head. No, the face that kept popping into her mind was Danny Hastings'. What would it be like if they were raising Lindsey together?

Yeah, right. The guy would never, ever live in a little backwater town like this. He'd just come back from surfing in Hawaii. He spent his time flitting from place to place, buying up people's property. No, a rolling stone like Danny was the last thing Lindsey needed in her life. And Lindsey would always be Sam's top priority.

Sam and Mike stepped out onto the dock and Lindsey barreled out of the house, Mama hot on her heels.

"Lindsey honey, you come back in here this minute," Katharine called, bursting through the screen door behind her granddaughter.

Sam scooped her daughter up before she could knock them both into the river. "Hey, Linds. Why aren't you inside with Memaw like you're supposed to be?"

Lindsey's green eyes widened. "But I wanted to see you, Mommy, 'cause I love you."

Sam laughed. "Nice try, Linds. But the eyelash batting was overkill." She set her daughter back on her feet. "Deputy Sanchez and I need to go catch a gator and you, young lady, are going to stay inside with Memaw like I told you, or you will be hating life for a long time. Understand?"

Lindsey sighed, defeated. Then her head came up. "Wait. What about the cell phone? Did you find out who lost it?"

Sam tread carefully. "Sheriff Porter is working

on it. He'll probably want to talk to us some more about it, but not right now."

Lindsey's green eyes filled with genuine tears this time. "I'm sorry I took it, Mommy. And sorry I snuck out."

Sam tilted her daughter's chin up and brushed the tears away. "It's good you're sorry, Linds, because what you did was wrong." She leaned over and kissed her forehead. "But for now, just remember I love you, always and forever. Now scoot."

She waited until the screen door closed behind Katharine and Lindsey before she headed for the marina and grabbed her gear. Several minutes later, she and Sanchez were putting down the river in her johnboat toward the spot where she'd last seen the gator.

Chapter Seven

Jeremy was dead. Danny sat in the SUV sipping coffee someone had handed him and tried to wrap his brain around the fact. There was no body yet—the divers were waiting until Sam and the deputy caught the gator. Guess they wanted to be sure it was the right one, and make sure the reptile didn't take out a diver.

He looked across the river to where Sam and Sanchez had tied off the johnboat. Just as she had earlier in the day, Sam had her gloves on and a long pole in her hand, duct tape looped to the utility belt at her waist.

He still couldn't figure what Jeremy had been doing way out here. Jeremy was not an outdoorsy kind of guy. He hated bugs of any kind and his only appreciation for nature was in seeing its potential to become something else. He would not have been out here without a compelling reason.

Was Sam Collins the reason? Danny knew she'd been furious with Jeremy for wanting her land, even more so with the city commissioners threatening to take it by eminent domain. Stupid, stupid move. That should only have been contemplated as a last resort. Those goons had shown their hand way too soon. Had Jeremy somehow paid the price for their stupidity?

Danny watched Sam sneak up on the riverbank above the gator and tried to picture her killing his friend in cold blood. His mind refused to conjure it up. It didn't make sense. Was the woman stubborn and protective of her land? Sure. Nothing wrong with that. Did she love her family? Absolutely. But would she kill to protect them?

It was the one question Danny couldn't answer. He knew, given the right provocation, people could do anything, but there was a core of decency about Sam making it impossible to picture her as a killer.

Unless it was self-defense. But that would put Jeremy in the position of physically threatening her, and that picture didn't gel either. In a fight, he'd bet Sam could take his partner in hand-to-hand combat. Jeremy was slight, never worked out; said he didn't believe in unnecessary sweat. Sam, on the other hand, was in top physical condition.

No, he couldn't picture Sam in the role of killer.

As he'd done countless times over the years, he pulled out his wallet and removed the tattered snapshot from behind the twin's latest school photos. It was the one from Annie and Jimmy Wayne's wedding. He stood in the middle with Annie on one side and Sam on the other; he had no idea why he still carried it. He just couldn't seem to part with it. He peered closer. The lighting was terrible, but the faces were clear enough. Though Annie glowed with happiness, Sam's smile couldn't erase the longing in her green eyes.

As he had so many times before, he ran his finger over her face. Even in this grainy photo, her eyes called out to him, making him want to hold her close and take away the loneliness reflected in those green pools. No, he couldn't finger Sam as a killer.

Danny heard a loud splash and shoved the photo back into his wallet. He stood and watched. Sam had looped the rope over the gator and now she and Sanchez were braced against a tree, holding the gator as he rolled and tried to escape the noose around his neck.

In minutes, it was all over. The gator was roped,

tied, and hauled up on the bank so the current couldn't carry him away.

"Should I open him up here, Sheriff, or wait until we get him to Rupert's?" Sam called across the water.

"Come get me and the coroner," Porter called back. "Sanchez, keep an eye on that reptile."

Danny sipped more coffee, watching as Sam ferried the two men across. Porter nodded and a moment later Sam's single shot to the creature's head echoed off the water. They crowded around the gator and he saw Sam pull the knife out of the sheath at her waist. He couldn't see her cut the gator open, but suddenly, she jumped to her feet, whirled around, and vomited in a nearby clump of ferns.

Danny's hand shook as he set the cup down on the dashboard. They'd found the gator that killed Jeremy.

****

That night, Sam was tired to the point where staying upright was a struggle. Yet when she'd gone to tuck Lindsey in, her daughter had thrown herself into her arms and started sobbing. Sam instinctively cradled her close and rocked her, just like when she was just a little slip of a thing.

When she'd finally cried herself to sleep, Sam wiped away her own tears, and took a shower before heading over to Haven House. Katharine had promised to keep one ear on Lindsey.

With the top down on the Jeep, the wind whipped around her. Sam was operating on two levels. The physical part of her went through the motions and did what came next, while her emotions chased each other round and round like squirrels in a live oak. As soon as she thought she had a handle on what she was thinking and feeling, her mind charged off in another direction. She should try to sleep, but she knew she wouldn't be able to. Maybe a dose of Emma Jean's practicality would help her sort it out.

Though it was after eleven, lights blazed in the old house as Sam pulled into the gravel driveway. She squinted at the peeling white paint. It was time to scrape off the old and repaint, but she couldn't do it right now, and it made her feel guilty. Not only was the home perpetually short on cash, but the pregnant girls who lived there couldn't breathe paint fumes while perched on ladders. So Sam had said she would take care of it. But that was before the whole eminent domain thing came up.

At the reminder, her stomach clenched. Before she could knock on the massive double front door, it swung open. Libbey, one of the newer girls, stood there, wide smile on her freckled face. "Hi Sam, come on in. Emma Jean said you were coming by. We just finished a round of Monopoly."

Sam crossed the threshold, surprised as always, by the warm welcome she always received. It was such a contrast to the way folks in town responded to her, she was never sure how to react. "How are you feeling, Libbey?"

The sixteen-year-old patted her rounded middle. "Me and Junior are doing fine. He's getting feistier every day."

Sam raised her brows. "You know it's a boy?"

Libbey laughed, tossing her red curls. "No, but only boys can be so annoying on a regular basis."

Sam laughed, amazed again at the serenity with which this young woman faced her circumstances. Her boyfriend had abandoned her, her father threw her out of the house—calling her a whore—and yet...she was at peace, smiling and laughing. Sam hated to admit it, but part of her was jealous. She wanted the same thing in her own life.

"Hello, Sam. Welcome, child," Emma Jean said,

grasping both of Sam's hands in her work-roughened ones. She led her to one of the mismatched sofas in the living room. "I heard you've had quite a day."

Sam glanced at Libbey, who raised both palms and stepped back. "I get it. My cue to leave." Once Libbey was out of earshot, Sam realized she didn't know where to start, so she gave Emma Jean a quick rundown of events.

When she finished, Emma Jean merely looked at her and raised a brow. "And?"

"And what?" Sam asked, though she knew what was coming. She fought the urge to squirm.

"And how are you handling all this, emotionally?" When Emma Jean wore her teacher-face, Sam knew there was no escape.

"It's hard. Lindsey cried herself to sleep. I haven't rocked her like that since she was a baby. I am so afraid for her."

"And rightly so. But how are you handling the speculation by our ever narrow-minded townsfolk? I heard several convoluted interpretations while I was in town this afternoon. "

Sam flinched. Emma Jean always did go for the jugular. Her voice came out a whisper. "That's hard, too. I've been looked at with suspicion my whole life. You'd think I'd be used to it by now."

"We don't ever get used to it, girlfriend. We all want to be loved and accepted the way we are."

"But it doesn't change anything. My priority is saving the fish camp."

"Why?"

Sam's head snapped up. "You know why. It's our home." She waved a hand. "It's your home, too."

"And it's what your father wanted."

"Right."

"What do you want?"

"To save the fish camp." When she saw more words forming on the other woman's tongue, Sam plowed on. "You said you'd help me."

Emma Jean nodded firmly. "And I meant it. Those bungling bozos are not taking this property away, not without a fight."

"And who is going to fight them?" Sam's laugh was bitter. "Me? You and a bunch of pregnant girls?"

Emma Jean pierced her with a look. "Child, please. You know these girls are about more than their bellies just like you're about more than your father."

"So what are we going to do?"

Emma Jean went into her office just off the living room and returned carrying a yellow legal pad. She sat down in the armchair, legs tucked under her. "We've come up with a few ideas."

"Who's we?"

Emma Jean slipped on her reading glasses and peered at Sam over the rims. "The girls and I. First, you need to see a lawyer."

"I can't afford a lawyer."

"I know. Which is why you're going to call a friend of mine who does pro bono work. Then, we're going to host several fundraisers."

As Emma Jean outlined the list, Sam sat back, stunned. "Why would you do all this?"

"Because this is important. You're important, the property is important, and we can't let them get away with this. One of the basics our country was built on is property ownership. They aren't going to trample those rights just because they want more tax money." She shook her head emphatically. "Oh, no. Not if we can help it."

By the time she walked out to her car a while later, Sam's head was spinning. Was it possible? Could they really take on the commission and win? Sam had always considered them a harmless bunch of bumbling idiots, but this time, they were hitting too close to home. What if they lost?

"We'll win, you know," a voice said and Sam spun around. Libbey leaned against the Jeep, arms folded over her belly.

Sam smiled. A girl who'd been through what Libbey had and could still maintain such a pie-in-the-sky naïveté was a treasure. "How can you be so sure?"

Night sounds filled the air around them. Crickets chirped and palm fronds clattered in the breeze. Libbey snorted in disbelief. "What? Have you no faith? Come on, Sam, Emma Jean told us how you two made this place happen. We're all going to help you save it."

"And if we can't?"

"Of course we can. It's just going to take work." She paused and brushed the thick curls from her forehead. "This is God's house, just like a church. He's not going to abandon us now."

Sam shook her head, amazed. "I wish I could be as sure as you are."

"Why aren't you?"

Sam finally looked Libbey right in the eye. "I don't think my faith is as strong as yours."

Libbey smiled. "You know it only takes faith the size of a teensy little mustard seed, right?"

Sam couldn't help smiling back. "I've heard that."

They listened to the wind in the trees for several moments before Libbey broke the pensive silence. "Can I ask you a question?"

"Sure. Shoot."

The young woman took a deep breath and looked away before she spoke. "Do you think I should give my baby up for adoption, or raise him myself?"

Oh, my. "Ah..." Sam wiped her hands on her shorts to buy time. "Why don't you ask Emma Jean?"

"I will. But I want to know what you think."

Past and present merged in a weird

kaleidoscope in Sam's mind. *What should I do, Annie?* She'd asked. *I can't tell you what to do, Sam. You have to follow your heart.*

Was that the right answer for this young girl? Sam had been twenty-two then; Libbey was only sixteen. It was different, and yet it wasn't.

"Look, Libbey, I'm really the wrong person to ask for advice."

"But you've been through it. You know." There was desperation in her voice.

"Emma Jean talks too much," she muttered. She chose her words with extreme care. "First, if Emma Jean told you my story, I expect you to keep it confidential. For my daughter's sake."

Libbey nodded. "Of course. I'd never tell anyone. And really, Emma Jean didn't tell me. I figured it out."

Sam took a deep breath. "When I found myself pregnant, I was a lot older than you are."

"You were twenty-two. I know. Did you love Lindsey's father?"

Did she? Could you love someone you'd only known for seventy-two hours? Sam settled for, "I cared for him very much. But even more important, I believe all babies are precious, no matter how they get here."

"So abortion wasn't an option."

"Never. The only question was whether to raise her or not."

"I heard about your dad."

Sam saw the sympathy and understanding in Libbey's eyes. "He was not a nice man when he drank. I heard something similar about yours."

"Yeah."

"Look, Libbey. I can't tell you what to do. Only you can decide, because you will have to live with your decision forever."

"Were you scared?"

"Of giving birth?"

"No. Of being a mother."

Sam laughed. "Terrified. Sometimes I still am. I've never been mother material, but I'm trying."

"You're doing a great job. Lindsey's awesome."

Emotion welled in Sam's heart like a physical pressure. It tried pushing its way out in tears, but she blinked them back. "Thank you, Libbey. Listen to your heart on this one, okay, and do what's right for your baby. Whether it's raising him or letting someone else raise him. Whatever choice you make, do it out of love."

Libbey threw herself into Sam's arms and burst into tears. Sam wrapped her arms around her, realizing again how very young she was, and murmured soothing words as she stroked her hair. She glanced over the young woman's shoulder and saw Emma Jean peeking through the curtains, white teeth gleaming in her dark face.

Finally, Libbey pulled away. "Sorry."

Sam tipped up her chin. "Don't be sorry. Hormones are crazy things. You'll figure it out, okay?"

"Thank you." And she turned and disappeared into the house.

****

When Sam pulled up in front of the marina a short time later, she was surprised to see Danny Hastings sitting on her porch steps. He stood as she approached and by the light of the security lamp, he looked exhausted and drained.

"Is everything okay?" she blurted, then shook her head. "I mean, has something else happened?"

"Don't worry, I know what you meant. No, there's no more news—good, bad, or otherwise."

"Then what brings you out here this late?"

He massaged the back of his neck and averted his gaze as though he wasn't sure himself. Then he stopped and stared at Sam like a wolf sighting his prey. He didn't move, didn't blink. The breeze ruffled the branches overhead, bringing with it the marshy scent of the river.

Under his scrutiny, awareness skimmed along Sam's nerve endings and hummed deep in her belly. Because of the shadows, his eyes looked black, dark with longing. Conflicting emotions raced through her. The intensity reflected in his eyes made Sam want to leap into his arms and never let go. Or, run screaming in the other direction. Maybe both.

Mouth dry, she didn't move, just watched. And waited.

He cleared his throat, fiddled with his watch a moment, then shrugged before he met her gaze again.

"I just wanted to be sure Lindsey was okay. And I heard your husband died. I wanted to offer my condolences."

Sam looked away. "It was a long time ago."

"I know. But it's never easy to lose someone you love."

Sam met his eyes and once again found she couldn't look away. Did he know? Could he possibly understand, how much losing him had hurt?

He stepped towards her and before Sam could back up or figure out his intention, he cupped her face between his palms. Trapped, Sam stood still, too shocked to move; too warmed by his gentle touch to pull away.

"You're so beautiful," he murmured. "I'd forgotten just how much."

He stared into her eyes as time stretched between them, a fragile thread neither wanted to break. Slowly, inch by inch, he leaned closer and Sam found herself straining to meet him halfway. Up close, his eyes burned with blue flame, warming her from the top of her head to the soles of her feet.

But inches before his lips touched hers, he caught himself. With obvious regret, he placed a gentle kiss on her forehead and stepped back, his hands hanging awkwardly at this sides. He cleared his throat. "Let me know if there's anything I can do for you, all right?"

Stunned, Sam could only nod. His best friend was dead, yet he wanted to know if he could help her? Unable to find any words, she stood in the moonlight and watched as Danny got into his car and drove away.

****

It was after one in the morning when Luke Porter plopped down in his ancient leather chair and gulped another slug of coffee, hoping to revive a few more brain cells. He was exhausted. But tired he could deal with. It was having a problem with no solutions that nagged at him.

Jeremy Castle was dead, the apparent victim of an alligator attack. Not out of the realm of possibility along the Withlacoochee River. Except gators were opportunistic feeders. It was unusual for one to attack a grown man. They usually went for smaller prey, since they were easier to manage.

The other piece of the puzzle was where the body, or at least the first body part, was found. All along that stretch, the bank was above the river, a small ledge hollowed out by the water underneath and supported by tree roots. No way on earth could a short-legged gator lunge up from the water to reach someone standing along the riverbank. The angle was too steep.

Luke tapped his pencil on his desk. So Castle had to have been in the water for some reason. But Luke wouldn't get any more answers until the divers found the rest of the body. If they found it. Their best hope was that the gator had wedged it under a submerged rock or tree root so he could come back for it later. If it had broken loose, the current would carry Castle's body to the Gulf and they would never find him.

They'd found the guilty gator, which was a start. Porter knew the district attorney would chew him out for letting Sam catch the gator, but he hadn't had a lot of options. Besides, he'd had Sanchez with her the whole time. If she was guilty, and that was a great, big gaping IF in Porter's mind, she wouldn't have had an opportunity to destroy any evidence.

Luke swallowed more coffee and grimaced. The stuff could peel paint off a car. The biggest question now was how—and why—Jeremy Castle had gotten into the river.

He checked his watch and stood, stretching the kinks from his back. Might as well get a few hours shut-eye. The divers would be out at first light and he'd head over to interview Sam and her daughter. He'd known Lindsey all her life and didn't want to scare her, but his gut was telling him she either knew more than she was saying or had seen something she shouldn't. In either case, he'd have to tread lightly, or Sam would go mother-bear on him. But he had a suspicious death here and he intended to get to the bottom of it.

Actually, he had more than one. Hastings words ran through his mind. *This is too small a town to have this many deaths.* Luke scrubbed the stubble on his chin as a greasy churning started in his gut. He couldn't dismiss the man's words. First, he'd get to the bottom of Castle's death; then he'd figure out what else was going on in Riverlake. And pray like hell the two weren't connected.

The gleam of headlights flashed in his office window. Luke peered out between the metal blinds and groaned as a news van drove up. When one came, the rest weren't far behind. Great, despite his warnings, someone in the department had let the news slip to a spouse or family member and he was about to become the main course of a media feeding frenzy. Definitely time to go home.

He grabbed his Stetson and walked out the back door into the alley. Maybe, just maybe, he could catch an hour-long nap.

****

Danny sat in his room at The Azalea House with his cell phone pressed to his ear. On the other end, Laurie sobbed and hiccupped trying to talk, but he couldn't make out a word of it, so he just made soothing sounds and waited. He had no clue what else to do. He'd told Laurie what they'd found, but in reality, there was no concrete news. They had discovered a body part, not a body, though he knew Sam had found more evidence. Still, until the medical examiner made a positive identification and listed a cause of death nothing was certain. Danny had only his gut to go on, and his gut was telling him this was Jeremy's body. He suspected the sheriff agreed, but was bound by protocol.

Danny stared at the blue morning glories marching across the wallpaper and squirmed in the blue-cushioned white wicker chair, trying to get comfortable. He felt like he could suffocate in all the girly stuff. How did men get themselves talked into staying in these places?

Suddenly, a picture of Sam, blonde hair spread across the flowered pillowcase, arms open in welcome and wearing nothing but a smile popped into his head. His blood heated and he shifted in the chair again. Okay, yeah, he could see why men stayed in places like these.

"What are we going to do?" Laurie wailed. Or at least that's what it sounded like.

"Look, Laurie, I'm going to stay here and find out all I can. The divers will be out in the morning."

"Oh, my poor baby," Laurie sobbed, drowning

out the rest of his words. "This just can't be happening. It can't."

"Are the girls asleep?" he asked softly, hoping to encourage her to lower her voice.

She sniffed. "Yes, I tucked them in a while ago."

"What did you tell them?"

"What do you think I told them?" she demanded. "What do you take me for?"

"Whoa, Laurie. It was just a question. If I talk to them in the morning, I don't want to say the wrong thing."

He waited while she sobbed some more, the sound muffled as though she had something over her mouth. "I told them they think Daddy might have gotten lost in the woods, but they have people looking for him."

Danny stood and paced. Not the sort of answer to help the girls sleep, but he supposed there wasn't a good one, short of flat-out lying. But the girls were smart. They'd be more worried if they thought the adults were trying to hide something from them. "Try to get some sleep. I'll keep you posted, all right?"

"Do you really think I can sleep when my husband is dead?" she wailed.

Danny bit back his frustration. "Try to lower your voice, Laurie. You'll wake the girls. Besides, there is no proof it's Jeremy." Not yet, anyway.

Once he hung up, Danny booted up his partner's laptop. He wasn't sure what he was looking for, exactly, but he figured he'd know it when he saw it.

Danny swallowed hard as he scrolled through Jeremy's list of files and folders. He stopped when he came to one Jeremy had password protected. Didn't take him long to figure out the password. Jeremy was a creature of habit, so after he'd tried his and Laurie's birthdays, Danny hit pay dirt with their anniversary date. *Not smart, buddy. Too easy to figure out.*

He opened one of the protected files and started reading. Several minutes later, he flopped back in the chair, his blood running cold.

Oh, Jeremy. What have you done? Danny scanned the files again, hoping he was wrong, but he wasn't. His friend had leveraged all his personal assets on this deal. If it didn't go through, Laurie and the girls would have nothing. Absolutely nothing.

Danny lunged to his feet and started pacing again. Eventually, two thoughts forced themselves to the front: For Laurie and the girls, he had to make sure the deal went through. He had no choice.

And he had to figure out if Jeremy's death was an accident—or murder.

Chapter Eight

Lindsey sat on the edge of her bed and tried to calm her racing heart. She'd gotten dressed, brushed her hair—three times—packed her backpack and even made her bed and put her clothes away. She couldn't stall any more.

Her stomach cramped and she wrapped her arms around her middle, rocking back and forth. How could she tell them what she saw when she couldn't remember?

She leaped from her bed, raced down the hall and made it to the bathroom just in time to throw up in the toilet.

"Lindsey, are you okay, honey?" her mom asked through the door.

Lindsey's hands were shaking as she grabbed a towel and wiped her face. "I don't feel so good."

Mom poked her head in and wrinkled her nose at the smell. She leaned over and flushed the toilet, then felt Lindsey's forehead. "No fever. Good." She gave her one of those Mom-looks and Lindsey turned her face away. "Are you upset over what's been happening, Princess?"

Lindsey nodded, deciding it was the best answer. That way, she couldn't get into any more trouble. Maybe she'd just never say anything again, ever.

There was a knock on the bathroom door. "Lindsey, Sam, Sheriff Porter is here."

"We'll be right out," Mom called, then turned to her and cupped her chin. "Just tell the sheriff the truth, okay? We'll sort everything else out later."

Lindsey launched herself into her mother's arms. "I'm sorry. I'm so sorry."

Mom rocked her back and forth, patting her back and for once, Lindsey didn't care, didn't pull back and tell Mom she was too old for mushy stuff. She just wanted someone to make her feel safe.

****

"Is there anything else you want to tell me about the other night, Lindsey? Did you see or hear anything else? Anyone else?"

Lindsey seemed to shrink into herself at the question. Head down, arms wrapped around her middle, she kept shaking her head. All of Luke's police instincts screamed for him to push just a little harder. Was it possible she'd been a witness to Castle's murder? Or was Lindsey simply rattled by all the questioning?

For the investigation's sake, a witness would be good. For the girl's sake, simply finding a phone while sneaking out at night was safest.

Luke sighed. He pulled a card from his pocket and slid it across the table. "Thanks for your help, Lindsey. I want you to take my card and if you remember anything else about that night, anything at all, I want you to call me, day or night. All right?"

She nodded, gingerly picking up the card as though it were live ammunition. "Can I go now?"

Sam kissed her forehead. "Go, or you'll miss the bus. I love you," Sam added as Lindsey dashed from the room.

As soon as she was gone, Sam turned to him with shrewd eyes. "What do you think she knows?"

"I'm not sure, but I think there's something she's not saying. If you find out, will you let me know?"

Hesitating, Sam nodded as she studied him a long moment. "I know you didn't just come here to question my daughter, Sheriff, so you might as well

90

get on with it. I have things to do."

Luke sighed. "Look Sam, you know I have to ask. I have a death to investigate."

Her chin came up defiantly and Luke saw her father reflected in her eyes: a hard stare daring anyone to mess with her family. That stance, and Katharine's staunch refusal to press charges were the only things that had kept Luke from arresting the sorry son-of-a-bitch years ago. Thankfully, the old buzzard was dead and couldn't cause any more trouble.

But was his daughter capable of violence to protect what was hers? Luke couldn't make the image gel in his mind, but after a lifetime in law enforcement, he knew he needed more than gut instinct to go on.

He pulled out his notebook and made her go over the night of Castle's death one more time, ignoring her impatience. He was almost done when his cell phone rang. "Porter."

"Sheriff, this is dispatch. Got a call from Rupert. Says he found a fancy car in the woods not far from where we found the body."

"Thanks, Alice. Tell me where."

"Rupert said it was too well hidden to find on your own, but he'll meet you at his place and take you there on foot."

"Tell him I'll be there in twenty minutes."

He tucked the phone back into the case at his belt, stuck his notebook in his shirt pocket and stood. "I'll just check in with your mama before I go."

Sam led him out to the front porch, where Katharine sat in a wooden rocker, knitting on her lap.

"Good morning, Ma'am. Wondered if I could ask you a few questions."

Katharine looked up, but wouldn't meet his eyes. Behind him, Sam cleared her throat. "I'll be

91

down at the marina if you need me, Mama. Joe's working this morning, right?"

Katharine nodded and kept knitting. "Have a seat, Sheriff, and ask your questions." She looked over at him then, her eyes hot. "Though understand I won't help you charge my daughter with something she didn't do."

Again there was fierce protectiveness. No wonder Sam was so tough. He cleared his throat. "The night Jeremy Castle showed up here, did you hear the conversation?"

A faint blush tinged her cheeks and she wouldn't meet his eyes. "It isn't polite to eavesdrop."

"It's even more impolite to evade a question from the sheriff," he returned.

Her head snapped up and she met his gaze squarely. "I overheard him again try to buy our property and I heard Sam tell him again that no, she wasn't selling. He told her this wasn't over."

"What did Sam have to say?"

Katharine looked away and sighed. "She said if he kept harassing us, he'd be sorry."

Luke's eyebrows shot up.

"She meant she'd hire a lawyer to protect our family, she told me so," Katharine added in a rush, obviously realizing how such an admission sounded.

"What happened then?"

"Mr. Castle got back in his car and drove off."

"Did Sam come back inside afterwards?"

Katharine picked up her knitting and studied her hands as she worked. Her voice, when she finally answered, was soft. "I don't know. I went to bed and didn't see her until the next morning."

"Did you hear her leave?"

She shook her head.

Luke studied her a moment and played a hunch. "Do you want her to sell the property, Katharine?"

Silence. Then a shrug, nothing more. Luke

waited, then glanced at his watch. He stood, and reached into his pocket. Drawing out a card, he scribbled on the back and handed it to her. "My cell number is on the back. If you ever need—or want—to get in touch with me, call. Any time, day or night."

She met his eyes for one brief second. He thought he caught a fleeting glimpse of longing, but it was gone too quickly for him to be sure. What would it take to break through the barriers she'd constructed around her heart? After the hurt he caused when they were young, would she ever give him another chance?

Luke jammed his Stetson on his head as he headed for his SUV. Not trying to pin a murder rap on her daughter would probably be a good start.

Muttering over his own wayward thoughts, he roared out of the gravel driveway and made tracks to Rupert's shack. Maybe Castle's car would provide some clues.

****

After Porter left, Sam waited a while for her heartbeat to slow. Somehow, she couldn't get past the idea Lindsey knew more than she was saying. Maybe if they spent a little time together…

She walked out onto the porch, where Katharine was absentmindedly knitting and staring off down the road the sheriff had just traveled. "Mama, could you take care of things here for a while? I thought maybe Lindsey and I would take a ride into Dunnellon, do a little shopping." Sam's smile was wry. "She says she missed the bus."

Katharine met her gaze squarely. "Might give you a chance to find out what's really going on with our young-un."

"Exactly what I'm thinking."

Sam went back inside and knocked on Lindsey's door. She found her daughter lying on her pink bedspread, staring at the ceiling. "Want to do a little shopping? Pick up a few groceries?"

Lindsey sat up and wiped the tear tracks from her face. "Okay."

They were halfway to town when Lindsey turned to her and asked, voice tentative, "Why don't we stop and buy you a skirt, Mommy?"

Sam froze. Her heart started hammering and racing, trying to outrun her fear. She swallowed. "Um...we'll see."

Lindsey crossed her arms and sighed. "You always say that."

Sam forced a smile. "Well, it's better than 'no,' right? So, we'll see."

It's only a skirt, it's only a skirt, it's only a skirt.

Sam kept repeating the words in her head the rest of the trip into town. She really needed to get a grip. Clothes couldn't hurt her and Pop couldn't either. The time in third grade when Pop had caught her wearing that pretty flowered Goodwill dress was ancient history. He couldn't hurt her now. Knowing the truth didn't slow her heart rate one iota or keep her from having to wipe her sweaty palms on her shorts.

Beside her, Lindsey kept her face to the wind, staring out at the pastures racing by. When she finally turned towards her, Sam braced for the question she knew was coming.

"Why don't you wear skirts? I know you work outside and everything, but I think you'd look nice."

Oh, what to say. She'd always tried to keep some of the uglier truths about Amos from his granddaughter. She knew Lindsey would hear the local gossip sooner or later, so she'd never lied, but she'd left out volumes about the past. Maybe it was time to tell her part of the story, at least.

"A long time ago, Memaw and your grandfather had a son named Robert. He died when I was seven, but your grandfather never got over it, I guess. He really, really wanted a son and he, um, sort of expected me to take Robert's place."

While Sam searched for the right words to continue, Lindsey said, "Is that why he taught you boy's stuff, like hunting and fishing and catching gators?"

Sam smiled. "Yeah. And I didn't really mind, 'cause I love to be outside."

"Was it hard, killing things?"

Sam sighed. "Yeah, it was — still is. But here's the thing, Lindsey, we never took down an animal just for sport. Every single time we went hunting, we ate the meat. There's a big difference between sport killing and hunting for food. Do you understand?"

"Sure. So did Grandpop not like it if you wore a skirt?"

Ah, trust a child to grasp the heart of the matter. Sam unconsciously rubbed a hand over her rib cage, remembering how Pop showed his opinions with his fists, and then caught herself. "Yeah, you could say that. I think it was hard on him to be reminded I wasn't Robert and dressing like a girl did that, so I avoided it."

Lindsey nodded and turned her face into the wind for the rest of the trip. Sam slowly released a pent-up breath and continued her mental pep talk all the way into the women's section of the local discount store.

"Oh, Mommy. Look at this one," Lindsey exclaimed, racing over to a rack of filmy skirts in watercolor shades. She pulled one out and thrust it at Sam. "Feel this. Isn't it soft?"

Sam ran a tentative hand over the fabric, remembering another skirt, another time. *"But isn't it pretty, Pop? I won't wear it anywhere except church, I promise."* In her ears, Pop's roar still echoed through the years, bunching her hands into fists.

"Mommy? Here's another one. Try this one, too. Oh, and look at these shirts. They go with the skirts."

Sam blindly reached out, desperate to focus on the present, to keep the past from reaching from beyond the grave and paralyzing her.

She found herself standing in the dressing room, an armful of skirts draped over her arm and her daughter watching her with a hopeful, yet wary, expression.

"You're going to look really pretty, Mom."

Sam swallowed hard, pulled off her shorts and yanked on the skirt, carefully avoiding the mirror. The fabric slid over her legs and swirled softly around her calves. Sam couldn't breathe. Her hands shook and her throat went dry. She stripped off the skirt and scrambled back into her shorts. "We'll take them. Let's go."

"But Mommy," Lindsey said, scrambling to keep up with Sam who was almost running towards the check-out counter. "You didn't try on the others. Or the shirts."

"They're all the same size. I'm sure they'll fit. We have to go."

They stood in line, Sam's chest heaving and Lindsey watching her warily as if she was a bee that had bumbled into the house. "Are you okay, Mommy?"

Sam's smile was all teeth. "I'm fine, really. I just remembered something I need to do."

****

He sat at the counter at the Lady Bug and listened to the rise and fall of voices all around him. The main topic on everyone's lips was the discovery of a body—or at least part of a body—down by the river. Everyone was sure it was the missing developer.

He frowned. This was not good. They'd found Castle too quick, before time and nature could finish the clean-up process.

Newspaper reporters sat in clusters at four different booths, while several television vans lined the sidewalk, their cameramen shooting footage of the sheriff's office across the street, though Porter had not made an appearance this morning.

Speculation on the cause of death ran from a random alligator attack—his personal favorite—to premeditated murder.

In their usual booth, Tommy Sooner, Rudy Emerson and Bill Farley watched the goings-on. He could tell Sooner was itching for an opportunity to stand in the spotlight. The man had political pipe dreams, and this situation fed right into his delusions of grandeur. Sure as shooting, within two minutes, he stood and scanned the room as though he were giving a press conference and patted the air with his hands until the noise died down.

"Ladies and gentlemen of the media, my name is Tommy Sooner and I'm a city commissioner. I heard several of you asking about the missing man, Jeremy Castle. Since he was a developer from California and my colleagues and I had just met with him hours before his disappearance, perhaps I can answer some questions for you."

The room erupted into chaos the likes of which the Lady Bug hadn't seen since 1984, when the rival high school's football team made the mistake of stopping at the diner after defeating the local boys.

An ear splitting whistle sounded and everyone fell silent. Carl, the Lady Bug's cook and a former boxer, stood with his arms crossed over his beefy chest. "You all either do this nice and quiet-like, or you do it outside. Your choice." He scanned the room at large, then disappeared behind the swinging door.

Immediately, hands shot up around the silent

room and Tommy Sooner began calling on reporters like a teacher choosing his favorite students to answer questions.

The man kept his eyes averted, looking up just often enough to match voices and faces. You never knew when such information would come in handy. The police had squat at this point. Or at least, the reporters didn't know anything. Luke Porter could be close-mouthed as a clam.

Satisfied, he shrugged. So far, there was lots of speculation with no real information.

"What about the phone?" A perky little blonde reporter asked Sooner the question he'd hoped no one would ask.

He stiffened. They'd found Castle's phone?

Sooner frowned. "I'm afraid I don't know anything about a phone, young lady."

"My source tells me a local kid, a Lindsey Collins, found it in the woods near where the...ah...body was found."

While Sooner hemmed and hawed, the listener aligned his silverware with military precision, his mind clicking through a list of possible scenarios. Lindsey found Castle's phone?

"If you have questions about an active investigation, young lady, I suggest you ask them of the right people."

All eyes turned to the Lady Bug's front door, where Sheriff Porter stood blocking the entrance, scowling under his Stetson.

The young reporter didn't miss a beat. "What can you tell us, Sheriff?"

He scanned the room before his hard gaze returned to the blonde. "I can tell you if I catch any one of you anywhere near the Collins girl, you will answer to me." He waited a beat. "Do I make myself clear?"

Heads nodded. Then the blonde spoke again.

"Have you made a positive identification on the, ah, remains yet, Sheriff?"

He nodded once. "They belong to Jeremy Castle." When more hands shot up he said, "That's all. Now, if you're done eating, I suggest you move along."

"Are you going out to the Collins place, Sheriff?"

"I'm going to conduct my investigation. I'll brief you here at four p.m. If you get in my way, I'll have you locked up."

"What about the power of the press?" One older reporter growled.

The sheriff acknowledged him with a nod. "You know me well enough by now, Dutch, to know I mean what I say. Good day, ladies and gentlemen."

Once the sheriff disappeared, the room erupted in angry conversation. From the kitchen, Carl banged on the little silver bell he used to signal the waitresses. The reporters took the hint and formed a line in front of Darla at the register.

They'd identified the body.

Lindsey Collins had found Castle's cell phone. What else did she know?

He needed to find out.

****

Sam sat on the dock, repairing one of the pontoon boat's lines. As she scanned the bright sky, she had a queasy, unsettled feeling in the pit of her stomach that just wouldn't go away—and it had nothing to do with their earlier trip to town. Like an approaching storm, something menacing hovered in the air, not yet visible, but moving towards them nonetheless.

What if Lindsey had been attacked by the alligator, instead of Castle? What if someone had killed Castle and—please, God, no—Lindsey saw it?

Sam forced the last part away for now. It was too terrifying, too incomprehensible. Gators she understood; murderers, she did not. Instead, she thought about Castle. As far as she knew, no one had any reason to kill him. Her stomach flip-flopped. Except her. Surely Porter didn't believe she'd murdered anyone, did he?

A car pulled up the gravel drive and stopped. Sam didn't need to look up to know who it was. Danny Hastings' rented Mustang had a distinctive growl. Plus, her body radar buzzed any time he came within twenty yards.

Sam kept her eyes trained on her task as he approached.

"Hello, Sam."

When she looked up at him from her sitting position, he looked haggard, even though dark sunglasses covered his eyes. He held out a hand and she eyed it warily before accepting his hand up. It would be childish to refuse and she didn't like looking up at him.

"What brings you here, Mr. Hastings?" she asked formally, once they were eye to eye.

A half smile glimmered, then disappeared. "Why not call me Danny? The Mr. makes me think you're talking to my father."

She shrugged and gave in. "What do you want, Danny?"

"I'd like to talk to Lindsey."

"Why?"

"Because she found Jeremy's cell phone."

Sam crossed her arms over her chest. "Sheriff Porter questioned her this morning."

"I'd like to talk to her myself."

She shook her head. "Sorry. No."

"Why not? I'm not going to bully her."

"I don't know that," Sam shot back. "I don't know you at all."

"You did, once."

And only once. And it had taken her years to get

over him. "The past is off limits. I won't discuss it with you."

His voice lowered intimately. "Don't you ever think about what might have been?"

Only every time I see Lindsey. "Look, that should never have happened. You know it. I know it. I don't want to rehash it with you."

Silence stretched between them, broken only by the rustle of wind in the treetops. "You're even more beautiful now than you were then."

He'd said the same thing before. The quiet words pierced a long-hidden corner of her heart, but she refused to let him see the way they affected her. "I have a daughter to raise and a business to run. I'm not interested in a relationship. Certainly not another one-night stand."

His smile was charmingly boyish. "Neither am I, but would it hurt to have a cup of coffee with me?"

More than you know. "I'm not interested. I'm sorry." Sam turned back towards the marina, but a hand on her arm stayed her.

"The ring was Jeremy's."

Sam sucked in a breath. For a moment, she'd forgotten about his friend, about the investigation. She'd let herself be lulled by his wonderful voice and apparent interest in her. But he was Jeremy Castle's partner, part of the team determined to destroy her family's marina. They were enemies, in the truest sense of the word. So why was it so hard to walk away from the warmth in his eyes?

"I'm sorry. I was hoping he was merely lost."

"But after you cut open the gator yesterday, you knew he wasn't."

Sam heaved a sigh. "I knew the remains were human. I was hoping they didn't belong to your friend."

"Did you kill him?"

Sam met his gaze head on, speechless. She

couldn't believe he'd asked such a blunt question. But she understood. So she answered in kind. "No. I was angry at him for pushing me, angry for the way the commissioners were trying to get my property by force, but I didn't kill him. I have a daughter. I can't raise her from a prison cell."

A sudden chill ran down her spine and raised gooseflesh on her arms. If, in fact, she went to prison, would this man take Lindsey from her? The idea was too horrible to contemplate.

"If you didn't kill him, then who did?"

"Who says anyone killed him? Has the medical examiner announced his findings?"

"I don't think so, but I have a hard time believing he went swimming alone in the dark, way out there. Don't you?"

"I don't know. Anything's possible. I didn't think my daughter would wander out there alone either, but she did." As soon as the words left her mouth, she wanted to call them back. She didn't want him thinking about Lindsey. Not now, not ever.

"I think somebody murdered him. And I intend to find out who. And why."

"Sheriff Porter will figure it out. He won't stop until he has answers."

"I'm not going to sit around waiting for a small-town sheriff to get his team of Barney Fifes organized. I'm going to do what I need to figure this out."

He paused, studying her in a way that made her cheeks heat. "Will you help me?"

Sam's heart thundered in her ears. "I'm sorry; I can't." She looked away.

The silence lengthened.

"Can't? Or won't?"

Heart pounding with regret and fear, Sam started up the dock. "Both. I'm sorry."

****

At one o'clock the same afternoon, Danny walked into the city commission's conference room and shook hands with the men gathered across the sagging table from him. "Mr. Sooner, thanks for setting this up so quickly." The other man's capped teeth reflected the overhead light, nearly blinding him.

"Mr. Emerson, Mr. Farley, thanks for coming." Danny sat down on a metal folding chair and pulled documents and a yellow legal pad from his soft-sided leather briefcase. At the head of the table, Tommy Sooner made a great show of removing a pad from a locked briefcase the size of an orange crate. Across the table, Emerson and Farley exchanged glances and pulled pens from their shirt pockets.

"As I told Mr. Sooner over the phone, since I wasn't here for your meeting with my partner, I'd like a recap of your conversation with him, if you would."

The three men exchanged looks. Sooner spoke up first. "Mr. Hastings..." he cleared his throat, "What are your plans with regard to the development?"

Danny had expected the question. So much of what he did was bluffing, with a smidge of Academy-Award acting thrown in. This was one of those times, despite his personal feelings. "I am going to proceed, Mr. Sooner." He looked the other man straight in the eye. "Why wouldn't I?"

Sooner flushed and looked away. The question was whether the pompous idiot had something to hide, or if he found the idea of focusing on business right now repugnant, given the current investigation.

Sooner ran a finger along the collar of his shirt, then eyed his two cronies. "What with Mr. Castle's, er, demise, we thought you might reconsider, but..."

And under normal circumstances, he'd be

absolutely right, Danny thought. But these were not normal circumstances. Danny was beginning to think the answers to Jeremy's death were far more complicated than they appeared. If he kept the development plans in play, he had the perfect excuse to stick around and look for answers.

Danny's trained eye noticed Rudy Emerson's upper lip was beaded with sweat and Bill Farley refused to meet his eyes. Something was definitely up.

"In light of Jeremy's death, the plans will develop more slowly of course, but they will continue."

Sooner cleared his throat. "Mr. Hastings, you have our heartfelt condolences on your loss, but...ah...you can't slow things down."

Danny raised a brow. "Why not?"

Again, the three exchanged looks. "We had an agreement with Mr. Castle, and part of it entailed a strict timeline."

Danny flipped through the pages he'd printed from Jeremy's computer. "Was this outside the official paperwork?"

Sooner nodded once. "It was an additional incentive and reward package designed to benefit both parties. We've upheld our part of it and we, ah, expect you to uphold your company's." Sooner rooted around in his huge briefcase and handed over a two-page document.

Danny read the document, his frustration growing with every sentence. If he reneged, or even slowed things down by a week, these bozos would sue Castle Development for breach of contract and he'd owe them even more money. He couldn't believe Jeremy had signed something so incredibly stupid. Slowdowns and delays were the rule in development, not the exception. Danny felt the noose tighten around his neck.

He stood and shoved his papers into his briefcase. "Gentlemen, you've been very helpful. I'll be in touch."

****

Bill Farley ran a hand through his thinning hair and said exactly what Tommy was thinking. "That boy's got something up his sleeve, but I don't know what."

Rudy snorted. "You think everybody's up to something. You need to quit watching Law & Order re-runs."

"He may be right this time," Tommy agreed. "I think he wants out of the deal. It's up to us to make sure he doesn't." Tommy casually stuck his hands under the table and wiped his sweaty palms on his slacks.

"You think he can get Sam to sell?" Rudy asked.

"He sure is a charmer," Tommy commented. "He could, if anyone can." And he'd better. Tommy ran a finger around his suddenly too-tight collar. Time was slipping away like sand through an hourglass. His situation got more precarious with every passing day.

"What about Katharine? Think he can convince her to sell?"

Tommy tapped his chin. "Maybe. Or maybe I'll give it a shot. Tell her how much easier her life could be without so much hard work."

"And if she won't?" Rudy asked.

Tommy considered his options for a moment. "We need to schedule a hearing on eminent domain right away. It will give us a little insurance. We'll get the property either way."

"Sam will fight," Rudy said.

Tommy smiled. "She will, but what good will it do? She'll have to get a lawyer, and she can't afford one. And she'll need community support and, well..." he let the thought trail off. Everyone knew Sam was an odd one. A misfit.

"You think we'll still be able to fish out there once this development goes through?" Bill asked.

Rudy whapped the back of his head. "Course. It's part of the deal. We get free use for the rest of our lives. We told Castle, and we'll make sure Hastings knows it, too."

Bill looked from him to Rudy and back again. "You think Sam killed him?"

"Wouldn't put it past her. Her old man turned up dead in the river, too. Seems too convenient, if you ask me," Rudy responded.

The men nodded and rose.

"I'll schedule the hearing." Tommy walked out with them, but he ignored their banter. The CPA would be coming to audit the commission's books soon. They were running out of time.

Chapter Nine

The lawyer Emma Jean had recommended worked out of a renovated Victorian in downtown Ocala. John Brantley, Esquire, had been an old college chum of Emma Jean's late husband Henry. The minute Sam pulled into the parking lot, she realized she was completely out of her league. This gleaming structure was the epitome of what Haven House used to be.

Sam parked the Jeep and got out, rubbing her hands on her khaki slacks. Maybe today would have been a good day to wear one of those skirts still lying in their shopping bag against the back wall of her closet. She glanced around the discreet parking area. Where was Emma Jean?

Just as Sam was ready to hop in her Jeep and leave, Emma Jean's ancient Toyota came chugging into the parking lot, belching black smoke.

Sam waved the smoke away from her face, opened the door and helped her friend out of the car. "I can fix this, you know."

Emma Jean smiled widely and patted Sam's cheek. "I know, honey, and I appreciate the offer, but right now, you have your hands full. Besides," she added with a coy smile, "there's a certain gentleman mechanic I am hoping will take an interest."

"In you, or in the car?" Sam responded, laughing.

"Both, of course," she said primly, heading up the walk without a backward glance.

Sam was still laughing as she caught up to her

on the expansive front porch. She stopped abruptly and leaned closer to her friend. "I think this may have been a very bad idea."

"Nonsense. It'll be fine. You'll see."

"Emma Jean, this place reeks of money. Which I don't have."

"We want the best, honey. Brantley is it."

"But I can't afford him."

"Let's deal with one thing at a time, okay?"

They walked into a reception area of gleaming woods and antique furnishings, their footsteps muted by a thick Persian rug. A perfectly groomed young receptionist ushered them into an office dominated by a desk large enough to seat eighteen people comfortably. Behind it, a portly man wearing horn-rimmed glasses glanced up and a smile dimpled all three chins.

He rose and rounded the desk, his immaculately tailored jacket straining the buttons. "Emma Jean. So very lovely to see you, my dear. How are you?"

Emma Jean performed the introductions amidst a flurry of handshakes. "You know why we're here, John, and I'm hoping you can help us."

Brantley waved them into seats across from him and opened a folder on his desk. For the next hour, he spouted legalese and precedents until Sam lost what little hope she had. The only thing she really understood was how community support was the key to saving the marina. If what he said was true, they were wasting everyone's time. No one would help her. Many of them still thought she'd killed her own father, and others saw only dollar signs and progress with this development. No, she was on her own.

She tuned back into the conversation in time to hear Emma Jean say, "You know we don't have that kind of money, John."

"For what?" Sam blurted. They both looked at her in surprise.

Emma Jean sent her a sympathetic look. "John will represent you pro bono, but he thinks step one is to get the marina and Haven House in top shape so they can't declare the property blighted."

Sam thought of all the repairs she'd been putting off, from new roofs on the outbuildings to updating the outdated electrical system. And that was just the marina, never mind Haven House.

The meager hope flickering in Sam's heart died. She stood and offered her hand. "We're sorry for wasting your time. But thank you for your advice."

"Look Ms. Collins, I'd really like to help you. I feel strongly about this case and I think we can win if we—"

"We'll have a fundraiser," Emma Jean interrupted. "We'll raise the money, do the work and keep having fundraisers as we go. We'll get the community involved."

Sam stared at her as if she'd grown another head. "The people of Riverlake aren't going to help me, Emma Jean. And you know most of them don't think much of Haven House either."

Emma Jean's face took on its sternest expression. "Where is your faith, girlfriend? This situation stinks to high heaven. God will intervene and rally the good citizens of Riverlake. I firmly believe it."

Brantley smiled, his eyes bright with zeal. "I'll get the preliminary paperwork started, find out when the hearing is going to be. You ladies work on things from your end, the most important of which is community support, all right?"

Sam mumbled something she hoped was polite and walked out in a daze.

"We're going to fight, Sam, and we're going to win."

"How can you say such a thing? You heard the man!"

109

"God has a plan. He always does. But He also expects us to do our part. Are you with me, girlfriend?"

Sam sighed. What choice did she have?

You'll never make it work, Sam. You're just a girl. Girls are worthless.

It's not over yet, Pop. We've only begun to fight.

"Okay, Emma Jean. Tell me what you're thinking." She checked Emma Jean's watch. "You'll have to hurry, though. I have a river cruise scheduled in a bit."

By the time she reached the marina, Sam's head was spinning.

****

Luke pulled up at Rupert's dilapidated shack and climbed out of the SUV, feeling every one of his fifty-eight years. The humidity wrapped around him with the same heavy certainty he felt about this case. It was going to get worse. He'd been a cop too long to assume the easiest answer was the right one. Conversely, he'd also learned the right answer often sat squarely in front of everyone's face.

He jammed his Stetson on his head and turned, blinking as Rupert suddenly appeared in front of him. "Geez, old man, you got to quit sneaking up on people, especially people toting guns."

Rupert grinned, revealing his two remaining teeth. "I figured if you're a good cop, you shoulda heard me."

Luke beetled his brows, enjoying their little game. "Didn't need to hear you; I could smell you at twenty yards."

Rupert laughed, then spit a stream of tobacco juice inches from Luke's cowboy boots. "I always hit what I'm aiming at."

Luke casually settled his hand on the holster at his hip. "Me too, old man. Me too."

"Come along, Sheriff, and I'll show you what I

found." Rupert darted down a path into the woods and disappeared.

Luke grimaced and hurried to keep up with the wily Cajun. Rupert had settled here back in '65, but he'd never lost his Cajun speech patterns, or his knack with a skinning knife. As a taxidermist and gator processor, he was the best around. Given that everyone, Luke included, overlooked Rupert's penchant for making whiskey in the still behind his shack.

He caught up to the other man and they tromped through the dense underbrush for about a quarter mile before Rupert stopped and pointed. "There."

Luke squinted and even knowing what he was looking for, it took a moment to make out the shape of the car. This was no rental haphazardly parked by a tourist heading off on a hike. This car had been deliberately hidden.

Luke sighed. Much as he'd been hoping Castle's death had simply been an accident, every piece of evidence pointed towards murder. He walked up to the BMW, but didn't get too close, in case there were footprints near it.

He pulled out his cell phone, scowling when he realized there was no signal. He walked all around the car, then squatted on his heels to study the ground. Only one set of prints leaving the car.

He walked around to the other side. No tracks.

"What you think, Sheriff? This de car of our missing developer?"

"Too soon to tell, my friend." He straightened. "I can't get a signal, but I need my crime scene tech out here. Will you bring him?"

"But of course." Rupert led the way back to Luke's SUV.

Luke had one foot in the vehicle when Rupert said, "Sam-Sam didn't do this, Sheriff."

He met the old man's eyes. "I have to look at all the evidence."

"If you look in that girl's eyes, you'll have all the evidence you need."

Luke nodded. "But we both know it isn't enough for a court of law."

"Maybe not," Rupert agreed. "But it is where you start. With the heart."

Luke got in and started the engine. "Thanks for the help, Rupert. I'll be in touch."

****

Sam closed the door to the couple's rental car and forced a bright smile. "Thanks for coming. Enjoy the rest of your trip to Florida."

She waited until the little station wagon disappeared in a cloud of dust before she heaved a sigh. The seventy-something Nolans from New Jersey had just finished their river cruise and not a moment too soon. Another ten minutes of Mrs. Nolan's shrill harping on her husband and she'd have tossed the overweight woman over the railing without a moment's remorse.

"Delightful couple, aren't they? And so affectionate."

Sam turned towards the lazy drawl, but she already knew who it belonged to. Seconds before Danny spoke, an unwelcome little quiver had traveled through her, alerting her to his presence. "What are you doing here?" she demanded. "I told you I don't want you around."

"No, actually, you said you couldn't help me investigate Jeremy's, ah, disappearance. A different matter entirely."

Sam stalked past him. "Go away, would you?"

"Well, now, that might be difficult, seeing as how I'll be staying here a while."

She whirled on him, studied his lazy stance, which was just shy of smug. "Not in this lifetime. Do

I have to call the sheriff and have you physically removed?"

He pulled off his dark sunglasses, let them dangle from the strap around his neck. "Might want to talk to Katharine first. Lovely woman, your mother. So nice of her to rent me one of those little cabins for a couple weeks."

Weeks? Sam stared up at him, forcing her jaw shut. "We'll just see about that."

She was in high temper when she burst through the door of the marina and found her mother deep in conversation with Tommy Sooner.

"Mama, could I talk to you a moment?" With clenched teeth, her words came out more growl than question.

Katharine's chin came up as though bracing for battle. Her eyes were tentative, but she wasn't backing down. "Now's not a good time, honey. I'm a bit busy at the moment."

"Don't put me off." Sam leaned across the counter. "What were you thinking, renting a cabin to Danny Hastings?"

Katharine leaned closer. "I was thinking we could use the money. And I was thinking it'd be nice to have a man around for a while."

"Not that one," Sam retorted. The minute the words were out, she wanted to call them back.

"Why not?" Her mother's eyes narrowed speculatively. "What's wrong with him?" Suddenly, speculation turned to fear and her eyes took on their haunted look. "You don't think he'd hurt us, do you?" she whispered.

Not in the way you think, Mama. "I just don't want him around."

Katharine studied her, then straightened her spine. "Well, want him or not, he's paid for a month in advance, plus breakfast and supper, so you're going to have to get used to the idea."

"I'll tell him we changed our minds."

Sam turned, but Katharine reached out with a grip a hairsbreadth shy of painful. "You'll do no such thing. He's paid. I agreed. It's the way it is."

Sam stared at her mother in wonder. Now she decided to be forceful? After all these years? Danny couldn't stay here. If he did, it was only a matter of time before he discovered Lindsey's identity. And it was a secret Sam planned to carry to her grave.

She whirled around and collided with a strong chest. Hard arms reached out to steady her, and a smile lurked around his mouth. "I'll try to be on my best behavior, I promise."

The rat. He'd been standing right behind her and heard every word. She poked his surprisingly hard chest. "Stay. Out. Of. My. Way."

Then she stormed out of the marina, barely registering the wide-eyed look on Tommy's face. She had to walk. Clear her head. Too much was happening, too fast.

****

Danny watched Sam disappear into the woods by the river, liking the smooth rhythm of her gait, the way her braid swung with every step. Even furious, she was beautiful.

He leaned back against one of the dock pilings. So, the lady really, truly didn't want him around. Why? Couldn't be because of his sparkling personality. Women loved him. Couldn't be because she didn't need his business. Based on what he'd found on Jeremy's laptop, it was taking everything they had to keep the place afloat.

What was Sam hiding? He wasn't sure. But he intended to find out.

Satisfied, he turned and headed back inside. Katharine looked up from behind the counter and smiled, the same welcoming smile he hoped Sam would give him again.

"Your daughter doesn't want me here."

Katharine waved away his concern. "She may not want you, but she'll put up with you. She has no choice."

Suddenly, inexplicably, Danny didn't want to be tolerated, he wanted to be welcomed. Usually, people begged him to stay and he was the one who pulled away, following the next thrill, looking for the next adventure. Yet here, in this little no-name dot on the map, he had an irrational urge to settle in, put down roots, become part of the fabric of the place. Crazy. Must be Jeremy's death, bringing on all this unexpected sentimentality.

Yeah, that was it. As soon as he figured out what had happened, he'd be ready to move on. He always did.

****

When Sam marched into the Lady Bug a short time later, she was still in high temper. If Danny Hastings had the poor judgment to cross her path right then, she'd skin him alive. Well, maybe not skin him. It would be a shame to ruin so much male beauty. She rammed a hand through the strands of hair floating in front of her eyes. She'd gone certifiably nuts, no question about it. Otherwise, why, in heaven's name, hadn't she tossed Danny Hastings back into his Mustang and shoved him back onto the highway. He wasn't much taller than she was. She was fairly certain if she had the element of surprise on her side, she could take him.

Sam sighed. The lowering truth was no matter how much she was afraid of him staying, part of her didn't want him to leave. The irresistible dimple in his cheek made her abandon every shred of common sense she'd ever possessed.

"Hello, sweetheart," a familiar voice greeted.

Glad for a distraction, Sam smiled as she turned towards a back booth. She plopped onto the red vinyl across from Jimmy Wayne and raised her eyebrows. "Loafing, are you?"

He grinned. "It's been a slow day. Thought I'd come over here and see what's new on the gossip-meter."

"And?"

"You're big news, sweetheart. So was Lindsey—"

At her narrowed eyes, he held both hands up, palms out. "Let me finish before Mama Bear gets her claws out. I said Lindsey was big news, too, until our friend Porter told them if he caught anyone sniffing around your place or your daughter, they'd answer to him." Jimmy Wayne took a sip of his coffee. "His bark is worse than his bite, but those news flunkies don't know that."

Sam's eyebrows rose again. "You don't think Porter would take on someone who went after Lindsey?"

He shrugged. "Maybe. But I get the feeling he doesn't want to be bothered too much."

Sam disagreed, but she held her tongue. She and Jimmy Wayne had never had much use for Porter, but she'd seen the way he spoke to Lindsey, treated her with care.

"So Lindsey found the dead guy's cell phone, huh?" he asked.

Sam's irritation spiked at his cavalier attitude. "Show a little respect, Jimmy Wayne. The man is dead."

He shrugged. "These developers are like vultures, Sam. They won't stop until every square mile of Florida is paved and landscaped." He cocked his head and sent her a quizzical look. "Thought you felt the same way."

"I do. And I want them to go away and leave us alone. But it doesn't mean I want them dead."

"How long is Hastings staying?"

Sam sipped her coffee before she answered.

"Claims he won't leave until he finds out what happened to his friend."

"I'm sure the news will send Mrs. Mertz into seventh heaven. This isn't exactly her busy season."

For some reason, Sam didn't want to correct him. While she tried to decide what to say, Jimmy Wayne studied her like a bug under a microscope. "Wait. He is staying at The Azalea House, right?"

"Nope."

"There aren't too many other options, Sam. Don't tell me he's staying out at the fish camp."

"Yup."

"Why?"

Sam started to tell him her mother made all the arrangements, but something about Jimmy Wayne's sudden intensity warned her to tread carefully. "We need the money, you know that."

"How long is he staying?"

"Couple of weeks. Less if he gets the answers he's looking for."

"Does our beloved Sheriff Porter have any likely suspects yet?"

"Yeah, a twelve foot gator currently at Rupert's."

"Funny. Besides him."

"How would I know? He doesn't tell me what he's thinking."

"But you're still a suspect."

Sam huffed out a breath. "Of course. How could I not be? Think, Jimmy Wayne. I was one of the last people to see Castle alive. And when I saw him, I threatened him."

Jimmy Wayne patted the air with his palms. "Easy, girl." He paused, then asked, "What about Lindsey?"

Sam's maternal radar buzzed. There it was again, a certain...something, when he asked about her daughter. "What about her?"

"Did she find more than just a cell phone?"

Sam swallowed hard, terrified at having the question she'd been trying to ignore stated so flatly. "I don't think so. No."

"You sound like you're not sure."

Her chin came up. "I'm sure. She said she didn't and I believe her."

"Does Porter?"

She hesitated a beat. "He didn't say." But she knew he had his doubts. If she was honest, so did she. And that, more than anything else, was keeping her up nights. If somehow Lindsey had seen a murder...Sam swallowed hard. It didn't bear thinking about.

She reached over and checked the expensive leather-banded watch on Jimmy Wayne's wrist. "I've got to go, Jimmy Wayne. Game starts in less than half an hour."

As she stood, he grabbed her wrist, rubbed his thumb over the plain band on her ring finger. "You haven't been wearing my ring."

Sam met his disappointed gaze, deciding honesty was the best approach. "I can't, Jimmy Wayne. Not right now. There's too much else going on for me to think about it, okay? Give me a little time. Please."

She waited while his jaw worked and he wrestled his frustration under control. Finally, he nodded and smiled. "Sure, Sam. Take all the time you need."

She kissed the top of his head. "Thanks, Jimmy Wayne. You're the best." She tossed a couple of singles on the table. "You playing today?"

Jimmy Wayne's smile was warm, his earlier frustration gone. "You know I never miss a chance to help my favorite girl beat the tar out of the Catholics."

Sam kept her tone light. "I'll have to be on my toes, though. Father James throws a wicked curveball." She waved and hurried out to her Jeep.

****

Danny carefully dodged bodies of all shapes and sizes as he climbed to the top row of the metal bleachers and sat down, wincing as the heat scorched his backside. He wiped sweat from his face and grimaced. Five thirty on a Tuesday evening in September and he could make a fortune cooking burgers on the bleachers. Speaking of burgers, the scent of beef sizzling over an open flame made his stomach rumble.

Katharine smiled from beneath the brim of the straw hat perched over her bun. "Go ahead and order a snack. I figure you'll still be able to do justice to my cooking when we get home."

On Katharine's other side, Lindsey turned imploring blue eyes towards her grandmother. "Can I have a hot dog, pleeeaase? I'll still eat, I promise."

Katharine smiled. "You say the same thing every time."

Lindsey giggled. "I know. But I always eat, don't I?"

"Yes you do, honey. You're about ready to eat us out of house and home."

"Oh, Memaw. I will not."

"Why don't you wait just a little while, honey. These old knees don't like climbing the bleachers too much any more."

Lindsey leaned around her grandmother and pierced him with a pleading look. "Maybe Mr. Hastings can take me."

He saw Katharine's hesitation and smiled reassuringly. "Sure. As long as it's okay with your grandmother."

Katharine had barely nodded when Lindsey bounded down the bleachers without slowing an inch. He followed carefully, mumbling excuses as he went. She was a delightful sprite, similar to Laurie's girls.

He sobered at the reminder. He was here to do a job, find out what happened to Jeremy and make sure the twins were taken care of. He had to keep his priorities in mind.

Lindsey slipped her hand into his and he stopped, startled. "Are you okay, Mr. Hastings? You look sad."

Danny leaned down to her level. "I'm okay, Lindsey. Thanks for asking. I'm sad because Mr. Castle was my best friend."

Her eyes widened and then filled with compassion. "I'm sorry he died."

"Yeah, me too." He looked out over the field without seeing it, then brought his gaze back when she tugged on his hand, leading him towards the concession stand.

Once he paid for their food, Danny started back towards the bleachers. He shouldn't push, especially after Sam clearly told him no, but he had to know.

He lightly pulled his hand back and drew her to a stop beside him. "Lindsey, I need to ask you a question."

He saw the trepidation cross her face, but forged on anyway. "Did you see or hear anything the other night out in the woods? Anything that might help the sheriff figure out what happened?"

All the color drained from her tanned face. "Why does everyone keep asking me the same thing?" she whispered desperately. "I don't know, okay. I don't know." She whirled and ran back to her grandmother.

Way to go, Hastings. Scare the poor kid to death.

Except he wasn't sorry. Sam's little girl knew something. The look on her face was a dead giveaway. A chill chased down his spine. Had she seen a murder?

Danny swallowed hard and scanned the lively

crowd filling the bleachers. Had one of these friendly, small town people killed his best friend in cold blood? He huffed out a breath. If they had, and if Sam's little girl had somehow seen it happen or seen who did it, the child was in grave danger.

Sam would tear a strip off his hide for questioning Lindsey, but he could care less. He'd make her see what was at stake, and maybe, just maybe, she could get Lindsey to tell all. Because if what he was beginning to suspect was true, Sam's little girl could be next to die.

Chapter Ten

From her position behind first base, Sam smacked her fist into her glove and watched the batter from St. Luke's take his position. Nine times out of ten, Marco Juarez hit a line drive straight to her. At well over six feet and muscled from dishwashing at the Lady Bug, Marco hit hard and straight. The choice was catch or duck. Sam chose to catch.

Feet slightly apart, knees bent, she waited, avoiding Marco's unsettling stare. Her eyes darted to the bleachers; she wrenched them back. *Keep your eyes on the ball, Sammy. Eyes on the ball.* It wasn't easy. The pitcher seemed to be in no hurry and her gaze kept straying to where Danny sat chatting with her mother as though they'd known each other for years. What were they talking about?

Danny threw his head back and laughed at something her mother said. Sam swallowed hard and told herself she didn't care. How could he manage to look so carefree, so comfortable? And why did the sound of his laughter reach so deep inside her, call to a part of her she'd carefully locked away more than ten years ago?

Crack!

Too late, Sam wrenched her eyes back to the field. Marco's line drive sizzled straight for her, the white ball filling her field of vision. Without conscious thought, she sidestepped the ball and stuck out her glove, stunned when it hit the leather with enough force to knock her on her backside.

Cheers erupted from the stands and Mike Sanchez, who played shortstop, jogged over and offered her a hand up.

"Nice save, Sammy. Had me worried there for a second."

Sam wobbled to her feet, her arm tingling. *Yeah, me too.* She pulled off the glove and shook her hand, wincing. "The boy hits hard."

Sanchez grinned. "Yeah, but he always hits straight to you. And you always stop him."

The rest of the team offered congratulations as they headed for the dugout and their turn at bat. Sam refused to give so much as a glance in the direction of the bleachers. Distraction had almost gotten her a line drive to the midriff.

She sat down on the bench and flexed her fingers. Her arm would be sore tonight, no question.

"Nice catch, Ace. Your hand okay?"

Sam sternly admonished her heart to slow down before turning to face Danny. He leaned against the chain link fence, arms folded over his impressive chest, feet crossed lazily at the ankles. It was completely unfair, how good he looked. But he was so not right for her. She had to remember that. Unfortunately, the part she kept remembering was the night she'd met him, the way he'd drawn out her carefree side, the way he'd gotten her to shed her usual restraint and laugh with abandon.

Or maybe it was the alcohol. Sam gave an inward snort. She'd never lied to herself and she wouldn't start now. The wine she'd sucked down to calm her nerves might have played a part, but the truth was it was Danny himself. He was the one who saw past the girl who always did what was expected of her to the unfettered one screaming to get out. In one weekend, he'd drawn her out, had seen the real Sam, the one who laughed and joked and tossed the "shoulds" aside and enjoyed every moment. He'd met that Sam, and he'd liked her. He'd made her feel beautiful and cherished and for the first time in her life, proud to be a woman.

And on Monday morning, he was gone, leaving nothing but a rose and a note on her pillow.

Once Sam realized he'd taken off, two emotions settled in with a vengeance: guilt and fury. But beyond her indignation at being used, her anger burned hot. He'd made her think—for the first time in her life—that being herself was not only okay, but wonderful. That glimpse of what could be was the part she couldn't forgive.

To be honest, some of her fury lingered still.

"Sam, you're on deck," Mike called.

She took a moment to remember where she was, then sent Mike a thumbs-up, and turned back to Danny.

His lopsided smile made her heart ignore all her warnings. It raced and whispered for her to take a chance. Maybe this time, he'd stay.

"Go get 'em, Ace."

Sam couldn't decide how to react, so she said nothing, simply picked up her bat and forced her body to go through a few practice swings while she waited her turn.

Once she stood at the plate, she struggled to collect her focus, but it slithered just out of reach.

The pitcher released the ball. She swung.

"Strike one!"

Focus, girl. Come on. Don't let him get to you.

Release. Swing.

"Sttttrrrrike two!"

The crowd shouted encouragement.

Danny's voice carried above all the others. "Eye on the ball, Ace. You can do it."

Darn right she could. And not because he said so either.

Sam took a deep breath and closed her mind to

everything but the ball in the pitcher's hand. She saw him signal the catcher, but she'd been taking pitches from him long enough to know what he was planning.

He wound up. Sam shifted her stance the slightest bit to the outside. She watched, every cell poised, and then swung with all her might.

Crack!

The ball sailed right past the startled pitcher's outstretched glove, past the shortstop's heroic leap and dropped just over the fence behind the outfield.

The crowd cheered. Sam jogged the bases, smiling as the other team threw down their gloves in disgust. As she rounded third, the third-baseman mumbled, "Geez, Sam, have a little pity, would you?"

"Sorry, Charlie. Gotta keep you boys on your toes."

She crossed home plate and looked right into Danny's blue eyes. He was behind the fence, beaming a smile that ought to be illegal. "Way to go, Ace. You always hit like that?"

"Of course," she tossed back, surprised at the saucy tone coming from her mouth.

"How's the hand?"

His unexpected concern, coupled with his support, tangled her tongue. Generally, she took care of everyone, offering support and encouragement. She wasn't at all sure how to accept it. Especially from Danny.

"No worries. It's fine."

****

Danny watched confusion cross Sam's green eyes. His question seemed simple enough, yet she seemed surprised he'd asked. He thought about it for a moment and realized nobody pampered Sam, nobody took care of her.

His eyes narrowed as Jimmy Wayne Drake sauntered over, offering his congratulations. His smile turned to a frown when Jimmy Wayne brushed a proprietary hand down Sam's braid. Danny didn't miss the way she carefully restored the distance between herself and the other man, though. Good.

Conversation swirled around him as he watched Sam interact with her teammates. One of the only women players, she was treated like one of the guys, except they patted her back instead of her backside in congratulations.

In the stands, the women stood in clusters and talked. But once the congratulations were done, Sam stood alone. Isolated on the crowded field.

Danny had taken one step toward her when a snatch of a nearby conversation stopped him.

"...arm like that, yeah, she coulda done him in," an older male voice said.

"Don't make sense to me, though, why she would. I mean, you know she'd be the first name on Porter's list," a second male voice argued.

"Don't you remember what happened to her drunk of a father?"

The second man made a dismissive sound. "Never was any proof she had anything to do with it. We all know the fool could have fallen and hit his head, just like she said."

"Just seems mighty coincidental, is all I'm saying."

"Amos was a no-good, mean drunk. I say good riddance and let the dead rest in peace."

The first man harrumphed and the two of them wandered away. Danny caught up with Sam as she was walking towards her Jeep and hefted her equipment bag from her shoulder.

"Hey, what are you doing?" She tried to take the bag back. "I can carry my own stuff."

"No doubt. But this time, I'd like to carry it for you."

She stopped, hands on hips. "Why?"

He grinned. "Why do I want to carry it for you? Because it's what gentlemen do."

Her eyes shot sparks. "You are no gentleman."

"True enough," he admitted with a lighthearted chuckle. "But under your uniform, you are very much a lady."

Sam blushed and turned away. Danny caught her arm and slowly turned her to face him. "I meant no disrespect, Sam. You're a beautiful woman, and every inch a lady. Don't let anyone tell you different."

Her only response was to pivot on her cleats and march over to her Jeep.

Danny's smile faded as he remembered the conversation he'd overheard and the one he'd had with Lindsey. It was a good thing Sam was strong, because he had a sinking feeling things were going to get worse before they got better.

He saw Sheriff Porter exit his SUV and headed in his direction. He had more questions now than ever. Maybe Porter had answers.

****

Sam's hands shook as she tossed her bag into the Jeep. Why, oh why, did the man have such an effect on her? She had told herself that... that...chemical reaction she'd had to him the weekend of Annie and Jimmy Wayne's wedding was due to alcohol. Or maybe because she was all dolled up and not looking or acting like herself. But none of it seemed to be true. The fact was, every time she was near the man, every cell in her body wanted to move closer, smell his spicy aftershave, bask in the safety his strong arms promised.

She tossed her head in an effort to clear him from her memory. All of it was ridiculous and childish. She was a grown woman, a strong, independent woman with a child to raise and a homestead to protect. Even if—and it was a big if—she was interested in a relationship with a man, which she wasn't, he would be completely the wrong man. Which she'd always thought was why he'd appealed to her years ago, too. He couldn't be permanent. He was a good-time guy, though she figured both of them got way more than they bargained for that night.

Another blush crept up her cheeks. She couldn't think of that night without blushing. Part of her still couldn't believe they'd done what they'd done. Part embarrassment, part longing, she didn't know how to behave whenever he was around. Would it always be between them, the filter though which every conversation was viewed? Every time he said something, she wanted to scowl, "What do you mean?"

"Sam. Wait up."

Sam huffed out a breath and turned. Was there no escaping him? She folded her arms and waited.

Danny reached her and adopted a similar pose. He leaned against the Jeep's front fender. "Tell me about your father's death."

Of all the things she expected him to say, this one didn't even make the top one hundred. Her mind scrambled to keep up. "What about it?"

"How did he die?"

She narrowed her eyes, trying to decipher what was going on behind his mirrored sunglasses. "It was a long time ago. Why?"

He shrugged. "Just wondered."

Oh, she'd just bet. "Been listening to local gossip, Hastings?"

Another shrug. "Something like that." He looked away, then met her gaze again. "You don't find it strange to think he died not far from where Jeremy did?"

"He fell and hit his head on his johnboat."

"Near where Jeremy was found."

Sam nodded. "What's your point? Or do you just have a morbid sense of curiosity?"

"I'm trying to understand what happened."

"Not much to understand. My father was a drunk, a mean drunk, if you must know. Locals said the only surprise was that it hadn't happened sooner. End of story."

"Must have been hard on you and your mother."

He hadn't phrased it as a question, but Sam knew what he was asking. "His living was much harder on us than his dying, if that's what you want to know."

"Locals wonder if you helped him die." His tone was matter-of-fact, giving no hint to his feelings.

Sam mopped sweat from her brow, wondering what he thought. Knowing people still speculated about it shouldn't prick the carefully guarded corners of her heart, but it did. She suspected it always would. Especially with Danny. "They've been wondering since it happened. Guess some of them will go to their graves wondering."

"It bothers you." He stated it as fact.

Sam adjusted her ball cap and opened the Jeep's door when she saw her mother and Lindsey heading their way. "It was a long time ago."

"Can I hitch a ride home with you?"

Home. What a dangerous word. "You can hitch a ride back to the fish camp," she replied, extra emphasis on the last two words.

With a wide grin, he gallantly helped Lindsey and Katherine into the Jeep before climbing into the passenger seat beside her.

It was going to be a long ride home.

****

By the time she roared into the driveway, Sam felt like she was going to jump out of her skin. Danny kept sending her these knowing looks—

growing desire mixed with a tender longing which knotted her insides and made her palms slip on the steering wheel.

Anxious to get away, she leaped out of the Jeep almost before she stopped. "I'm going for a run." She leaned over and gave Lindsey a hug, then looked toward Katharine. "Mama, do you mind—"

"I'll be happy to get my favorite granddaughter tucked into bed."

"Memaw, I'm your ONLY granddaughter," Lindsey complained.

"Well, now, you might be right, but you're still my favorite. Now scoot. Off to the bath with you."

"Thanks, Mama."

Katharine made a shooing motion with her hands. "Go, you're jumpy as a cat on a hot tin roof. Scat."

Relieved, Sam took off at a slow jog, heading for the river and her cave. Maybe a swim would help her work off this tension.

She gradually increased her pace and ran several miles, her tension draining away with every step. Finally, sweat pouring off her skin, she stopped at the water's edge and toed off her running shoes. Next, she peeled off her wet team T-shirt, then shimmied out of her soggy shorts. Once she'd shed her sports bra and panties, Sam stopped to take a deep breath. The cool air felt wonderful on her damp skin. She stretched her arms over her head, took a deep breath and dove cleanly into the water, straight down to her cave.

****

Fifteen feet away, Danny stopped and closed his mouth, afraid his tongue was hanging out. Damn, she was gorgeous. When she'd taken off running, his only thought had been to follow her, talk to her, see if he could ease some of the tension between them.

But now, he realized part of his problem—and

hers—was tension of a whole other sort. When she started peeling off her clothes, he knew he should look away, but he couldn't force himself to do it. She'd had an amazing body all those years ago, and it was even more mouth-watering now.

When she reached her arms over her head and stretched, he stifled a groan. And when she dove into the water and disappeared, his groan turned to a cry of alarm. He watched the widening ripples where she disappeared, waiting for her to surface. When she didn't, he raced toward the spot, calling her name while he stripped off clothes and shoes.

He dove and headed for the river bottom, the moonlight shimmering through the cypress trees providing only bits of scattered light. Panic built in his chest when he saw or felt no trace of her. He popped to the surface and called again, chest heaving. "Sam! Where are you?"

He dove again, straining to find her, trying to figure out if she were caught on the bottom in a tree root, or whether the current had dragged her away. Back on the surface, he spun this way and that. "Sam! Sam! Damn it, answer me!"

"What are you doing here?" She looked stunned. And angry.

He spun around and there she was, treading water beside him, wet hair slicked back, looking like a water nymph. Relief stole his breath as he lunged for her and dragged her into his arms, seeking the warmth of her lips. "Oh, thank God you're okay."

The contact of warms lips and cool water sent need flaring through his system. She squirmed in his arms, trying to break free, then went totally still, as they both became aware of their bodies touching, sliding against each other as they tread water.

Again, she tried to inch away, but he didn't let her go. He needed to keep a hold on her, make sure she was okay.

"What are you doing here?" she asked again, the same combination of shock and annoyance in her tone.

"I followed you—"

She cut him off. "I don't like to be followed."

He nodded. "I'm sorry. I only wanted to talk to you."

She squirmed again and he let her go. She moved a safe distance away, as though she needed the distance to feel secure before she asked, "About what?"

The reasons had seemed so clear when he set off down the path. Now, he couldn't put his finger on a single one. So he settled for, "I was worried about you."

"No need. This is my home."

He jutted his chin toward the river behind her. "Where did you go? No one can hold their breath so long."

Sam didn't say anything for a minute, as if considering how much to say. "I went to my cave."

Danny spun around and looked, but he couldn't see anything. "Here? In the river?"

Sam nodded.

"But you don't use SCUBA gear to get there."

"No, I can dive down and come up inside without needing it."

"Will you take me there?" Danny watched the play of emotions across her face in the moonlight. Fear, hesitation, longing. The same tangled stew of feelings he was dealing with.

In the end, all she said was, "Maybe someday."

"I've missed you, Samantha." The words slipped out.

She smiled, a sad little half smile that broke his heart. "I've missed you, too."

Slowly, he eased up to her and pulled her back into his arms, sighing as their bodies touched. He kissed her then, slow and deep, savoring the feel of her tongue tangling with his, the taste that was hers alone.

Being with her was like coming home. There was something so right, so calm and peaceful, when they were together.

And there was desire, too, no doubt about it. The minute her bare skin touched the front of his jockey shorts, she jumped back as though she had touched a hot poker.

"Turn your back, Hastings, so I can get out of here."

He saw her panic, understood it, and grinned despite himself. "I've seen you naked before."

"I was young and dumb then."

"But beautiful—then and now."

She splashed water in his face. "Flattery will just make me mad. Turn your back."

He did, still grinning, listening to every sound as she dragged her clothes back over her damp skin. At the sudden silence, he turned—and realized she'd fled.

He was grinning like a fool when he climbed out of the water and reached for his own clothes. She would quit running. All in good time.

Though what he'd do with her once he caught her, he had no idea.

She was a homebody. He was a rolling stone. They had no future.

Yet, he couldn't imagine his future without her.

Chapter Eleven

The day of the "Save Riverlake" fundraiser was unbearably hot, even for Florida. A breeze would have been nice, but nothing stirred. The smoke from the barbeque grill hung like fog over the town square, blurring everything around the edges. Sam was tempted to walk off into the mist. Nobody would even notice her absence.

"Come on, Sam, smile. It's going to be okay," Emma Jean admonished, coming up behind her carrying a pie in each hand. Giving Sam a hard look, she set the pies on the dessert table. "Where is your optimism, girl?" She leaned closer and lowered her voice. "The girls have worked their tails off for this. They need your support."

What about what I need? Sam wanted to cry. But as soon as the thought formed, she felt ashamed. She was the adult; most of them were kids. They needed her to act like a grown-up. Whether or not Sam felt she had anything to give was beside the point.

She smiled and returned Emma Jean's quick hug. "You're right." Then she turned to the tent where Libbey and three of the other girls were setting out plates and napkins. "Hi, ladies. I wanted to thank you for all your hard work. Being out in this heat isn't easy."

The new girl, what was her name? Belinda, Sam thought it was, straightened and pressed her hands to the small of her back. "It's hotter than this back home, so we'll be fine." Then she wrinkled her brow, white teeth gleaming against brown skin. "We're going to save your property, Sam, we really will. Try not to worry."

Sam fiddled with the stack of napkins to hide her emotions. How was it these girls, with every reason to gripe and feel sorry for themselves, constantly cheered her up?

She glanced at the clock tower at one end of the square. "It's almost lunchtime. Let's hope everyone in town is hungry for a burger or hot dog today. And the fabulous potato salad you girls whipped up."

"Oh, my, would you look at that?" Libbey suddenly whispered, awestruck.

Sam spun around and her mouth dropped open. Danny Hastings had just stepped out of a huge pickup truck, which he'd backed up right next to their tent. He and another man were busy removing the bungee cords securing something that looked like a tent in the bed.

Libby fanned a hand in front of her face. "Even in a ratty T-shirt and jeans, the man can raise my temperature."

"Libbey," Emma Jean admonished.

"Sorry," she mumbled, but her smile didn't waver. "He's just nice to look at, Emma Jean, is all."

"Well, stop gawking and get back to work."

"Yes, ma'am." Libbey gave him one last glance before turning back to what she was doing.

Sam hadn't moved. She watched, fascinated by the play of muscles in his arms and shoulders as he and the other man slid this huge blob of plastic onto the grass. Next thing she knew, what sounded like a generator came on and the blob began to unfold.

"A bounce house!" Belinda squealed. "Did he really bring a bounce house?"

He most certainly had. Well, he wasn't going to upstage her fundraiser—no matter how cute he looked in jeans. Sam marched across the grass and hissed in his ear. "Just what do you think you're doing?"

He turned and grinned over his shoulder. Really, that slow grin should be illegal. "Hi, beautiful. Isn't this cool?" He indicated the slowly inflating bounce house. "The kids will love it."

Sam was so angry she was quivering. "Is it not enough to know Castle Development has way more money and horsepower than we do? Do you have to sabotage this, too? I can't believe you would do such a thing." She spun around and stomped away. After the way he'd treated her at the ball game she'd begun to think maybe he was a decent guy after all. But no, he was like all men—only after his own agenda.

A strong hand grabbed her arm and spun her around. "Whoa. What's going on here, Sam?"

"Oh, don't give me that. You knew we were having a fundraiser today. You had to have seen the signs all over town."

"Of course. That's why I'm here."

Sam stared at him, dumbfounded. "I can't believe you can be so callous as to destroy what we're trying to do." She tried to leave, but he refused to relinquish her arm.

"How is my helping you destroying what you're trying to do?" he asked.

"How is setting up a competing event helping us?" she shot back.

"Competing—" his breath whoshed out of him and he shook his head. "I'm not competing with you Sam. I'm trying to help. I figured the bounce house would draw more people down here. Any money goes toward your fundraiser."

For the second time in fifteen minutes, Sam's mouth dropped open in shock. "You're doing this for us? Why?"

He looked away, then back at her. "Damned if I

know. It looked like you could use a hand, so I'm offering one."

"But...but, we're on different sides."

He raked a hand through his hair. "I know. But since I can't back out of the deal, I'm trying to make it a fair fight."

****

Later that night, Sam sat on the porch with Katharine and Lindsey, each of them nursing a glass of iced tea.

"I'm sorry it didn't go better today, Samantha."

Sam sighed and took another swig of her tea. "Actually, it barely went at all. People just wouldn't come. After expenses, there was only two hundred dollars profit."

Katharine rocked slowly, her head against the back of the chair. "It was nice, what Danny did with the bounce house."

Lindsey's smile lit up her sunburned face. "It was awesome."

Sam frowned. "I still don't get why he did it, though."

Katharine turned to face her, voice low. "Don't you?"

"No." She wouldn't let herself think about it. If he started caring about her, and she started caring about him...no.

"Come on, Samantha. The man is sweet on you."

Sam looked over at the cottage where Danny was staying and panic fluttered in her belly. She knew it was dangerous to have him in such close proximity. Not only was her heart at risk; the real threat was what would happen if he found out about Lindsey. She had to keep them apart. Though she couldn't quite get the picture of him jumping in the bounce house with her daughter today out of her mind. He was amazing with kids. If only...

Before she finished the foolish thought, his

cottage door opened and he headed in their direction.

Katharine leaped from her chair. "Come on, Lindsey."

"Mama..." Sam warned.

Katharine paused with her hand on the screen door. "Give him a chance, Sam. He's a good man. Come inside, Lindsey."

But Lindsey stood frozen in place, her smile suddenly gone.

Sam glanced from her daughter to Danny, watching him walk towards her, a mason jar of wildflowers tucked in one hand. He moved with a loose, easy stride, as if he had all day to get where he was going. But she knew looks were deceiving; under all his apparent laziness beat the heart of a predator.

"Evenin', Samantha. Lindsey."

"Hi." Sam wanted to roll her eyes at how breathy her voice came out.

"Don't ask me any more questions, okay?" Lindsey burst out. "I don't *know* anything." She ran inside and the screen slammed shut behind her.

Sam stood, fury surging through her veins. "When did you question my daughter? Before or after I told you to leave her alone?"

Danny sighed. "After. At the ball game."

"You had no right." Her jaw ached from gritting her teeth.

"She knows more than she's saying, Sam. Or maybe she saw more than she knows, but either way, I needed to ask."

"I told you not to."

"I know. And I'm sorry I went against your wishes. But do you understand my need to know what happened to Jeremy?"

She did. She'd felt the same frustration after Annie's death. But to have him spending time with Lindsey...

"Stay away from her, Hastings."

He nodded and thrust the jar at her. "How about a peace offering? I saw these by the side of the road and thought of you."

Despite herself, one corner of her mouth kicked up. "I remind you of unkempt wildflowers?"

He stepped closer and Sam fought the urge to back up a step. "No, not unkempt. But individual. And beautiful. Not artificial."

"Is that really how you see me?" As soon as the words left her mouth, she wanted to call them back.

He leaned closer, and for one terrifying-yet-wonderful moment, Sam thought he was going to kiss her again. Instead, he ran a gentle finger down her cheek. "I didn't figure you for the hothouse flower type. Besides, I heard someone call these Redneck roses."

Sam smiled. "I think the term only applies if you're actually a Redneck."

He glanced down at his jeans and T-shirt. "And I'm not."

"Not in a million years."

He shrugged. "Oh, well." He paused, then said, "I'm sorry the fundraiser didn't do as well as you'd hoped." Before she could respond, he leaned close and tucked a loose strand of hair behind her ear before he lightly cupped her cheek.

The sudden motion made her stiffen in surprise. He stopped and looked at her. "Why do you always look braced for a blow?" His face darkened. "Never mind. I can guess. But you need to know I don't hit. Ever."

Sam risked a glance at his blue eyes and saw the truth there. This man was many things, but violent towards women wasn't one of them. "I know. But old habits die hard, I guess."

"Well, how about making some new ones? Have dinner with me tomorrow night."

"I don't date."

"So do something different. Go out with me."

Images of the two of them, talking over a nice dinner, maybe a moonlit stroll afterwards brought up yearnings she could never give in to. Certainly not with this man. "I'm sorry. I can't." She grabbed the jar of flowers. "I have to go."

Just as the screen shut behind her, she heard him whisper, "Coward."

****

From his position in the woods, The Exterminator put down his binoculars and scowled. Oh, no. This was not good; this was not good at all. What was Hastings doing, looking like he wanted to kiss his Samantha? Nobody but him put his hands on her.

She was his. Always.

It was about time everybody knew it.

Chapter Twelve

The week before the public hearing passed in a blur of endless work and preparations, interspersed with moments of total panic. Work around the marina, flyers and notices posted around town, huddled meetings at Haven House. Though the sun shone, to Sam it seemed a black cloud obscured the light and covered everything in dark gloom.

The day of the hearing, she tried focusing on the river cruise and the customers at the bait shop, but based on the puzzled looks aimed her way, she wasn't sure she succeeded. At lunchtime, she asked Katharine to cover for her and headed for the river. She was too restless to sit, too frantic to pray. A hard run through the woods, followed by a swim to her cave was the only way she could deal with the panic churning inside her.

After checking to make sure she was alone, Sam stripped off her shorts and tank top, and dove into the river. Because the Withlacoochee was spring fed, the water was 72 degrees year round. In winter it felt warm, but today, with temperatures in the 90s, the cold sent a shock wave through her system. She popped up in the cave gasping. Once she had the flashlight on, she scrubbed at the goose bumps pebbling her skin. Anything to keep her fear from swallowing her whole.

Huddled in the threadbare green towel, Sam finally opened the floodgates in her mind and let the thoughts come. She tried to gather them into some coherent order, but it proved impossible. Disjointed snatches of conversation and memory fought for position at the forefront of her mind.

You're nothing but a worthless girl. A son would keep the fish camp going, but you'll lose it for sure.

I won't, Pop. I promise.

She's strong enough to have killed her drunken father.

What did you see out in the woods the other night, Lindsey?

We'll fight them, Sam, and we'll win.

Do you ever wonder what might have been?

Sam wrapped her arms around her middle and rocked back and forth. Emma Jean and the girls from Haven House had promised to be there in force tonight to support her. But would it be enough? The turnout at the fundraiser—or lack thereof—was not a good sign. She supposed she should be relieved her lawyer would be there, too, but only IF he got back in time from another hearing out of town. Otherwise, he'd send a representative from his office, whatever that meant.

She took a deep breath and glanced upwards. "God, you know how hard it is for me to ask for help, but I'm asking. Please, don't let them declare our property a redevelopment zone. Don't let them take it away."

After a quick glance at her watch, Sam tossed off the towel, doused the light and dove out of the cave. By the time she ran back to the marina she was no more settled than when she'd left.

She couldn't eat dinner; nausea churned in her stomach. Her hands shook as she braided her hair, and she had to run to the bathroom twice. She reached into the closet for a clean pair of khakis and froze. The shopping bag stuffed in the back seemed to call out to her. Slowly, she reached in and pulled it out. Would it make a difference if she showed up in a skirt? Could she?

She jammed her hand into the sack and pulled out one of the skirts. The silky feel against her palm instantly sent her back in time.

I'll only wear it to church, Pop, I promise.

Boys wear pants. Don't ever let me see you looking like a sissy girl again. It's an abomination.

Sam shivered. It wasn't the words so much as the beating which had followed that still sent chills down her spine. But Pop was gone. She had to keep telling herself he was really gone. He couldn't hurt her any more. And wearing a skirt might help her save the marina.

Slowly, she pulled the skirt up over her hips. The slippery fabric seemed to float around her legs. The feeling was so foreign, so...feminine, it terrified her and she bolted for the bathroom.

After she'd emptied her stomach for the third time, her knees felt rubbery, but she glanced in the mirror, straightened her spine and locked her knees. "Suck it up, Collins. Now is no time to be a wimp."

Still, she'd just as soon not stand up in front of all these small-minded people and beg for help. She'd spent a lifetime on the fringes, the misfit quietly longing for acceptance. She was kidding herself to think it would change now. Her father's death and later her return as a "widow" with a newborn had only added fuel to the gossip fire. She twisted the plain gold band on her finger, hating the lie like never before.

Annoyed with her dithering, Sam snapped a rubber band on the end of her braid as she marched down the hall. At Lindsey's door, she caught her reflection in her daughter's cheval mirror and stopped. The skirt flared out and then settled around her legs as she stepped closer. Her heart rate sped up as she whirled back into her bedroom and yanked off the skirt. She couldn't do it. Not today.

Once back in a familiar pair of khakis, she raced

through the kitchen towards her Jeep. One glance at the clock and she groaned. If she didn't put the pedal to the metal, she'd be late, and that was unacceptable. Mama had left with Lindsey almost fifteen minutes ago.

Sam pulled the door shut behind her, and at the last minute, reached back in and locked it, something she'd never done before.

She slid behind the wheel of her Jeep, pumped the gas a few times and then bounced over the gravel drive to the paved road. It was tempting to speed, but if she did, her tires would spit gravel off the road and she'd have to have more brought in. Which she couldn't afford.

Once she hit county pavement, she gripped the gearshift, stomped on the clutch and let her rip. She flew down the road, questions and worries vying for dominance.

What if nobody will help you? A little voice whispered. *Folks round here don't trust you or like you. Why should they help you?*

Annie was the only one she'd ever told about the condemning loop that played in her head. Her friend had laughed and said, "What, you think you're the only one with negative tapes wearing a groove in your mind? We all have those. The question, Sam, is what you're doing about it. Are you going to yank those old tapes out and replace them with new ones? Or are you going to keep listening to this nobody-likes-me-think-I'll-go-eat-worms recording?"

She missed Annie, missed her smile and carefree attitude, her straight-on way of looking at the world. Sam wondered again what had been bothering her friend before her death. It was a question that still nagged Sam at odd moments. Something had clearly been wrong, but no matter how much Sam probed, Annie wouldn't say. Sam had always thought it had to do with her and Jimmy

Wayne. Maybe they'd hit a rough patch. It was the only thing she could think of which Annie would have kept from her. But Sam had never worked up the nerve to ask Jimmy Wayne about it, either.

Alabama's *"Born Country"* came on and Sam pushed everything from her mind but the upcoming meeting. Nobody was going to get away with stealing her property. She'd fight for their home with everything she had. If they thought she wouldn't, they were in for one heck of a surprise.

****

He crouched behind a huge live oak, hidden behind low branches draped in Spanish moss. He'd checked the spot earlier and knew he couldn't be seen from the road. His palms were damp, so he wiped them on his slacks. Again. Must be hotter than he thought out here, because he just couldn't seem to stop sweating. Mosquitoes buzzed around his head and sweat rolled down his back. Good thing he'd thought to throw an extra shirt into his car before he left home. It wouldn't do to show up at the meeting looking like he'd been swimming in his clothes.

He stopped to listen. The squirrels had finally forgotten about him and gone back to whatever they were doing. Their scolding chatter was distracting and he couldn't afford distractions. He checked his watch, then wiped his hands on his slacks again before he raised the rifle and looked through the scope. He had one chance; he had to get it right the first time.

Heart pounding, he forced himself to take deep breaths. He could do this. He had to. There was no one else who could solve this problem.

When he heard the Jeep whip around the corner and pick up speed on the straightaway, he smiled. She was behaving true to form. Everyone in town knew Sam drove too fast.

Elbow braced against the tree, he held his breath as he sighted the rifle, then counted off the seconds and slowly squeezed the trigger.

By the time the Jeep skidded off the road, he was sprinting back to the car he'd safely hidden out of sight.

****

The high school cafeteria was packed to the gills. The tables had been folded and stored to make room for rows of metal folding chairs, while a podium had been set up in the middle of the stage.

Danny stepped through the doorway and spied Katharine manning the refreshment table with several of the church ladies. Apparently, nothing happened in this town without coffee, cakes or cookies to go with it.

As he stepped further into the room, a heavyset woman in a flowered dress stopped and poked him in the chest with one finger. "We don't need your kind in this town. So you just head on back to wherever you come from—"

"Now, Vonette, you'll get your turn later." A lanky older man sent Danny a wink before he steered his wife towards the refreshment table, while she continued her muttering.

Danny sighed. He didn't want to be here and resented Jeremy putting him in this position. As soon as he had the thought, guilt swamped him. Jeremy was dead and he wouldn't speak ill of his best friend. Besides, his concern tonight was on the living, namely Jeremy's two daughters. It was his job to make sure they had a future.

He spotted Lindsey scowling at him and sucked in a deep breath before heading her way. "Hi, Lindsey. How's it going?"

"Like you care," she snapped. Tears suddenly swam in her eyes as she pierced him with a look that could have cut glass. "You want to take the fish camp away."

Danny sighed, wishing there was another way. If he could have walked away from this deal, he would have done so as soon as he realized the woman Jeremy had wanted him to "make nice to" was Samantha Collins. He didn't want to hurt her or her daughter, but his loyalty was to Jeremy's girls. Unless and until he could find another solution, he had to keep moving forward.

He crouched down so they were eye level. "I'm not trying to take it away, Linds. I'm trying to buy it. It's business, not personal."

She folded her arms over her chest. "You made my mama cry."

The accusation in her voice pierced his heart. He'd bet his convertible it would take a lot to make Samantha cry. "I'm sorry. If there was another way, Lindsey, I'd take it. But there isn't."

"I hate you," she spat in a loud whisper, then whirled and ran to her grandmother's side.

Danny got to his feet in the sudden silence. Everyone in the room had stopped what they were doing to watch him, their looks ranging from sympathy to outright fury. Had one of them killed Jeremy?

There was a flurry of activity near the door as Emma Jean Tucker and about twelve pregnant girls from Haven House filed into the room. Emma Jean's piercing gaze dared anyone to get in her way. She sent Danny a disgusted look, then lifted her chin and led the girls to a row of chairs at the front.

She sat down beside a young man wearing an expensive suit which hung on his lanky frame. His gaze darted around the room, like a kid at the dentist's office hoping for a last-minute reprieve. He seemed uncomfortable around the girls, for when one of them tried to make a joke, he turned red and ducked his chin.

A screech sounded from the microphone and all eyes turned towards Tommy Sooner as he cleared his throat. "Ladies and gentlemen, thank you for coming. If you'd take your seats, we'll get started."

The crowd began to move and Danny followed, looking for Sam. She had to be here somewhere, but he hadn't seen her since he walked in. The seats filled quickly, so he joined the clump of men leaning against the back wall, still scanning the room for Sam.

He found Katharine and Lindsey in the second row, with an empty seat beside them. A niggle of worry slid down his spine. Where was she?

Katharine turned in her seat and he raised his eyebrows in question. She shrugged in response and scanned the room. When she looked back at him, he saw his own worry reflected in her eyes. Sam wouldn't miss this meeting. Not for anything.

On the platform, Tommy Sooner worked his way through the preliminaries. Like any good politician, he'd saved the juiciest item on the agenda for last. From across the room, Jimmy Wayne Drake made his way to where Danny stood.

"Have you seen Sam?" Danny asked.

Jimmy Wayne's look darkened. "That's what I came to ask you."

"Haven't seen her, and it has me worried."

"Well, if she's not here, it'll certainly make your job easier."

Danny turned and faced the other man squarely. He kept his voice low. "Watch your step, Drake. I know you're her friend, but if you think I'd do something to keep her away, you're crazy."

"You'd have the most to gain."

Danny took a firm grip on his temper. Taking a swing at Drake and landing in jail was not the outcome he needed tonight. He tuned in as Sooner finally moved into a discussion of the fish camp.

"As most of you know, Castle Development—tonight represented by Danny Hastings, business partner to the unfortunately deceased Mr. Jeremy Castle—wants to buy the old Collins place and surrounding property and develop it into a beautiful waterfront community, complete with marina and golf course."

"What about Newton's Folly?" Someone interrupted from the back.

Sooner scowled at the man. "Wait your turn, Jim Bob, I'll get to questions. But yes, Newton's folly—currently known as Haven House—would be included in the deal and the developer plans to turn it into a fancy restaurant. Maybe even a classy five-star place."

A collective gasp emanated from the crowd.

"I heard Sam doesn't want to sell," someone else yelled.

Sooner's smile widened. "I think Castle Development just hasn't made her an offer yet she can't refuse."

Lindsey shot to her feet. "My mama doesn't want to sell our fish camp. For any amount of money."

Sooner looked down at the girl. "If that's the case, honey, where is your mama? Why isn't she here to speak for herself?"

Danny straightened and shot Sooner a look. He didn't care for the man's patronizing tone.

Katharine pulled Lindsey down beside her, frantically whispering in her ear. Then she cast him a desperate glance, but Danny wasn't sure what he was supposed to do.

Up front, Sooner slipped into legalese so deep most of these folks had no idea what he was saying. He finally wound down with, "As your city commission, we propose the Collins place be designated a redevelopment zone and we will continue our discussions with Ms. Collins in hopes she will sell us her property."

"And if she won't?" A big man hollered from the back of the room.

"We'll discuss the ramifications at the next meeting. Now then, if there are no further questions or discussions at this time, I move we designate—"

"Not without Sam here."

The faces which snapped his way were no more shocked by his outburst than Danny himself.

Sooner narrowed his eyes. "What did you say, Mr. Hastings?"

Danny stepped forward and met Sooner's gaze squarely. "I said, nothing happens without Sam here."

Sooner laughed, the sound ugly. "If this was really so important to Ms. Collins, don't you think she would have shown up tonight?"

Certainty pumped through Danny's veins. "I think the only thing that would have kept her away was an emergency of some sort. I'm going to check on her. No decisions get made unless she's here."

Sooner straightened to his full height. "Mr. Hastings, you can't walk in here and tell the city commission what to do."

"I just did. And if you want to do business with Castle Development, you'll remember what I said."

He slammed through the outside doors and hopped into his car, tires squealing as he sped towards Sam's place.

Something was not right.

Chapter Thirteen

"Ma'am, can you hear me? Ma'am?"

The muffled voice came from far away, buzzing in Sam's head like an annoying fly. She tried to raise her hand to swipe it away, but fire raced up her left side and made her moan.

"Ma'am? Ma'am?" the voice was young, male, and getting squeakier with every repetition.

Sam forced words out. "I'm okay," she shouted, but the kid must be deaf, because he wouldn't stop yelling. She tried again. "I'm okay."

"Thank God you're not dead," the kid breathed.

Sam couldn't pry her eyes open, but the kid must be leaning right over her because she caught a whiff of nacho chips. The smell didn't help her queasy stomach.

"I'm going to be sick," she moaned, struggling to open her eyes and lean forward at the same time. Something was holding her back and she struggled to free herself.

"Ma'am, please stay still. The paramedics are coming. Please, don't move."

Hands tangled with hers, trying to still her movements. Sam finally forced her eyes open and immediately wished she hadn't. Three images of a young kid swirled in front of her face.

One look and she turned her head and threw up.

"Oh, man," the voice groaned. "Those are my new shoes."

"Sorry," Sam mumbled.

Sam felt napkins dabbing at her mouth and

151

murmured, "Thanks."

"Everything's going to be okay, Ma'am. Just stay still. Everything's going to be okay."

The kid sounded like he was scared to death. "I'll be fine, really."

"Just don't die on me."

Sam managed a smile. "Wasn't planning on it. How bad is it?"

He dabbed at the wetness that kept trickling into her eyes. "You hit your head pretty good, looks like, and your side is bleeding."

Sam heard a muffled siren in the distance. The kid heaved an audible sigh of relief. "They're almost here. They'll take good care of you."

"Thank you for helping me," Sam whispered.

"Uh, yeah, sure. No problem."

Sam thought maybe he was saying something else, but the words were muffled and then faded altogether.

****

Danny flew down the two-lane highway, scanning both sides of the road for signs of Sam's Jeep. It was the first thing he thought of, the only thing he could imagine that would keep her from the meeting.

He rounded the curve and muttered a curse as his fears were confirmed. He skidded to a stop beside assorted emergency vehicles. On the shoulder, a rust-dotted old Camaro sat by the sheriff's SUV. A lanky young man of about eighteen leaned against it, arms wrapped tightly across his middle.

Danny spotted Sam's Jeep wedged between two water oaks and took off running. Porter and one of his men were circled around it, taking pictures and making notes.

"Where's Sam?" he demanded as soon as he got within earshot.

The sheriff eyed him with one brow raised. "On

her way to County General."

"What happened?"

"Don't know yet."

Danny growled low in his throat. Porter held his hands up, palms spread. "Easy, Hastings. All we know at the moment is that Sam's Jeep hit the tree and she suffered a nasty concussion."

"Will she be all right?"

"Paramedics think so." Porter turned to Deputy Sanchez and both men ignored him while they scanned the area around the crash site. "Let's start across the road," he told Sanchez. The other man nodded and walked away.

Danny fell into step beside them as they crossed the blacktop. "What are you looking for?"

"Evidence." Porter used his flashlight to pierce the deepening gloom, sweeping it back and forth. Not far away, Sanchez did the same.

Danny reached out to grip the man's arm, thought better of it and stepped in his path, instead. "What are you looking for?" he repeated.

Porter sighed and rubbed a hand over the back of his neck before he turned back and met Danny's gaze. "It's possible someone took a shot at her."

"What?" Danny reared back and cursed. "You'd better find out who did this, Porter."

"I plan to. Make no mistake." Porter's voice was hard and in his eyes, Danny glimpsed a fury and determination he'd not seen there before.

Danny sprinted back to his car and put the pedal to the medal all the way to County General.

****

Shouting voices pulled Sam back from the darkness. One was male and angry, the other female and soothing. She pried her eyes open, squinting against the fluorescent light.

"Get out of my way."

"Sir, you can't go in there. Not unless you're

153

family. Sheriff's orders."

"Don't make me bodily move you, honey," the male voice warned.

"I'm calling security."

"You do that. Call Porter, too. In the meantime, get out of my way."

The curtain around Sam's bed was yanked open and Danny strode to the bed, towering over her like an avenging angel. He stopped short when he got to her side, eyes widening as he looked her up and down.

"That bad, huh?" she mumbled.

He grabbed the chair next to the bed and slumped into it, then gently took her hand in his and just sat there, looking at her. Sam's eyelids felt like they were weighted by bricks, so she let them close. Gradually, she heard his breathing go back to normal and his breath came out on a long sigh.

He raised her hand to his mouth and placed a gentle kiss in her palm. "Are you okay?"

Her hand tingled where his lips had touched it. It was unnerving, but she didn't pull away. "Yeah. Feel like a truck hit me, but I'll live." She forced her lids open.

He smiled, dimples flashing. "Glad to hear it."

Sam tried to return the smile. Then Danny paused, as if choosing his words carefully. "Do you remember what happened, Sam?"

"Not really. One minute I was driving along and the next some kid kept asking if I was okay."

Her eyes widened suddenly and dread washed over her like icy water. "I missed the meeting." She knew only too well that Sooner would take advantage of the situation.

"Yeah, you did. But they're not doing anything without you."

Hope flared briefly, but she snuffed it out. No sense getting excited over nothing. "How can you be sure?"

"Well, for starters Emma Jean gave them the what for, with lots of verbal support from the girls with her, and then some young pup from your lawyer's office offered his two cents."

"And Tommy backed off? That doesn't sound like him." Even in her groggy state, she knew that.

Danny glanced away, then back at her, his look sheepish. "I also told them they couldn't."

Her eyebrows shot up and she winced at the pain in her skull. "You what?"

"You heard me." He stood and brushed her hair back from her forehead where several strands had escaped her braid. "Right now, you just have to worry about getting better. We'll talk more later."

He turned to go. "Wait. I need to know—"

"Mama!" Lindsey raced into the room and then skidded to a halt when she saw Sam. "Oh, Mama," she whispered and then burst into tears.

Sam patted the space beside her with her good arm. Lindsey tiptoed over and perched on the edge of the bed. She leaned over to give Sam a hug, but lost her balance and bumped into her.

The impact ignited the flames in Sam's side and blackness swallowed her whole.

****

Sheriff Porter was not a happy man. The closest thing they'd ever had to a crime spree was the summer several of the local high school kids decided to TP a different house every night of the week.

But this? This was a whole other kettle of fish. First Castle went missing and turned up dead. Now someone took a shot at Sam. Not in his town. He wasn't sure about Castle's death yet, but he'd bet his pension the bumbling fools on the city commission were responsible for Sam's gunshot wound. He'd lay money on Tommy Sooner, but could be one of the others did it. Or paid to have it done. Thank heaven the shooter was a lousy shot.

Telling Katharine Sam had been shot was one of the hardest things he'd ever done. The second hardest was being here at the station when he wanted to be at the hospital offering Katharine a strong shoulder.

But he could help the family best by figuring out who tried to kill Sam. Which meant dealing with Sooner and company.

He sighed and headed for the interrogation room where Tommy was cooling his heels. He didn't have enough rooms to put one of them in each, so Sanchez had Rudy treed in Luke's office with Bill Farley mumbling next to his desk, where Sanchez could keep an eye on both of them.

Luke opened the door and marched into the interrogation room, face and tone all business. He slammed the door shut behind him, slapped his notebook on the table and then leaned forward, getting right in Sooner's face.

"We can do this easy or we can do this hard, but you're not leaving here until I know exactly what you boys did to Sam Collins tonight."

Chapter Fourteen

"Mr. Hastings, you have to leave now," the nurse said. Danny glanced over his shoulder, but didn't relinquish his chair. Behind the nurse, a security guard loomed in the doorway, arms crossed over a belly straining to pop out of his tan uniform shirt.

The nurse tapped her rubber-soled shoe, but Danny ignored her as he rubbed Sam's hand. She didn't have girly hands; hers were calloused and strong, competent, like their owner. Danny found he didn't want to let go. Ever.

"Sir, you must leave *now*. Please don't make a scene."

Much as he didn't want to leave, he knew the best way to protect Sam was to figure out who tried to kill her. Between the overprotective nurse and the security guard, she would be safe enough tonight.

He started to get up when Sam squeezed his hand. "Stay." He leaned closer, thinking he'd imagined it. Her eyes fluttered open and he saw confusion in their depths. She blinked several times as though trying to clear hr head.

Attila-the-nurse bustled to her side, elbowing Danny out of her path. "Good, you're awake." She took Sam's vitals then turned to Danny and arched a pencil-thin eyebrow. "Why are you still here?"

"I want him to stay," Sam murmured.

"Sorry, honey, family only." The nurse patted her hand.

"Stay."

Nurse Brenda narrowed her eyes and glanced

from one to the other. Then she wagged a finger under his nose. "Okay, but only for thirty minutes. And only because the sheriff okayed you."

Danny smiled and winked. "Whatever you say, boss."

One corner of her mouth kicked up. "Smarty pants."

Nurse Brenda motioned the security guard out ahead of her, letting the door swish shut behind her. Danny resumed his seat, again taking Sam's hand.

"Is Lindsey okay?"

"She will be. Your mom took her home."

"Not easy to see your parent in the hospital."

Danny studied their clasped hands. He wasn't sure which topic to broach first, but he decided it didn't matter. Neither was going to make her happy. He met her eyes. "Sam, somebody shot you tonight."

He watched the emotions play cross her face in rapid succession: shock, horror, disbelief, anger. She reached a hand out and gingerly touched the bandage at her side. "How bad is it?"

"I'm not sure, but the good thing is you didn't need surgery."

She swallowed hard, fists balled at her sides. "You're telling me somebody tried to make my daughter an orphan tonight?"

"That's the sheriff's theory, yeah."

She clenched her jaw. "I'd bet my last dollar it was the three stooges."

At his puzzled expression, she added, "Our beloved city commissioners."

"From the gossip I overheard at the nurse's station, Porter is questioning them as we speak."

"I'm not giving up my property," she snapped, chin raised.

"I know." He paused, "But it's not worth dying over, is it?"

"So what, I should just give it up? Oh, wouldn't

that be convenient for everyone, especially you!"

He tried to grasp her hands again, but she snatched them out of reach. "Listen Sam, if I get the property in the end, it'll be done fair and square and legal. I'm not going to do anything underhanded. I told you that." He paused and waited until she was looking at him again. "I think there's something else going on in this town, and it's about more than just tonight."

"You mean your friend's death."

He nodded, then chose his next words with extreme care. "What if Lindsey was the target tonight?"

Sam gasped, eyes wide with fear. "Oh, God."

"We need to talk to her, see if we can help her remember exactly what she saw the night Jeremy died. Otherwise, we don't know who, or what, to protect her from."

She cocked her head and he realized he'd said "we." He wasn't sure what it meant, but he wasn't taking it back. Lindsey needed a champion, and right now, he was it.

"This isn't your problem, Danny. I'll take care of it."

"Ordinarily, I wouldn't argue with you, but you're going to be here a while and I don't think you want Lindsey here the whole time."

She scowled, but didn't argue.

"Look, Sam. Let me help, okay?" When she started to speak, he held up his hand. "Yes, I want to know what happened to Jeremy, I won't deny it. But Jeremy is dead. I want to make sure nothing happens to your daughter." He wondered at the pained expression that flitted across her features, but pressed on. "I know this whole property situation is hard on everyone, but I'm willing to put it aside for the moment so we can keep Lindsey safe. I think whatever she knows has her scared to death.

We need to find out what it is."

Sam's eyes suddenly filled with tears and he leaned over and brushed them away with the backs of his fingers.

"It's going to be okay."

Her eyes were huge, filled with frustration and fear and...something else. "You're a good man, Hastings," she whispered.

He smiled. "Yeah."

Then he leaned over and kissed her gently on the lips. He meant it to be a simple kiss, a promise of help, maybe a bit of comfort. But once his lips met hers, everything changed. The past receded and it was the night of Annie and Jimmy Wayne's wedding all over again. She still kissed with the same combination of strength and innocence he couldn't resist all those years ago.

He couldn't resist it now, either.

Sam was the first to pull away, though she seemed as reluctant as he did. It took him a moment to clear his head.

"One kiss is never enough with you," he murmured. He hadn't meant to say it aloud, but the words slipped out anyway.

Sam's chin came up. "It's going to have to be, Hastings."

He cocked his head, studied her. "Do you ever think about that night?"

Sam looked away. "It was a long time ago. I was a different person then."

"Maybe outwardly, but you're still the same."

"Yeah, and we all know what a draw that is."

He didn't miss the pain behind the sarcasm. "People are skeptical of what—or who—they don't understand. They're the ones missing out."

"Sure, which is why you skipped out after our weekend with just a note."

Now it was his turn to look away. He rubbed his

neck, then forced himself to look her square in the eye. "I felt guilty. Not only did we get in over our heads, but I took advantage of the situation."

Sam winced. "You mean I was drunk."

"Yeah. And I got the idea it wasn't something you did regularly."

"First and last time, actually."

"I'm sorry, Sam. For all of it. But—"

"No buts, Hastings. The past is over and done with. And if you think for a second I'm going to pick up where we left off while you're in town, I'll have them check you for a concussion, too. I have a daughter to raise."

"Doesn't mean you can't have love, too."

She arched a brow. "Is this the same guy Annie called 'No-strings Hastings'? Not interested." Sam turned her face away. "Now go away and let me rest."

Danny opened his mouth. Closed it. Some irrational part of his brain wanted to offer her forever, to beg her not to send him away. Before he could utter such idiocy, he turned and walked out. But as he pulled the door shut, he saw one lone tear roll down Sam's face before she swiped it away.

****

Danny almost tripped over the security guard lounging in a chair right outside Sam's door. "Sheriff Porter asked me to keep an eye on her until he gets here." He looked Danny up and down. "Told me to keep an eye on you, too."

"She's fine. Did you want to check?"

The man poked his bald head around the door, then gently pulled it shut again. "You can go."

Danny turned the corner and ran smack into Jimmy Wayne Drake, the last person he wanted to deal with at the moment.

"Where is she?" Drake asked, eyes wild. Normally immaculate, the man looked rumpled. And desperate.

"Easy, Drake. She's just down the hall. But she's resting."

"What happened?" Drake asked, his stance belligerent.

Danny folded his arms over his chest, kept his voice matter-of-fact. He didn't want this local yokel rushing in there and upsetting Sam any more than she already was. "Not sure yet, but Porter thinks somebody tried to kill her."

"What?" Drake asked, voice rising with every syllable.

Danny kept his voice low. "She was shot."

Jimmy Wayne shook his head in disbelief. "That's what made her drive off the road?"

Danny nodded. "It's the current theory."

Drake's eyes narrowed. "So what are you doing here?"

"Same thing you are. Making sure she's okay."

Jimmy Wayne stepped closer, too close. "Be mighty convenient for you if Sam was out of the picture."

Before he thought it through, Danny grabbed the other man by his arms and shoved him up against the wall. "You want to be careful about making accusations like that, Drake."

Jimmy Wayne squirmed, but Danny refused to let go. "Getting too close to the truth, am I?"

"You wouldn't know truth if it bit you in the ass."

"Hastings. Back off."

Danny looked over his shoulder and saw Porter and Sanchez bearing down on them. He let Drake's feet touch the floor. "I'll be watching you. So be careful."

"Are you threatening me?" Jimmy Wayne asked loud enough to be sure the sheriff heard him.

"Consider it a guarantee." Danny released his

grip and turned to leave.

"Not so fast, Hastings. I want to talk to you," Porter said.

"It's about time, Sheriff," Jimmy Wayne began, only to be cut off by Porter.

"Stuff it, Jimmy Wayne. You're next." He motioned to Sanchez. "Keep him company while Mr. Hastings and I have us a little chat." Porter motioned Danny into an empty waiting room and pointed to a chair. "Have a seat."

Danny stayed standing, arms crossed. "What are you doing to keep Sam safe?"

Porter raised one eyebrow. "I'm investigating. I want to know your whereabouts today, starting with breakfast."

"You're serious?"

Porter pulled a pen and little spiral notebook from his shirt pocket. "You, more than anyone in town, had a reason to want Sam out of the picture."

"I'd never hurt her."

Porter shrugged. "So you say. I'm more interested in facts. So, outline where you were today."

Danny huffed out a breath. "I had breakfast in my cottage and then worked at the bait shop from nine until three p.m. From there I went to the bank and store and by five, I was back at my cottage. I called Laurie in California, showered, and went to the Lady Bug for dinner. From there I went to the meeting."

Porter looked up from his notes. "You own a gun, Hastings?"

"I do. It's in California."

"Then I assume you know how to shoot it?"

Danny nodded.

"Make and caliber."

Danny paused, but then told him. "It's a Remington 30.06, Buckmaster 270, to be exact."

Porter raised his brows. "Same kind as the shell casings we found tonight."

"Doesn't mean I shot her." He was getting tired of Porter's attitude.

"True. Doesn't mean you didn't, either."

"Give it a rest, Porter. This is nothing but a waste of time."

Porter raised a brow. "From where I sit, Hastings, I'm interviewing all possible suspects."

Danny leaned forward and braced his arms on his thighs. He met Porter's look squarely. "Sam and I are worried about Lindsey." Danny lowered his voice. "What if she was tonight's target?"

Porter bit the inside of his lip, and replaced his notebook in his uniform pocket. "Then we have a real problem and little Lindsey may be in a heap of trouble."

****

Lindsey didn't say a word on the ride home, just stared out the window with tears streaming down her cheeks. Katharine brushed tears from her own cheeks, watching her granddaughter hurt.

"Your mama is going to be just fine, Honey-lamb, you heard the doctor say so." She tried to keep her voice upbeat, but it was hard.

Lindsey nodded but didn't look at her.

"She'll be home before you know it."

Katharine turned on the local gospel station because the silence was oppressive.

"Are we going to have to move?" Lindsey finally asked.

"If the city commission has their way, could be. But I thought you wanted to live in town?"

Lindsey shrugged. "I thought I would, but now I think I'd rather just stay here."

The silence stretched and Katharine saw Lindsey's throat work and tears run down her cheeks.

"It's my fault Mama got hurt," Lindsey whispered.

Katharine gripped the steering wheel. She wanted to shout "What?" at the top of her lungs, but it would make things worse, so she forced her voice into a calm she didn't feel. "Honey, why do you think this was your fault? How can that be? You weren't even there?"

"God is punishing me."

Katharine's heart stuttered at the pain in Lindsey's voice. Where had the child come up with such a thing? "What do you mean, honey? I don't understand."

"I messed up and now God is mad at Mama."

Katharine pulled into the gravel drive leading to the fish camp and stopped halfway down. She turned and faced her granddaughter, pleading for guidance from on high. "Lindsey, God doesn't work that way. If we do something wrong, we may have to suffer the consequences of what we did, but God doesn't hurt the people we love if we make a mistake."

Lindsey hurled herself into her grandmother's arms, sobbing. "I'm so scared, Memaw. I don't know what to do."

Katharine didn't understand what was going on, and Lindsey was crying too hard to make sense of what she was saying, so Katharine did the only thing she could: she rocked Lindsey in her arms, murmuring soothing sounds in her ears, just like she used to do for Sam.

****

He was not happy, not at all. Somebody had tried to kill his Samantha tonight. A fraction of an inch in either direction, and they might have succeeded. This would not do. Oh, no. This would not do at all.

He drove to town and went to the Lady Bug, where he spent the next hour listening to the

165

conversations swirling around him. Between the media swarm and the locals, the place was packed. Nobody told him exactly what he needed to know, but by the time he left, he was pretty sure he knew who to ask.

If he didn't get the answers he needed, well, sometimes bug extermination was a messy business.

Nobody hurt Samantha. He was furious someone had gotten so close to her tonight. He'd make sure it never happened again.

Chapter Fifteen

After two days in the hospital, Sam couldn't wait to get home. She squinted as the automatic doors *whooshed* open and the Florida sun blasted her eyeballs. Her vision was back to normal, but she still had a killer headache from the concussion. She cautiously opened her eyes and levered herself out of the requisite wheelchair.

Her side was still sore, but healing nicely. The nurses and doctor kept talking about how lucky she was, but Sam wondered. Hitting a moving target wasn't easy, unless you were a skilled marksman. So was the shooter actually trying to kill her, or simply scare her? Or, as Danny suggested, had Lindsey been the real target? Sam swallowed hard, pushing back the panic.

"You ready to go home, Mama?" Lindsey skipped beside her like a poodle on speed and Sam almost tripped over her legs.

"Come here, Princess, and let Mama lean on you." She tugged Lindsey snug against her side, as much to keep her from prancing as with the need to touch her. She had to make sure no one hurt her little girl. Ever.

The thought played and replayed in Sam's mind the whole trip home from the hospital as Lindsey chattered nonstop.

Once home, Sam rounded the corner of the house and found Danny manning the patio's barbeque grill. Wearing jean shorts and a sleeveless T-shirt, he looked like a commercial for summertime picnics. The muscles in his arms rippled as he closed the lid and turned, his slow, lazy grin sending a blush to Sam's cheeks. There was something about his smile that always scrambled her brain and left her tongue-tied.

"Welcome home. Dinner should be ready in a few minutes." He slowly looked her up and down, then hooked one of the Adirondack chairs with his foot and scooted it over. "Better have a seat, Samantha. You look ready to fall down."

"Gee, and here I thought I was looking pretty good."

"You always look beautiful, Mama," Lindsey countered. Then she wrinkled her nose as she looked at Sam. "Even if you do dress like a boy."

Danny laughed and offered Sam his hand, gently lowering her into the chair. If her knees hadn't suddenly felt all wobbly, she would have batted his hand away. But she decided she'd feel worse if she fell flat on her face.

Danny turned to Lindsey. "Lindsey, darling, your mama doesn't dress like a boy. She dresses like a very attractive, no-frills kind of lady."

Lindsey cocked her head as she considered his statement, while Sam wondered if there was any chance the brick patio would suddenly split open and let her slither between the cracks.

"I thought boys only like girly-girls."

Danny shrugged. "Some do. Some don't. Depends on the boy." He paused and sent Sam a smoldering look. "And the girl."

"Do you think my Mama's pretty?"

"Lindsey June Collins," Sam gasped. This had to stop.

Danny ignored her and kept his attention on her daughter. "I think your mama's beautiful. I always have."

Sam swallowed another gasp as Lindsey's brow

furrowed. She sent Danny a quelling look, but he pretended not to notice. "You mean you knew my Mama before? When?"

Danny leaned over and ruffled Lindsey's hair before he turned back to check the meat. "It was a long time ago, kiddo." He glanced at Sam. "A very long time ago."

"Are you coming to my birthday party?" Lindsey asked.

Sam gripped the chair's armrest until her knuckles turned white. *Oh, Linds. Don't go there. Please don't go there.*

"Well, it depends on when it is. If I'm still here, sure I'll come. Do I have to wear a tux and everything?"

Lindsey giggled and for a split second Sam wondered if telling him would be so awful. He was a natural with kids. "No silly. It's a cookout. A bunch of the kids from school and church are coming. There'll be lots of old people here, too, so you won't feel left out."

Danny threw back his head and laughed. "Thanks, Lindsey. So when is the party?"

"Next Saturday. But my birthday is really on Sunday."

Something shifted in his eyes and Sam held her breath.

"And how old are you going to be? Twelve?" he asked quietly.

Sam knew the exact moment he did the math and came up with their ill-fated weekend. He stood stock still, but his eyes scorched her with blue fire—rage, fury, stunned disbelief, but mostly, betrayal. His gaze shot to her left hand and the wedding band proclaiming the lie.

"Will your daddy be at your party, Lindsey?" Danny asked, but his eyes never left Sam's face.

"My Daddy's in heaven. He died before I was

even born."

At her blunt statement, Danny turned and faced the little girl. His voice was filled with genuine emotion. "I'm sorry. That must be tough."

Lindsey shrugged. "I want Mama to get me a Daddy, just like all my friends have, but she doesn't really want to. She says she's too busy." Lindsey paused and considered him. "Will you be my Daddy?"

Sam lurched out of her chair. She swayed dizzily, gripping the nearest porch column. "Lindsey, honey, that is not a question you can ask someone. If I ever do get married, sweetheart, it'll have to be something between the man and me, okay?"

"You mean if you ever get married *again*," Danny added from behind her. His voice was pleasant enough, but Sam could feel the fury rolling off him in waves.

Afraid she might fall down, Sam slowly turned her head and lowered her voice to a hiss. "We can discuss this later."

His voice was equally lethal. "Oh, you bet we're going to discuss it, honey. In fact, I guarantee it." Then he turned back to the grill and announced, "Dinner's ready."

****

Sheriff Porter was in his office, booted feet propped up on the desk, hands behind his head, staring up at the water-stained ceiling when his phone rang.

"Porter."

"Medical Examiner for you, boss."

"Thanks, Alice." He punched another button on his phone. "Porter."

"Hey, Luke, Joe Carter. This'll all be in my official report, but I wanted to give you a heads up. Bottom line: I can't make a determination on cause of death beyond alligator attack."

Luke groaned. That's what he'd been afraid of. "Was Castle alive when he went into the water?"

"Definitely. That much is clear from the remains we have."

"Signs of a struggle?"

"Harder to determine, though we did find evidence on one of the vic's wrists to suggest he may have been tied up."

"So it was foul play. Can you get me more?"

"I'll try. But don't get too excited, Luke. You know we don't have much to work with. The mark could just as easily have been from one of those rope bracelets."

"On a suit like Castle?"

"It's possible."

Luke sighed. "I hear what you're saying. So we know, officially, that a gator got him. Which we already knew. We know his body wasn't dumped there; he was alive when he went in the water. Anything else to suggest a struggle?"

"A gash on the same arm that appears too neat and tidy to come from a gator's teeth."

"Knife?"

"Possible. I have some people checking on that and the rope. I'll keep you posted."

"Thanks, Doc. I appreciate you rushing this."

"I'll expect dinner next time I get out your way. In the meantime, good luck."

"Thanks." Luke tossed the phone back into the receiver and resumed counting the ceiling tiles. He wanted to blame Castle's death on the gator and be done with it, but every cop instinct he had was screaming murder.

He was running through his list of suspects again when his office door banged open and Sanchez stormed in. "I hear you were harassing my wife and family. You got questions for me, Sheriff, then ask me. Not my family."

Luke's boots hit the floor and he stood and planted both fists on the desk. "Since, last I checked, I'm still in charge in this here town, I'll ask whatever questions I think need askin'. Fact is, you were supposed to show up at the town meeting the other night and you didn't, which was a surprise to your family. I'm checking on everybody who wasn't where they said they'd be at the time in question."

Porter leaned closer and caught a whiff of whiskey on the other man's breath. "Where you been, Sanchez? You been drinkin'?"

The other man looked away and visibly brought himself under control. "Look, I'm having some problems at home right now, but I'm handling it, okay? As for Tuesday night, I got in a fight with the missus just before the meeting, so I stopped off to have a drink and work some of my frustration off on a dart board."

"What'd you fight about?"

"Is that an official question?"

Luke narrowed his gaze at the other's man's lack of respect. This had to be the booze talking, because in fifteen years on the force, Sanchez had never acted this way. "Call it whatever you want."

Sanchez cleared his throat and studied his clenched fists. "Money. As always. We're working on it, like I said."

"Good. Now go home and sober up before your shift."

Sanchez opened his mouth to speak, then thought better of it and stormed out without another word.

Luke sat and drummed his fingers on his desk. His list of suspects kept getting longer, not shorter.

Chapter Sixteen

Strained was too mild a word for the somber group seated around the sagging picnic table. Katharine looked ready to bolt while the flames shooting from Danny's eyes could have melted steel. Lindsey, one sharp little cookie, looked from one adult to the other and finally blurted, "I'm sorry I made everyone mad. I didn't mean to. I just thought it would be cool to have a Dad." Her chin quivered and Sam's stomach knotted tighter. She wouldn't even glance in Danny's direction.

Sam reached over and patted Lindsey's hand. "It's okay, Princess. Just stop trying to marry me off, okay?" Her attempt at humor fell flat as Lindsey nodded glumly.

After several more minutes of awkward silence broken only by the sound of forks pushing food around on plates, Katharine cleared her throat and stood. "Thanks for grilling, Danny. I think I'll get started on the dishes. Lindsey, I could use a hand."

If Mama ever doubted Sam's story about her elopement and the death of her new husband, she'd never said. But as her eyes darted from Danny to Sam and back again, Sam knew she was connecting the dots now. Some lies, once put into place, were difficult to unravel. Sometimes, the truth wasn't kind, either.

As the silence stretched, Sam propped her elbows on the table and rested her chin in her hands, trying to figure out where to start, how to begin.

Danny beat her to the punch. He leaned across

the table, every muscle bunched, words ground out between clenched teeth. "Look me in the eyes and tell me she's my daughter. And then tell me what you were thinking to keep it from me."

Sam looked across the yard, unable to meet his eyes. When she opened her mouth, no words came out. Still, she had to do this — for his sake, as well as her own. Mustering up every shred of courage she possessed, she cleared her throat and tried again. "She's your daughter."

Danny reached across the table and raised her chin so she had no choice but to look at him. His touch was gentle, but insistent. "Now say it again."

Tears leaked out the corners of Sam's eyes. "She's your daughter."

"Why didn't you tell me? Why?" he demanded.

"Would you have wanted to know?"

There was a long moment of silence. "That isn't the point."

"Isn't it? What would you have done if I'd told you I was pregnant?"

He released her chin and rammed a hand through his hair. "I don't know."

"Besides, I didn't even know how to find you."

"Annie knew," he countered.

"Yes, she did. And she'd also just told me about your engagement to some socialite from an important family."

He scowled. "I still had a right to know."

Sam sighed. How could she possibly explain? "At first, I didn't realize I was pregnant. Then, I was completely stunned. I never thought it could happen after one time."

One corner of his mouth kicked up. "More like, one weekend, you mean. It was certainly more than once."

A hot flush raced up Sam's neck and she could feel her ears turn red. "Whatever, I'd never done

174

anything like that in my life, and I was scared spitless. I knew nothing about having a baby and given the childhood I'd been through, I wasn't sure I was a good candidate for parenthood."

He went stone still. "Did you consider abortion?"

Sam recoiled as though he'd slapped her. "Of course not. No. Not even once."

"Adoption?"

"Yes. I thought about it. A lot."

"What made you decide to keep her?"

Sam chewed her lip. Debated how much to say. "I fell in love with the little person growing inside me. Annie said she'd help me, and I decided I'd figure out how to do the motherhood thing right." *And I couldn't give up the one part of you I still had.* But Sam couldn't tell him such a thing. Not now with him scowling at her.

"So Annie knew, too. Who else?"

"No one."

"Not even your mother? Jimmy Wayne?"

Sam sighed. "Just Annie."

He reached across the table and snatched up Sam's left hand, pushing his thumb over the thin gold wedding band she wore. "And this? Who came up with this scenario? Or was there really some poor schmuck you talked into marrying you?"

"Annie suggested it, initially." When he snorted in response, Sam lost her grip on her temper. "Look, you weren't there. You'd flown off into the wild blue yonder and gotten engaged and I was alone and pregnant—and scared. I decided I wanted to raise my child here, where I'd grown up, but this is a small town. I didn't want her to grow up with the stigma of an unwed mother."

"Is my name on her birth certificate?"

Sam looked away and shook her head.

"Whose is, then? Or does it say 'unknown?'"

Sam had to clear her throat. "It says 'John

Halstead.'"

"The imaginary husband, I take it." He stood up and began pacing. "For a woman who's big on honesty and telling it like it is, that's one whopper of a lie to tell all these years."

Sam didn't like his tone. "I did it for Lindsey."

"And to protect yourself."

Sam tried to push up from the table, but found her legs wouldn't hold her, so she plopped back down. "Look, Danny, you don't have to like what I did, you don't have to believe me when I say I did it to protect her. These are the facts."

Squirrels chattered in the live oaks soaring above them, but down on the patio, the only sound was Danny's pacing across the aged bricks.

"She deserves to know she has a father."

"She knows she had one, once."

"Don't push me right now, Sam. You know what I mean."

"No, I don't actually. You tell her you're her father and then what? Will you stick around and be a part of her life? Go to parent-teacher conferences and tuck her into bed at night? Because if all you plan to do is drop a bombshell and leave, it'll be worse than what she's got now and I won't let you do it."

He crossed his arms and glared at her. "I'm not going to hurt Lindsey. She's a great kid." He paused. "Besides, you may not have a choice about all this."

Sam heart threatened to thump right out of her chest. "Meaning?"

"Meaning I have some thinking to do. And my lawyer to call."

He turned and started towards his cottage, then stopped and looked back over his shoulder. "This is not over, not by a long shot."

Wobbly knees or not, Sam lunged to her feet, gripping the table for support, every mama bear

176

instinct in full protective mode. "Don't you dare say anything to her without talking to me first."

He barked out a harsh laugh. "You've been calling the shots for too long, Sam. Now it's my turn. I'll get back to you."

****

The scene with Danny sapped what little strength Sam had left. She stumbled into the house and collapsed on the sagging living room sofa, too tired to sit, too wired to sleep. The old metal-blade ceiling fan lazily stirred the air and Sam flipped through channels with the ancient remote. There wasn't anything on worth seeing, but she didn't have the energy to get up and turn it off. Oh, for the simple luxury of a remote that changed channels *and* actually turned the TV off, too. But this was her reality—and another glaring difference between her life and Danny's.

He was going to call his lawyer. *Oh, God, no.* Would he try to take Lindsey totally away? Sam didn't think he would be so cruel, despite how angry he'd been tonight, but she really had nothing to base it on but a gut feeling. She really didn't know him at all.

Would he want visitation? Would Lindsey spend the rest of her childhood shuttling back and forth between Florida and California, with school vacations neatly divided between her two parents? Sam clutched the remote. She didn't want such a thing for Lindsey either, and yet...

Danny was her father. He was a good man and the two of them deserved to have a relationship. But was there a way to do it without causing Lindsey more pain?

Several cars rumbled up the gravel road and Sam struggled to a sitting position. A quick glance out the window showed Emma Jean's smoke-belching Toyota, along with two other cars she didn't recognize. Suddenly, the car doors opened and what seemed like dozens of women spilled out and up the porch steps, Libbey leading the charge. Not bothering to knock, she just opened the door and stuck her head around it.

"Oh, good. You're awake." She bounded into the room, casserole dish in hand.

"Lindsey in bed yet?" Emma Jean asked, coming in right behind her.

"I'll check," Libbey offered and then raised at brow at Sam, looking for directions.

Sam nodded towards the hallway. "Second door on the left."

Libbey leaned over and brushed a kiss on her cheek. "I'm so glad you're okay. We need you." Then she disappeared down the hall.

Mama appeared and helped Emma Jean direct the casserole brigade towards the kitchen, where Sam heard the fridge and cabinets opening and closing, along with light-hearted laughter.

Sam sat on the sagging sofa, speechless. What were they doing here? She recognized most of these women, but except for Emma Jean, none of them had ever been there before. Had something else happened? She wondered. But they didn't sound worried. Before Sam could make any kind of sense of it all, they trooped back into the living room and took up seats around the room. Mama and Emma Jean grabbed a few extra chairs from the kitchen and once everyone was seated, Emma Jean looked at Sam. Concern and affection shone from her eyes.

"I'm so glad you're okay, Sam. We were all so worried."

There were nods and murmurs of agreement.

Sam looked around the room, still unsure what to say, or do, or how to act. She'd delivered casseroles a few times for funerals and shut-ins, but had never been on the receiving end of such a delivery and show of support. A quick look at Emma Jean and Libbey's faces said they had something on their minds.

"What are you doing here?" Sam blurted. When she saw the stricken looks on everyone's faces, she tried to make amends. "I mean—"

"It's okay, Sam. We know what you mean." This from Gina Northrup. "I can't speak for everyone, but I know I've not been as friendly as I could have been." She shrugged and looked around the room for support. "I guess this is my way of trying to make up for the past."

More nods and murmurs of agreement. Sam was completely stunned. And shocked. After all her years of searching for acceptance, they were reaching out to her.

"Why now?"

Principal Dower piped up. "We're against what the city commission is trying to do and we're here to see if we can't help stir up some community support." She reached into her leather satchel and pulled out a clipboard. "While you were in the hospital, we formed a committee." She waved a hand to indicate the other women in the room. "We've also started a petition and have gotten a good response so far."

"And we're doing another fundraiser, but this time it's going to be a spaghetti dinner on a Friday night," Libbey added. "We've talked to all the churches in town about putting a notice in their bulletin."

"Just because your last name is Collins, doesn't mean you're like Amos," old Mrs. Wickers added with a snort. She and her husband had farmed melons just outside town for fifty years, but this was the first time she'd ever said two words to Sam.

There was dead silence.

The woman flushed and cleared her throat.

"What I meant was—"

"You don't judge somebody by their past," Libbey said.

Gina nodded. "We don't think you killed him, but even if you had, we wouldn't blame you a bit."

More nods and sheepish looks.

Sam swallowed the lump in her throat as she looked around the room. "Thank you," was all she could manage.

Emma Jean stood, all business. "Don't thank us yet, Sam. We've got a long road ahead of us." She looked around the room. "And now we need to go and let Sam get some rest." She leaned over and gave Sam a quick hug. "Don't lose faith, Sam," she whispered.

And as quickly as they came, they disappeared.

****

Katharine was sitting on the porch, rocking, just before ten o'clock when the sheriff's SUV rumbled down the gravel drive. She had been trying to absorb all that had happened tonight. The show of support for Sam after all these years... She sniffed and wiped her eyes. It was overwhelming.

But when she saw Luke's SUV, emotions of a whole different sort made her heart race into overdrive. She was never sure if her reaction was a conditioned response to a representative of the law, or a female response to the sheriff himself. Either way, it left her flustered and tongue-tied.

The sheriff climbed out of the SUV and ambled towards her, features shaded by his Stetson, his broad shoulders and muscled chest visible through his uniform shirt. Katharine's heart skipped a beat and she patted the bun at her nape. He was so handsome he always made her feel old and dowdy by comparison.

He stopped at the foot of the wooden steps and tipped his hat. "Evenin', Katharine."

"Sheriff."

"I know it's late, but I wondered if I might sit a spell."

"Certainly." Katharine leaped from her chair, then forced herself to slow down. She clasped her hands in front of her and took a deep breath. "May I get you some tea?"

"That would be mighty fine, thank you."

Half afraid he'd be gone by the time she got back, Katharine hastily poured two tall glasses of iced tea. She plunked a lemon slice in each glass, dumped a few cookies onto a plate and raced back to the porch, tray balanced between her sweaty palms.

The sheriff stepped over to hold the door open for her, then took the tray and carefully set it down on the white wicker coffee table. He sat in a facing rocker, took a sip of tea and sighed appreciatively. "Hits the spot. Your tea is the best in the county."

Katharine felt a blush climb her cheeks as she waved the compliment away. "What brings you out here, Sheriff?"

He set his Stetson on the chair beside him and leaned forward, hands clasped between his knees. "I really wish you would call me Luke."

"I-I," Katharine cleared her throat. "Why would I do such a thing, Sheriff?"

He raised a brow and sent her a charming half smile. "Tsk. Tsk. Are you going to make me spell it out?"

She nodded and croaked out, "Please."

"It's no secret I hold you in high esteem, Miss Katharine; I always have, since we were kids. You're a fine woman and I'd be honored if you'd let me call on you."

Katharine remembered the way he used to look at her in high school, before she got involved with Amos, before all her dreams died. Luke was wearing the same look in his eyes now, the one that said he thought she was beautiful and desirable, someone he wanted to spend time with. But she'd had her fill of men spouting pretty words. Her husband could talk his way around anything and her into anything when he set his mind to it. She didn't want to get caught in any man's snare again. "To what end, Sher—Luke?"

He sighed and met her gaze squarely. "My timing is terrible and I'm probably going about this all wrong, but I love you, Katharine. Always have. I'd like to make you my wife."

Katharine gasped. "Wife? You can't be serious."

"More serious than I've ever been in my life."

Katharine was tempted, oh, she was tempted. But her marriage had made her wary. "Being married wasn't an experience I'm eager to repeat."

"You were married to a lousy, no-good, son-of-a-bitch who didn't deserve one minute of your time." He paused. "I don't hit, Katharine."

Betrayal pierced her heart. "But if you knew he did, why didn't you help me?"

His expression turned fierce, frustrated. "Because you wouldn't press charges. How many times did I plead with you turn him in? I'm paid to uphold the law, Katharine, but part of my job is to follow procedures. And without your testimony, there wasn't a lot I could do to protect you."

"I was scared."

"I know. So was I." He looked away; then looked back. "I spent many a night watching your husband, especially if he was drinking."

"You kept watch? Here?"

He looked down at his clasped hands. "Yep."

"I didn't know."

"You weren't supposed to. Neither was he. Or anyone else, or my butt would have been in a sling."

Katharine blew out a breath. "I'm not sure I ever want to trust another man enough to get married."

Silence fell between them and Katharine debated taking the words back. There was no sound except the creak of their rockers and the night creatures rustling in the nearby woods. From down near the water, they could hear the faint lapping of the river against the dock. Had she blown her one chance?

Finally, he spoke. "Fair enough. And certainly understandable. How about if we spend time together, no strings. If at any time you want me to quit coming around, you just say so."

Katharine's heart thundered as she looked at him. When was the last time a man had asked her opinion? Given her options? "Can you live with that?"

He smiled, a slow smile that melted some of the fear which had kept her heart frozen all these years. "Miss Katharine, I've been dreaming about you from afar most of my life. I'd love the chance to do it up close. I'll take whatever you're willing to give and thank the good Lord for it."

He stood and held out his hand. Katharine got to her feet and slowly placed her hand in his outstretched one. He gazed down at it, nestled in his much larger palm. "I won't betray the trust you place in me, Katharine. Not ever."

He placed a gentle kiss on her palm, then scooped up his hat, tipped it in her direction and disappeared into the night.

****

Danny looked out the tiny window overlooking the cottage's front porch and saw the sheriff's SUV head down the drive. He'd bet his Rolex the sheriff was sweet on Katharine. Danny wasn't sure the sheriff had what it took to solve this case, but he had no doubt the man would protect those he cared about.

Danny went back to pacing, the wooden floor squeaking with every pass. He had a daughter. Several hours after learning the fact, he was still having trouble wrapping his mind around it. He had a daughter.

Not just any daughter, either, but Lindsey. A bright-eyed little spitfire who was very much like her mother, the one woman Danny had never been able to wipe from his mind or heart. The question now was what to do about it?

He might be furious with Sam for keeping the knowledge from him, but once the rage cleared from his eyes he realized there were more important things he needed to focus on. Like knowing he'd give his life to keep Lindsey safe. And her mother. He and Sam would deal with the rest later.

Great, a little voice in his mind said. *You'll protect them with your life, but you have no trouble stealing their property from them.*

Not stealing, he protested. Buying. There was a difference.

Except for the fact Sam didn't want to sell. Didn't want to see this place subdivided, manicured and landscaped. After being here a while, he really couldn't blame her. The peace of the place was growing on him. This was old Florida, the way it used to be before it was discovered by tourists and developers.

His cell phone rang and he checked the caller ID. "Hi, Dell. Thanks for calling me back. Listen, this deal down here? I think we should pull out. The holdout owner doesn't want to sell, is adamantly opposed, and I don't relish a drawn-out legal battle to get it through eminent domain. The city commission has a document saying Jeremy promised them a bonus to get it done quick, but we may have to eat the cost." He could sell off some personal assets for Laurie and the girls.

"Listen, Danny, um, I had promised Jeremy I wouldn't tell you, but...well, with everything that's happened—"

"I know about his personal debts, Dell."

There was a pause and Danny heard her sigh. "I'm afraid it's worse than just personal debts, Danny. All the company assets are tied to this, too. And you know as well as I do that Overland Investments isn't patient when it comes to getting their money."

Danny reared back as though he'd been punched in the jaw and stood there, shaking his head in disbelief. What had Jeremy been thinking? Why had he done this? "Let me make sure I understand, Dell. He sunk everything he had—business and personal—into making this deal happen. Why?"

Another sigh. "I have no idea. He wouldn't say, just said to trust him and not say anything to you. He'd work it out."

Danny gripped the back of his neck as he paced. If he tried to back out, Laurie and the girls ended up penniless. And if he went through with it, Sam lost the property she'd spent a lifetime trying to save.

"Okay, Dell. Here's what I need. Get me a list of the exact numbers we're talking about here. Then I want a complete list of Jeremy's assets. I'll take it from there."

"What are you going to do?" she asked.

Danny shrugged, even though she couldn't see him. "No idea. But I'll think of something. Jump on this, okay?"

"You got it, boss."

Danny sucked in a breath. "Boss was Jeremy's title. Let's leave it that way, Dell. Stick with calling me Danny."

A pause. "Sorry. Sure, whatever you say, Danny."

"Thanks. I'll be in touch."

Once he disconnected, he punched in the number for his financial advisor. Maybe, if he liquefied all his assets, he could find a way out of this mess.

****

If Sam didn't get out of the house, she was going to crawl straight out of her skin. Her legs were twitching with the need to walk. She pushed up from the couch and then slowly walked across the porch and down towards the dock. She wanted to dive to her cave, but with this bandage, it wasn't a good idea. So she settled for the short walk to her pontoon boat.

She stepped aboard and slumped down onto the cushions, soothed as always, by the gentle lap of the water. She still couldn't get Lindsey to come out here with her. And her daughter still woke up screaming every night. Sam wasn't sure what to do about any of it, but for now, she'd just go for a little ride, try to clear her head. She stood up to start the engine and felt her knees begin their infernal wobbling again. Dang, she hated this.

Footsteps sounded on the dock. "You're not going out alone, are you?" Danny demanded from behind her.

Sam huffed out a breath, but didn't turn around. "Go away, Hastings."

"I asked you a question."

Sam glanced up. He stood behind her, arms folded, chin jutting out—the epitome of male stubbornness.

"What I do is none of your business." She checked the lines, prepared to start the motor.

"I'm making it my business."

Sam faced him and folded her arms. Just like his. "Give me a break. Where's all this concern coming from all of a sudden?"

"Lindsey needs you."

186

Sam bristled. "You don't think I know that? I'm her mother. I've been thinking about her needs her whole life. Now all of a sudden you show up all concerned—" Sam stopped, regretting where this was heading.

"I would have been concerned sooner had I known she existed!"

Sam's gaze darted up towards the house. "Keep your voice down," she hissed. "She is not going to find out like this."

"How is she going to find out?"

"I'm not sure yet."

Danny huffed out a breath. "Me either."

Afraid she was going to collapse in front of him and totally humiliate herself, Sam sank onto the bench seat. "Go away, Hastings. I can't deal with you anymore today."

He nodded and turned to go. "Just be careful. Don't let your fury with me override protecting Lindsey."

Sam shivered and rubbed her hands up and down her arms. She hated to admit it, but he was right.

Chapter Seventeen

At noon the next day, the Lady Bug was crammed to the gills. When Jimmy Wayne stepped through the door, Danny nodded to the seat beside him at the counter.

"What can I do for you, Jimmy Wayne," Danny asked. He'd been more than a little surprised when Drake called him and asked for a meeting.

Drake smiled, but it didn't reach his eyes. "I have a few questions; thought we should discuss them, man to man."

Danny took a sip of his coffee and waited. In negotiations, silence could work to your advantage.

Before either man spoke, a young girl scampered over. "Hi, I'm Julia and this is my first day. What can I get for you boys?"

Danny couldn't help smiling. She was so painfully young and trying so hard to seem older. "I'll have a burger, fries and a shake."

Across the table, Jimmy Wayne raised his brows.

"What?"

"Thought all you California types were vegetarians."

Danny didn't miss a beat. "Thought all you southerners were rednecks."

The diner went dead silent. Danny didn't take his eyes off Jimmy Wayne.

"Nope," was all Drake said.

"Same for Californians," Danny added, relieved

when the conversations around them resumed.

Jimmy Wayne didn't say a word until he had polished off his chili and cornbread. He pushed his plate aside and leaned forward. "You the one who took at shot at Samantha?"

Danny didn't blink. "No. You?"

Jimmy Wayne huffed out a breath and sat back. "Now why would I want to hurt my fiancée?"

Before he could control his reaction, Danny barked, "Your what?"

Jimmy Wayne's look turned smug. "My fiancée," he repeated. "Didn't she tell you we're getting married?"

"Must have slipped her mind," Danny shot back, wiping his hands on a napkin. Sam planned to let this jerk raise his daughter? No way in hell. But he'd discuss it with Sam.

"I don't like you staying out at the fish camp," Jimmy Wayne stated, his look hard.

"Tough. I'm not going anywhere until this situation is resolved."

The two stared each other down like junkyard dogs claiming territory.

"Okay, Drake, just for the sake of argument, suppose it wasn't me. Who else would have taken a shot at Sam?"

Drake obviously didn't want to answer, but finally said, "I'd say the city commissioners. The three of them couldn't fight their way out of a paper sack without help, so they would have had to hire someone."

"But if Sam died, it'd be even longer before the deal went through."

Drake shrugged and held up his coffee cup to Julia, signaling a refill.

"Who else?"

Jimmy Wayne nodded towards the open window to the diner's kitchen. "Marco Juarez has been watching Sam since we were kids. Makes me nervous. He disappeared for a few years and scuttlebutt says he did hard time. We don't need his kind here."

Danny studied Juarez. Clean-shaven and well-groomed, he still looked like a man who'd seen his share of trouble. "What reason would he have to take a shot at Sam? Especially if he likes her?"

Jimmy Wayne shrugged again, then stood. "I need to get back to the store. Thanks for lunch."

Danny's irritation spiked as he picked up both checks. For Annie's sake, he'd tried to like the man, but there was just something about him...

He was a hunter, his cousin had said. Could he have shot Sam?

Danny left Julia a nice tip and headed back to the marina, to be near Sam and Lindsey. He couldn't shake the feeling things were coming to a head.

****

Luke Porter waited for the diner to empty after lunch before he approached Juarez. The other man's eyes widened slightly and his chin hitched up a notch, but otherwise, he didn't react. Just kept wiping down the counter.

"Juarez."

The other man nodded. "Sheriff."

"I need to ask you a few questions." He looked up as Darla came through the swinging door. "All right with you if I borrow him for a few minutes, Darla?"

"Sure thing, Sheriff. We're done with the rush anyway. Go ahead and use the office." She pointed with her head.

"Thanks." Luke waved the younger man ahead of him into small room, no bigger than a coat closet. "Have a seat." Luke took the chair behind the desk, leaned back and regarded the other man solemnly. "You know we've had some trouble here lately, so

I've gotta ask you, where were you last Saturday night about ten p.m., and this past Tuesday about six-thirty p.m.?"

"I was here, working. Ask Darla. I'm here every night until closing, except Mondays."

"What happens on Mondays?"

Juarez looked away, then met his gaze squarely. "My meeting with my parole officer."

"Okay. Last Saturday, what time did you get off?"

"Usually, it's about ten-thirty before we're done for the night."

Luke wrote the time down, with a note to check with Darla. "Did you go straight home after you left here?"

"No. I dropped by the Clam Shell first. Had a beer."

"Anybody there who can verify it?"

Juarez snorted. "Come on, Sheriff. I'm invisible in this town. Nobody would notice if I was there or not, unless something bad happened. Then they'd all swear I was."

Luke nodded. Sad, but true.

"So, this about the guy went missing?"

"Yeah."

"I never met him. Besides, I hate water."

"Word is you like Sam Collins, though."

Even under his dark skin, a faint flush brushed Juarez's cheeks. "She's a nice lady, but I don't know what that has to do with anything."

"Don't feed me any bull, Juarez. It's been all over the papers and the news. He wanted to buy Ms. Collins property. She doesn't want to sell."

"Then she shouldn't have to."

"I agree, but it's beside the point. The point is, did you have something to do with Mr. Castle's disappearance?"

Juarez's eyes narrowed and his hands balled

into fists. "I did my time, Sheriff, paid my debt. I had nothing to do with any of this."

"Were you working Tuesday night?"

"Yes. Open to close."

Luke sat back and studied the man as a minute, then two, ticked by. Satisfied, he met the other man's eyes. "Okay. You're free to go. But don't leave town."

Juarez stiffened, then turned and marched from the room. Luke sat for another minute, idly tapping a finger on the desk. With a sigh, he stood, closed his notebook, and thanked Darla on his way out.

Juarez was hiding something, but his gut said it wasn't murder.

****

The inactivity was killing her by inches. But every time Sam stood for more than five minutes, her knees got wobbly and her vision did this weird blurring thing, forcing her back down into a chair. Luckily—or unluckily, depending on your perspective—they hadn't had any cruises scheduled today. Mama didn't swim, never had, and wouldn't go out in a boat unless she absolutely had to.

Sam propped her elbows on the counter in the bait shop and rested her chin in her hands. Lindsey had another nightmare last night. This was the third one in less than a week. You didn't have to be a shrink to know they started after Castle's disappearance.

How was his family taking it, Sam wondered. She was used to thinking of him as "that developer," but Danny had said he had a wife and twin girls. She remembered the agony of Annie's death and said a quick prayer for them.

With no customers in the shop right then, Sam flipped open the paper and then gasped at the sight of Lindsey's face on the front page, opposite Castle's.

Does the girl know more than she's saying? The

headline screamed.

Sam scanned the article, heart pounding. Who would write this? It was pure speculation. How could they print such total fabrication? They as much as said Lindsey knew what happened. Worse, if Castle's death was murder, it reminded the killer there might be a witness.

Fear and fury rolled over her in waves, fighting for control. Fury won out. She picked up the phone and dialed the number listed under the byline.

The minute the reporter answered, Sam took his head off. "How could you do something so completely irresponsible? Why on earth would you put the picture of a child on the front page with no warning, no thought for the possible consequences?"

"You must be Samantha Collins." Before she could confirm or deny, he raced on. "Listen, it's a great human interest angle. Did your daughter see more than she's saying, Ms. Collins? Or is it Miss?"

"You creep. Do you not realize you may have put my daughter in danger?"

He paused for just a moment, and Sam wanted to call the words back. "Why? I thought the sheriff said Castle's death was an accident. How could this story endanger Lindsey?" Sam could almost hear the wheels turning in his brain. "Unless it was murder and she was a witness. Is that what happened, Ms. Collins?"

Too angry with him—and herself—to speak, Sam slammed the phone down with a growl.

"What was that all about?" Danny asked, the screen door slapping behind him.

Too angry to speak, Sam merely turned the paper around and jabbed a finger at the offending article.

"Oh, hell," Danny murmured, sliding onto one of the stools, scanning the article.

When he finished, he looked up and there was a

world of understanding in his eyes. He didn't beat around the bush. "This idiot" he thumped the paper "just painted a bulls-eye on Lindsey's back."

"Don't say that," Sam snapped back, wrapping her arms around her middle. The trembling started in her heart and in seconds, her teeth started chattering and her whole body shook.

Danny was around the counter in the blink of an eye. He pulled her into his arms. "I'm sorry. I didn't mean it literally." He leaned back so he could look into her eyes. "But you know it's the truth. We have to keep her safe."

Sam's legs wouldn't hold her up any more and nausea rolled in her stomach. She gripped the counter. "We have to protect her."

"And we will." Danny scooped her into his arms and headed out the door. "I'll get Katharine to cover the shop."

Sam wanted to protest, wanted to say she was fine, but the words wouldn't come. She couldn't depend on a rolling stone like him for the long term, but for today, she welcomed the security his arms brought. She rested her head on his shoulder, savored the rhythmic beating of his heart. He felt like home.

They were almost to the house when Sam saw something that tripped her already frantic heart into overdrive. She gripped his arm.

"I—Danny, I saw something over there, under Lindsey's window."

"What?"

"I'm not sure, but it reflected the light."

"Let me get you settled and I'll go take a look."

"No, I need to see."

Once there, he gently set her on her feet, but kept his arm around her waist.

They both stared. Right below Lindsey's window were footprints, two sets. A smaller set and a deeper, larger set. And reflecting the sunlight was an unbent paper clip.

Sam reached for it, but Danny stayed her. "Don't touch. We need to call Porter."

While they waited for him to arrive, Sam collapsed into a wicker chair on the porch. "This can't be happening. It can't," she whispered. Someone had been outside Lindsey's window. She knew the smaller footprints were Lindsey's, from the night she snuck out, but the larger set...

Within minutes, Porter's SUV came bouncing down the drive, a crime scene unit behind him. He didn't waste time on preliminaries. "Show me what you've got."

Danny led him around the side of the house and Sam could hear Porter's muffled curse.

Several minutes later, he appeared on the porch, Danny right behind him.

"You know what this means, right?"

Sam nodded. "Did you see the newspaper article?"

Porter spoke through clenched teeth. "I did. And I'll have that cub reporter's job before nightfall."

"So, now what?"

Porter looked at Danny. "The techs are making plaster casts of the footprints. I'll need to see yours, for comparison."

"He didn't do this, Porter," Sam said.

Luke merely raised a brow. "You know I'm going to look at everyone, Sam."

Sam looked at Danny and he nodded. She cleared her throat. "I'm going to trust you to keep this confidential, Sheriff..." she began.

"As much as I can, since I'm investigating what appears to be a murder."

"This has nothing to do with your investigation, not really."

"Why don't you just spill it and let me decide."

Sam took a deep breath. "Danny is Lindsey's father."

Porter's eyes widened, but he quickly masked his shock. "Does she know?" He looked from one to the other.

Danny answered before she could. "Not yet. I just found out recently, myself."

"How recently?"

"Since the night I got out of the hospital," Sam said in a rush, eager to change the subject.

"We're counting on your discretion, Sheriff," Danny added. "We don't want Lindsey to find out through the grapevine. This is too important."

Porter studied them both, then cleared his throat. "Sam, I need your boots, too."

A chill raced down Sam's spine. This felt too much like Porter's investigation after Pop died. For weeks, he'd kept her at the top of his suspect list. Only after every possible lead had been exhausted, had Porter finally decided she wasn't a suspect. It wasn't an experience she was eager to live through again. Still, he was the law. Sam gave a terse nod and headed for the house.

Katharine's car barreled down the drive. She leaped out and raced towards them, panic on her face when she saw the crime scene unit vehicles. "What happened? Is everyone okay?"

It took a while to calm her down and longer still before Porter and his techs left. Exhausted, worried and overwhelmed, Sam collapsed across her bed, desperate for a few moments to rest and gain her bearings. In moments, she was sound asleep.

****

When Sam woke two hours later, the house was stifling. She took a cool shower and then wandered into the kitchen, stomach growling. Turkey sandwich in hand, Sam walked down the gravel path, much steadier on her feet than she had been earlier. When she spotted the trampled area under Lindsey's window, the bread turned to dust in her mouth and she had to struggle to swallow. Thank goodness, Porter hadn't insisted on yellow crime scene tape around the area. It would have scared Lindsey to death.

Or maybe a dose of extra fear would have prodded her daughter to break her stubborn silence. Where was the line between "didn't know" and "wouldn't say"?

Sam stepped into the bait shop and stopped. Danny lounged at one of the stools, looking too much like he belonged there for Sam's peace of mind. A slow grin spread across his face when he saw her. "Hey there, beautiful. Sleep well?"

The casual endearment momentarily threw her. "I'm fine. Listen, we need to figure out what's going on. When I think about how someone actually stood under Lindsey's window..." she shuddered.

"Katharine and I were just talking about the same thing. I'm heading to the library. Want to come?"

Sam cocked her head, curious. "What are you thinking?"

Danny raised his hand and started ticking names off on his fingers. "Amos, Annie, Jeremy—all died in or around the river. Then Mrs. Mertz told me about another developer who came here last year and vanished. No one ever heard from him again."

Sam couldn't wrap her mind around the picture forming in her mind. "What are you saying?"

Danny's eyes were hard and determined, but sympathetic, too. "I think we need to start digging and the internet and the newspaper archives are the best places I know to start."

"Mama, can you—"

Katharine waved them away, her face pale. "Go. You don't even need to ask. I'll take care of things here and meet Lindsey's school bus."

Without thinking, Sam leaned over and brushed a kiss on Mama's cheek. "Thank you."

****

When Sam and Danny walked into Sheriff Porter's office later the same afternoon, the man looked like he hadn't slept in days. The knowledge softened Sam's attitude. He was taking this seriously.

He indicated the two chairs in front of his desk, then leaned back and said, "I haven't finished investigating—"

"That's not why we're here, Sheriff," Danny interrupted. "We just spent several hours at the library. Do you remember a man named Brian Edison?"

When Porter furrowed his brow, Sam jogged his memory by adding, "Of Edison Development?"

"Wasn't he the developer who came sniffing around your property last year?" Porter asked.

"That's him. Only he's missing," Sam said. "This was the last place anyone saw him."

"Did his family file a missing person's report?"

"They did. Later. We talked to his mother. He was a bit of a loner and this was his first attempt at property development. They didn't communicate regularly, so it was several weeks before she realized he never came back to Minneapolis."

Porter slapped a palm on the arm of his chair and pierced her with a look. "And once again, you were the last person to see him."

Danny surged out of his chair, but Porter waved him back down. "I'm just trying to follow all the threads, Hastings, and every time I do, they all lead back to Sam. She's the knot holding this all together."

"I didn't kill anyone," Sam said quietly. "You know that. And why would I stand outside my daughter's window?"

Porter shook his head. "I don't have any answers. You two just brought me more questions."

"Which we wouldn't have done if either of us had something to do with this."

Porter gave a quick nod of agreement. "Has Lindsey said more about the other night?"

Sam shook her head. "I keep asking, but either she can't say, or she won't."

Porter looked from one to the other. "Don't let that little girl out of your sight until we get to the bottom of this."

****

They were halfway back to the fish camp before Danny spoke. "So when were you planning to tell me about your engagement?"

Sam's head snapped up at the controlled anger seething behind his casual question. "There's nothing to tell. He asked; I said I'd think about it."

"You're not marrying him," he said, spitting the words from between clenched teeth.

Sam's chin shot up in the air. "That's not for you to say, Hastings."

"He's not raising my daughter." Danny's hands clenched around the steering wheel.

Sam looked out the window and sighed. "Be nice to share parenting, sometimes." At his sharp intake of breath, Sam realized she'd said the words out loud. She shook her head. "Look, Hastings, you'll be gone soon. I have to do what's best for Lindsey."

He pierced her with a fierce look. "Drake isn't it."

She studied his profile, the possessive attitude, and fought back. "You offering, Hastings?"

He said nothing, just swallowed hard.

Sam leaned her head against the headrest and stared out the window. "That's what I thought."

Chapter Eighteen

Friday night's spaghetti dinner fundraiser was an emotional roller coaster for Sam. The Chamber of Commerce meeting hall was packed, but Sam wasn't sure if it was because they all loved Emma Jean's spaghetti, or because they really wanted to help.

Sam headed towards the cashier where Libby and Belinda manned the till and the petition list. "How's it going, ladies?"

Libbey grinned. "We're raking in the big bucks tonight, Sam."

"And they're all signing the petition, too," Belinda added.

Sam's eyes filled. After all these years as an outcast, their support was overwhelming.

There was a commotion at the door and Sam turned, shocked to see Father Patrick and the entire Catholic Church softball team walk in, all of them in uniform. Behind them came the team from Redeemer Lutheran and her own teammates from Christ Community. Their wives and children streamed in behind them, until the line stretched out the door and down the sidewalk.

"Oh, wow," Libbey murmured.

Sam stood rooted to the spot as they paid for dinner, signed the petition, and then turned to her, offering brief words of encouragement as they filed past.

"Rough deal, Sam. We'll help you fight."

"This community won't stand for this."

"Keep up the good work. We need your marina."

"Don't give up, Sam."

"We'll beat this thing."

"Hang in there."

"You can count on us."

Once they had all come through the line and were filling their plates at the buffet table, Sam escaped to the restroom. She walked inside and leaned against the wall, arms wrapped around her middle, heart pounding. She couldn't believe this. All the church-league teams? Here to support her? It boggled the mind.

I know the plans I have for you...plans to give you a future and hope.

The Bible verse Emma Jean had each girl at Haven House cross-stitch onto a sampler sprang to her mind.

On its heels, Pop's voice chimed in. *You're nothing but a worthless girl. Worthless.*

Confused, Sam swiped at the tears leaking from her eyes. She wasn't a crier. Boys don't cry. At that, she laughed out loud. She was completely messed up in the head.

Libbey stuck her head into the room. "Sam, Emma Jean is looking for you."

Sam ducked her head and turned on the water. "Thanks. Be right there."

When she walked out of the restroom, she walked right into Danny. He reached out and steadied her, his expression hard. "I've been looking for you. Why did you disappear? You can't leave Lindsey alone."

She shrugged out of his grasp, stung. "I didn't. She's here in a room full of people she knows. I just went to the restroom, for heaven's sake."

"So where is she, then?"

Sam gripped his arm, her heart pounding. "What?"

"She's not here."

Sam took off running. When she skidded to a stop in the doorway, she scanned the crowd, frantically searching for that familiar blonde head. On her second pass, she found what she was looking for. Lindsey sat at a long table next to Gina Northrup and her daughter. Sam turned accusing eyes on Danny. "She's right there. Why did you scare me like that?"

"She wasn't there when I got here." He paused. "I was worried." He leaned closer and looked into her eyes. "I'll do whatever it takes to keep her safe. I need to know you'll do the same."

She shoved him out of her way and started towards Lindsey. "That goes without saying, Hastings."

Sam threaded her way between the tables until she reached her daughter. She reached down and hugged her and then said, "Where have you been, Linds?" She tried to keep her tone level, but Lindsey must have sensed her fear because she immediately twisted around to scan the room.

"What's wrong?"

"Nothing that I know of, but right now, I always need to know where you are, okay?"

Gina leaned across the table. "I'm sorry, Sam. I brought some desserts and asked the girls to help me carry them from the car. I wasn't thinking."

Sam slowly let out her pent-up breath, realizing Danny was standing behind her and had just done the same. "It's okay. I just worry, you know?"

Gina lowered her voice. "Something scary is going on. Makes me want to hide in my house with the shades drawn."

Sam nodded. "I know. Me, too."

"I know Sheriff Porter will get to the bottom of this." Gina glanced up. "Speaking of the sheriff..."

Sam turned to see Porter striding their way. The look in his eyes made her blood run cold. "Sheriff.

Good of you to come." She looked past him and nodded to Sanchez. "Mike."

Porter noticed the avid glances cast their way and lowered his voice. "There've been some new developments. We need to talk and for Lindsey's sake, I'd rather not do it with an audience."

An icy chill raced down Sam's back, but she stood her ground. "What are you saying?—"

Porter cut her off. "Not here."

Emma Jean stepped up. "Lindsey, honey, why don't you come help me serve the rolls while your mama and Sheriff Porter have a little chat." She led the way to the buffet, with Mama close on Lindsey's heels.

Mama sent a worried look over her shoulder, and Sam tried to smile back. She faced the sheriff. "Tell me what's going on."

He indicated the little meeting room next to the kitchen. "Let's talk in there."

When Danny tried to follow, Porter stayed him with a look. "You stay here."

Danny folded his arms over his chest. "Not on your life, Sheriff. I've been part of this from day one."

Porter considered, then gave a brisk nod and led the way into the room.

Sam rubbed her hands up and down her arms and tried to slow her racing heart. "What's going on?" She looked from Porter to Sanchez, who leaned against the door. Was he blocking her in?

Porter removed his Stetson and ran a hand through his hair. Then he reached into the pocket of his uniform pants and pulled out a plastic bag. Inside was a pocket knife with the initials CMFC on it. Collins Marina and Fish Camp. "Do you recognize this?"

Sam's mouth went dry. "Yes. It's mine. It went missing a couple of weeks ago."

"And you didn't think to report it?"

Despite the metallic taste of fear in her mouth, Sam laughed. "Come on, Sheriff. It's a pocket knife. I own a fish camp. I use them all the time. If I reported in every time I lost one, you'd be hearing from me twice a week."

"When was the last time you saw this one?"

"I really can't remember, Sheriff."

"Where did you last see it?"

Sam thought back. "The last time I remember using it was to clean some fish for a couple of tourists."

"I know what the initials are for, but what about the number?"

"We order them by the box, to use and sell. The ones we keep we engrave with a number to give us an idea of how many there are floating around."

Porter drew himself to his full height. "I'm sorry Sam, but Castle's blood was found on it. And your fingerprints. I have to take you into custody."

"I don't believe this," Danny growled. "It's all circumstantial. You can't tie any of it to Sam."

"I can't discount it, either. She had means, motive and opportunity." Porter turned to Sam. "I don't want to make a scene in front of everyone, so why don't we all just walk out quietly."

"Lindsey." Her name was the only thing Sam could think to say, the only real consideration.

Danny stepped in front of her, his hands gripping her icy ones. "Katharine and I will take care of her, I promise. And we'll get you out. We'll get a lawyer and—"

"I can't afford a lawyer," Sam mumbled. She couldn't even afford to fight the city commission.

Danny gently gripped her face between his palms. "Don't lose faith, Sam. You didn't do this and we're going to prove it."

Both Porter and Sanchez looked like they'd

rather be anywhere else. Sanchez shifted uneasily when Porter said, "Let's go, Sam."

Danny whirled on him. "You know this is crazy."

Porter met him hard stare for hard stare. "Step aside."

When the four of them stepped back into the hall, silence fell.

"What's going on, Sheriff?" A man called from the back.

"Go on back to what you were doing, folks, and let us do our jobs."

"Mommy!" Lindsey screamed, running towards her.

Sam looked at Porter, who nodded. Sam knelt down as Lindsey barreled into her. "I need to go with the sheriff, Princess. Memaw and Danny will look after you until I get back."

Lindsey's eyes filled. "How long will you be gone?"

Sam glanced at Porter, who shrugged. "I'm not sure yet, but I won't be gone one minute longer than I have to be, okay?"

The crowd parted and Emma Jean and Mama marched through like Moses and Aaron leading the Israelites through the Red Sea. "What is going on here, Sheriff?" Emma Jean demanded.

"Let's not make a scene, Ms. Tucker," Porter warned.

"Are you arresting Samantha?"

Loud gasps were heard around the room and the crowd surged closer.

"Please step out of the way, Ma'am," Porter said, advancing on the two women.

"Tell us what's going on, Sheriff, please," Mama said, and Sam saw Porter cave.

"New evidence has come to light, so I'm taking Samantha into custody for the murder of Jeremy Castle."

The crowd erupted into angry exclamations. Porter and Sanchez each grabbed one of Sam's arms and blazed a trail to the outside, a sobbing Lindsey on their heels. Once on the sidewalk, Katharine and Danny held Lindsey between them. Emma Jean, Libbey and the rest of the crowd surged onto the sidewalk.

"Mommy!" Lindsey screamed.

"I'll take care of her," Danny said, arms wrapped securely around a struggling Lindsey.

"We won't give up," Emma Jean called.

"Stay strong, Samantha," Katharine said.

"We love you," Libbey cried as Sanchez helped Sam into the back seat of the sheriff's SUV.

At the last second, Jimmy Wayne burst through the crowd. "Stop this. This is an outrage. We won't stand for this."

Porter ignored him and got in the SUV.

As they drove away, Sam glanced over her shoulder and saw Marco Juarez standing apart from the crowd. His eyes pierced hers as though he was trying to tell her something, but Sam had no idea what.

Then reaction set in and her teeth chattered all the way downtown.

****

The sheriff's substation only had two holding cells. From there, prisoners were usually transported to the county jail. After she'd been read her Miranda rights and fingerprinted, Sanchez led her to the cell on the left. It had a cot like the ones at summer camp, complete with blue ticking-stripe mattress and pillow. There was a toilet in the corner and nothing else.

Sam sank down on the bed, her mind muddled. Thoughts raced around in her head like a pinball in an old-fashioned arcade game. Through the chaos, only one thought managed to make itself understood; she'd been arrested for Castle's murder.

Chills still wracked her body, so she wrapped her arms around her middle and rocked back and forth. She had to think.

She was in jail for murder.

Which meant Castle's death hadn't been an accident.

And whoever killed him was still out there.

And maybe after Lindsey.

Her breath came in short pants and her fingers started tingling. She put her head between her knees to stave off hyperventilating. Danny would protect Lindsey, with his life if necessary. Of that, she had no doubt.

A noise outside her cell made her look up. Sanchez leaned against the bars, his expression sheepish. "For what it's worth, Sam, I don't think you did this. And I don't think Porter does, either."

"Then why am I in here while the real culprit is still walking the streets?"

Sanchez checked behind him to make sure they were alone. His voice was barely a step above a whisper. "I think Porter is hoping once you've been arrested, the real perp will relax his guard and make a mistake."

Sam leaped to her feet. "Are you saying I'm being used as bait?"

Mike patted the air and glanced over his shoulder again. "Shhh. It's just a guess, okay. I just came by to tell you not to worry."

Just then Alice, the dispatcher, burst through the doorway. "Sam, honey, I just heard. You'll be out of here in no time, don't you worry. In the meantime, is there anything you need?"

What could she say? *I need out of here. I need to keep my daughter safe. I need the killer caught.* Finally, she merely smiled and said, "Thanks, Alice. I'm okay."

After they left, Sam paced the confines of the cell until she couldn't walk any more. Then she collapsed onto the narrow bed, but sleep wouldn't come. What was going on in their sleepy little town? How could she have been arrested for murder?

The biggest concern though, was Lindsey. She knew Danny was right. Whether Lindsey had seen anything that night or not, the fact someone thought she had, put her in danger. Sam didn't doubt Danny and Mama wouldn't let Lindsey out of their sight, but she wanted to do it herself. It was her job, her privilege, her responsibility as Lindsey's mother.

She tossed and turned until she saw the first lightening of the sky outside the high barred window. As she drifted into an uneasy sleep, her last thought was how she'd seen more support from the community in the last few weeks than she ever had in her whole life.

She wondered how long it would last.

****

When Porter's SUV pulled away from the curb, Danny scooped a hysterical Lindsey into his arms and headed for his car, Katharine following close behind.

Once he had her buckled into the passenger seat, he turned to Katharine. "Are you okay to drive, or would you rather ride with us?"

Danny saw Katharine straighten her shoulders and look him in the eye. "I'll follow you home." He wondered if she—or Sam—realized how very much alike they were. Not in stature, but in sheer strength of will. He nodded and climbed behind the wheel.

He watched Lindsey out of the corner of his eye as he drove. The sobbing had slowed to a trickle of silent tears, but she still looked much too fragile. He flipped on the radio and sent her an encouraging grin. "Normally, driver picks the station, but today I'll let you slide. Put on whatever you want."

Lindsey looked out the window. "It's okay. You can pick."

Danny didn't press, just kept driving. After a while, he tuned in an easy listening station. Silences always made him feel he needed to fill them, and since he didn't want to push his daughter—his daughter!!—he kept time to the music with his fingers. She'd talk when she was ready. He'd seen Sam wait her out more than once.

They were only a few miles from the fish camp when she whispered, "Will Mommy be okay in jail?"

"Your Mom is a strong lady, Lindsey. She'll be fine. Actually, she's probably more worried about you than anything else."

"Me? Why?"

Danny thought a moment, trying to find the right words. "Lindsey, you're a real smart girl, so you know something is wrong besides just the situation about the fish camp. Sheriff Porter thinks my friend dying might not have been an accident."

He waited while she digested his words. Even at her age, she'd seen and heard enough about murder on the news and elsewhere to know what it meant, but he didn't think she'd ever dealt with it in relation to her safe little world. He hated to shatter her innocence, but knew he had to, to some extent.

When it sunk in, Lindsey turned to face him, eyes wide. "You mean somebody," she swallowed, "killed him?"

"We don't know for sure, but it looks like it." He turned off the highway and onto the gravel drive to the fish camp. He parked, pocketed his keys, and then turned to face her. "I know people have been asking you this, Lindsey, but I have to ask again. If you saw anything the other night, anything at all that might help the Sheriff figure out what's going on, now is the time to say it."

"But I don't know!" she cried. She pushed her

fisted hands on either side of her head. "It's like...like...like a kaleidoscope Mommy bought me. Every time you turn it, it always looks like something else."

"You mean you see snatches of stuff, bits and pieces?"

She looked at him, agony in her eyes. "Yeah, but I can't put them all together. They just disappear."

He reached over the gearshift and pulled her into his arms while she sobbed. He murmured soothing words in her ear and slowly rubbed her back. Seeing her hurt tore open a piece of his heart he knew would never heal again.

Eventually, Katharine stepped up and gently herded Lindsey into the house, one arm tightly wrapped around her. Danny waited until they were out of earshot, then whipped out his cell phone and called his office. He needed expert legal help and he knew just where to get it. Sam wouldn't spend a second more in jail than she had to. Not if he had anything to say about it.

Chapter Nineteen

The next morning, Sanchez escorted a man Sam had never seen before down the hall. Sanchez unlocked the cell, let the man in, then locked it again before he left. "Says he's your lawyer."

A well-manicured hand was thrust in her direction. "James Roberts, Esquire, at your service."

Sam looked him over, from his crown of snow white hair, past the custom-tailored suit, to the tips of his shiny wingtips. "You are not from legal aid."

He threw his head back and laughed, a deep, belly laugh that boosted Sam's confidence like nothing else would have. "Not for a lot of years, no."

"I can't afford you."

"You don't have to. My fees are all taken care of."

She only knew one person in town who would go to such lengths for her. "By Jimmy Wayne?"

Roberts frowned. "I don't know a Mr. Wayne."

Now it was Sam's turn to frown. "Then who hired you?"

"Danny Hastings. I've known him since he was just a little shaver."

"But..."

He held up a hand. "Look, Ms. Collins. Danny said you'd probably protest, but I should ignore you."

"What?"

He smiled. "He also said you were a very sharp lady. The truth is, you need help and I'm here to provide it. Go after Danny later, in person." He sat down on the cot and pulled a yellow legal pad out of his briefcase. "Start at the beginning and tell me everything that's happened."

Sam wanted to argue, but he had a point. And besides, he was her means out of this place.

An hour later, Roberts stood and called for Sanchez to let him out. "They have nothing but circumstantial evidence, most of it flimsy at best. We'll have you out of here in a jiffy."

Sam wondered what "a jiffy" meant in lawyer-speak, and less than thirty minutes later, she found out. Instead of Sanchez, Sheriff Porter walked though the doorway, Roberts hot on his heels. Porter unlocked the cell and said, "You're free to go. For now. But don't leave town."

"Why the sudden change?" Sam asked.

Roberts grinned. "I'll explain outside."

As they walked out the back door of the sheriff's substation, they passed Sanchez on his way in, leading a handcuffed Marco Juarez.

Sam's eyes widened. Marco focused the same intent, unblinking stare on her as he had yesterday. As he passed her, he looked over his shoulder and didn't break eye contact until the station door closed behind him. Marco, the killer? Despite all the rumors over the years, it was hard to imagine. He'd always treated her with respect.

Sam shivered and forced her attention back on what Roberts was saying. "Besides nothing but a boatload of circumstantial evidence, I convinced the sheriff you weren't a flight risk. Second, the crime lab called with DNA results of some hairs found in Castle's car. They belong to the guy they just brought in, Juarez."

"What happens now?"

He smiled. "You go home and take care of your daughter and let me worry about the legal details."

"I really can't pay you." Sam felt the need to say it again.

"As I said, take it up with Danny."

****

Sam was unprepared for the sight that greeted her when Roberts pulled up at the marina. The parking lot was full of cars and draped across the front porch was a crayon-drawn banner that read: Welcome home, Mommy.

Before she was completely out of the car, Lindsey burst through the front door, raced down the steps and straight into Sam's arms.

Sam wrapped her in a hug so tight neither one of them could breathe, but she had to get as close as possible. She breathed in Lindsey's scent and stroked her hair and thanked God again for giving her this most precious of gifts.

Sam saw Danny over Lindsey's shoulder and her heart gave a funny little lurch. Oh, to have Lindsey and Danny both in her life. Was it possible? Even for someone as damaged as she was? Could a guy like Danny want someone like her?

Danny loped down the stairs and wrapped his strong arms around both of them. "Welcome home, Sam," he whispered in her ear.

She remembered what he'd done and pulled back. He must have known she was thinking about the lawyer, for he put a finger over her lips. "Let's deal with that later, okay? For now, enjoy being home." He pointed his thumb over his shoulder. "Lots of people have come to help you celebrate."

Sam turned and saw her front porch crowded with Emma Jean and the girls from Haven House, along with several of the church ladies, and quite a few of the guys from the softball league. In fact, many were the people who attended yesterday's fundraiser.

She looked at Danny in confusion and he ran a finger down her cheek. "They're all here for you, Samantha."

Afraid her knees would buckle, she allowed him to lead her towards the house.

"Sam, telephone," someone called.

Still stunned, Sam went in the house and picked up the living room extension. "Hello?"

"This is not over," a voice whispered.

Sam couldn't tell if the caller was male or female, but the sound sent chills down her spine. "Who is this?"

"Remember what I said."

Click.

****

Somehow, Sam got through the next few hours. Her hands shook and her voice tended to quaver at unexpected moments, but she figured most folks would assume it had to do with her night in jail.

Once they were all gone and Lindsey was tucked into bed, Sam headed for the porch rocker. Her eyes automatically looked for Danny and she gave herself a stern mental shake. It hadn't happened often enough to call it a routine, exactly, but they'd sat out on the porch together enough nights that Sam was starting to look forward to it.

And that was dangerous thinking. If—and this was still a big if in Sam's mind—Marco was behind everything that had happened, then Danny would be heading back to California within the week. She couldn't let herself get attached to him. It would be too hard when he left.

"Evening, Beautiful," he said.

Sam whirled around and there he was, gilded by moonlight and looking far better than he should. As always, her heart hammered and she fought the unwelcome urge to run her fingers through his hair. To keep her hands from betraying her, she crossed her arms and leaned against a porch post.

"Thanks for what you did today, organizing all this." Sam indicated the banner that still hung above her head.

He stepped closer. "I had nothing to do with it. It all came from the townspeople."

At her skeptical snort, he cocked his head and studied her. "Do you still not get it, Sam? There may still be a few who view you with suspicion, but the rest care for you. I suspect most of them always have."

Sam stood and let his words wash over her. Her heart absorbed them like a salve, soothing so many of the places which had always been raw and burning.

Then she remembered the phone call. She stiffened and eyed him through the deepening gloom. "During the party, someone called and said this was not over."

He stepped closer and gripped her shoulders. "What? Today?"

Sam nodded as a shiver rippled up her spine.

"Did you tell Porter?"

"I called him from my cell. They're going to get the phone records, see what they can find out."

He pulled her into his arms and rested his chin on top of her head. "I wish you'd told me right away. I'd have been there for you."

Sam sighed and snuggled closer, content to enjoy the moment. "You're here now."

She felt him smile, and then he began to hum in her ear. Memories crashed over Sam as he took her right hand and clasped it in his. Awareness shivered over her skin and heat pooled low in her belly. She placed her hand on his broad shoulder and looked into his deep blue eyes. His slow, intimate smile reached all the way to her soul and drew her closer. Slowly, they danced in the moonlight while he hummed song after song they'd danced to all those years ago.

He kissed her after a while, a slow, tender

melding of mouths and hearts. His obvious care for her and gentle comfort filled so many of the empty places in Sam's lonely heart.

Yet, even while sensation and emotion filled every corner of her mind, a part of Sam's heart stood off by itself, reminding her this couldn't last. He'd leave before long. Just like before.

Still, Sam couldn't pull away. Instead, she rested her head on his shoulder and stored up memories for the lonely days ahead.

Chapter Twenty

The day of the father-daughter outing dawned clear and bright, a fact Danny became acutely conscious of when Lindsey came bounding into his cottage without knocking just as dawn streaked across the sky.

"Why aren't you up yet, Danny?" She bounced on the end of his bed, two neat braids bouncing with her. "It's time to go." Sam said she'd still been having nightmares and was sluggish in the mornings, but today, Lindsey was raring to go.

Danny cracked one eye open and tugged the covers securely around his bare middle, keeping a tight grip on them. He'd been dreaming about Sam and the very last thing he wanted to explain to their precocious daughter this morning was why the covers were poking up like a tent pole. "I don't think we need to leave right this second, Princess. We've got a bit of time."

"Not much," she insisted. Lindsey made a grab for the covers and Danny tightened his grip.

"Sweetheart, go on back to the house and I'll be there in a bit—after I've gotten dressed and made some coffee, okay?"

Her eyes widened suddenly as she looked at him. "Where are your PJs?"

"Ah, I...it was too hot, so I took them off."

Lindsey cocked her head as she studied him, but before he had to say any more, footsteps pounded up the two porch steps. "Uh, oh," Lindsey murmured as Sam peered through the open front door.

"Lindsey," Sam called in a stage whisper.

Danny looked past Lindsey and met Sam's startled gaze. He grinned when he saw her eyes flare as they traveled over his bare chest and her breath hitch when she saw the bulge beneath the covers.

When her eyes flew back to his, he arched a brow. *Like what you see?*

A flush crept up her neck and Sam turned her gaze on Lindsey. "Back to the house with you, young lady."

"Why can't I wait here?"

"Because it'll take longer then."

"Probably not, 'cause Danny already has his PJs off," Lindsey countered.

"Lindsey."

Little Miss Princess hopped off the bed with a long-suffering sigh. Sam turned back to the bed and Danny hid a grin at the way she deliberately kept her gaze above his neck. "I'll put a pot of coffee on." Sam grabbed Lindsey by the hand and towed her down the hall, all but dragging the little girl back up to the house.

Not just any little girl, he amended. His little girl. And her amazing, adorably sexy mother. His body added its agreement and he grimaced as he headed for a cold shower. "Down, boy." Today was about protecting Lindsey.

He stepped under the cold spray, fists clenched as he tried to deal with the fact Lindsey was going with Jimmy Wayne as her "dad". Since she'd asked him weeks ago, he and Sam had decided to leave things as they were. They'd tell her about Danny another time. They didn't want drama today and Jimmy Wayne was inclined to pout. Besides, this would free up Danny to keep a close eye on things. He knew this was the best way to handle things. But he didn't like it.

****

While the rest of the world had been sleeping soundly under a full moon and a false sense of security, he'd been hard at work. He put down the drill and examined the neat hole in the bottom of the canoe. He'd filled it with a water-soluble plaster which would dissolve in water. Now he carefully covered it with a light coating of silver spray paint to match the aluminum canoe. Within minutes of launch, the canoe would fill with water and unfortunately, one less Brownie would return from their trip today. He sighed. Some days, an exterminator's job was very unpalatable. Today was one of those days.

But after he'd seen Hastings put his hands all over his Samantha last night, he'd known he had to take action. Lindsey's unfortunate demise would forever ease his worry over what she might have seen the night of Castle's death. And when Hastings went to jail for her murder, he'd be right there to help Sam pick up the pieces.

He packed up his tools and headed home. He couldn't lose sight of what was important.

After today, Samantha would again be safe from those who wanted to harm her and her heart would be free to love only him.

****

Sam's emotions were still rushing all over the place when Danny walked into her kitchen and headed straight for the coffee pot. Once he'd taken a few sips, he plopped into a chair and focused the full force of his blue gaze on her. "Good morning, beautiful. Sleep well?"

"Not too bad," she said, which was a bald-faced lie and she feared he knew it. Between worries about Lindsey and her inexplicable, totally inconvenient desire to spend the rest of her days as close to Danny as she could get, Sam hadn't slept more than a few minutes, tops. She feared the bags under her eyes gave her away, if nothing else.

As if he'd read her mind, he rose and stepped up beside her, running his finger across each cheek. "You look tired, beautiful." He tucked a strand of hair which had escaped her haphazard braid behind her ear. "I'll take good care of our girl today, Sam, I promise. I won't let anything happen to her."

He must have seen something in her face, because he pulled her close and wrapped his arms around her, tucking her close enough her breasts were flattened against his chest and she could hear the steady rise and fall of his heartbeat. She hesitated for just a moment, then laid her head on his shoulder and absorbed his strength.

They rocked together for several minutes before she raised her head. "I could cancel my tours today and go with you."

"Spoken like a good mom worrying about her chick. We'll be fine, Sam. Go, you need the money and between Katharine and me, Lindsey will be more tightly guarded than Fort Knox. She'll hate it."

Sam couldn't help smiling. "Thank you."

He leaned in and placed a gentle kiss on her lips. "You're welcome."

****

The Brownie troop was a wriggling, giggling, chattering mass of excited eleven-year-olds, surrounded by several candidates for sainthood who were trying to corral their unruly offspring into some semblance of order. Danny laughed at the din as he and Katherine unloaded coolers and supplies from vehicles onto nearby picnic tables.

Nestled among the live oaks on the shore of Lake Nadine, the county park was a popular spot. They'd reserved all the canoes for a few hours, as well as the covered pavilion for the cookout and end-of-the-year awards ceremony scheduled for early afternoon. They wanted to insure a typical summer shower didn't ruin the fun.

Jimmy Wayne Drake stepped under the pavilion in an outfit more suited to an afternoon on a yacht than a canoe. Polo shirt, crisply pressed khaki shorts, deck shoes and a blue and orange baseball cap completed his ensemble. Drake took in Danny's jean shorts, already-sweaty T-shirt and muddy tennis shoes and dismissed him with one condescending nod in lieu of a greeting.

Danny grinned. "You know this is a picnic, not a regatta at the yacht club, right?"

"I do, do you?" Jimmy Wayne retorted. He turned, scanned the noisy crowd for a moment and then headed towards Lindsey. "I'll just go claim my date for father-daughter day."

Score one for the jerk. Danny chewed the inside of his cheek and bit back the urge to tell Jimmy Wayne just who Lindsey's father really was, but he shrugged it off. Let Drake enjoy his little fantasy today. He'd soon learn the truth, and Danny would delight in telling him.

And then what? a little voice asked. Will you stay and make them your family, take care of them forever? Till death do us part and all the rest of it?

Even while his heart smiled at the idea, the rest of him broke out in a cold sweat. He just wasn't family man material. He'd always known it.

One of the dads came trotting up, already looking frazzled. He stuck out his hand, T-shirt straining over his belly. "Hi, I'm Jim Reddick, Ashley's father. I'm supposed to give you a hand getting the canoes in the water." He gestured over his shoulder, where another father was trying to call roll over the din. "The natives are getting restless."

Danny turned to where Katherine was smoothing a plastic tablecloth over one of the tables. "Katherine, you okay here for a few minutes?"

She waved him away and efficiently snapped

another cloth over the next table. "Go, everything's under control here."

The two of them muscled the rolling rack down to the water's edge and in no time had all the canoes lined up on the banks, complete with paddles and life jackets.

Mr. Al, husband of the troop leader and guy in charge—presumably because he could yell the loudest—gave the signal and suddenly the area was teeming with squealing girls all trying to get in the boats and out onto the water.

Though Danny was peripherally aware of the actions around him, his eyes were focused on Lindsey—and on Jimmy Wayne. No matter that Sam and Lindsey adored the man, Danny had disliked him on sight—from the moment Annie had first introduced them. He saw Lindsey gesture from a canoe and Jimmy Wayne gesture from another. From his vantage point, Danny couldn't hear what was said, but despite Lindsey's frantic gesturing and head shaking, she eventually abandoned her canoe choice for Jimmy Wayne's. Danny gave her points for not pouting longer than it took to walk from one boat to the next.

As soon as Mr. Al waved his hands over his head in some sort of signal, the swarm of canoes surged away from shore. Shouted instructions from the dads; shrieks from the girls and more than one canoe spinning in circles. Danny found himself laughing at the spectacle, caught up in the excitement and joy of the moment.

Mrs. Mimms, the troop leader, materialized at his elbow. "What a bunch, huh?" she asked ruefully.

Danny chuckled. "They do have energy." He watched a canoe rock precariously. "And what they lack in skill, they make up for in enthusiasm."

"And volume."

They laughed as one of the canoes flipped over

during a water fight.

"Could you help me get a few more boxes out of my car?" Mrs. Mimms asked, shaking her head.

Danny turned and scanned the water until he spotted Lindsey and Jimmy Wayne's canoe, with Lindsey in front looking like Pocahontas with her two tight braids. He nodded to Mrs. Mimms. "Sure. Lead on."

****

Katharine smoothed the last tablecloth in place and scanned the water for the umpteenth time. She knew she shouldn't worry, but she couldn't help it. Lindsey was not only her own precious granddaughter, but knew she was Sam's very reason for drawing breath. If Katharine let anything happen to her...she didn't even want to imagine such a thing. She didn't think Sam would survive it.

She tossed the extra sacks into the trash can and secured the lid, then scanned the water again. And again.

Lindsey and Jimmy Wayne were gone.

No. She looked again, counted all the boats, scanned the hair and profile of each little brownie. No Lindsey.

Without thought, Katharine sprinted for the water's edge as fast as her arthritic knees would allow. She grabbed the extra "emergency" canoe and clambered in, alarmed at how easily the thing threatened to capsize. Heart pounding with fear for Lindsey and panic over being in the water to begin with, she grabbed the paddle and headed for the cove along the western shore. It was the only logical place they could have gone; the only part of the lake not visible from the picnic area.

The canoe spun in a circle and she had to stop and calm herself. "Side to side, Katharine. Come on. Sam taught you how to do this." Though truthfully, Katharine hadn't wanted to learn. She'd always loved to watch the water, but always been terrified to be in it. Especially after Amos held her head under water during one of the swimming lessons he insisted on right after their marriage. She gripped the paddle more firmly. That was past and didn't matter. What mattered was finding Lindsey.

After a few more fits and starts, she finally got the canoe headed in the right direction. Paddling with all her might, she raced after her grandchild. "Please, God, let her be safe. Let her be okay. Let me get there in time."

****

Danny and Mrs. Mimms carted what seemed like the entire contents of someone's house, but between every trip, Danny checked on Lindsey. When he saw her splash the nearest canoe with her paddle, Danny turned back for the last load.

This trip took the longest, since he had to wait for Mrs. Mimms to round up all the stuff which had spilled out of the other boxes and bags, but eventually they returned to the picnic area.

As soon as Danny set the box on the nearest picnic table, he turned towards the water, looking for Lindsey. When he didn't spot her after three sweeps of the crowd on the water, the hair on the back of his neck stood up. He checked his watch. In total, they'd been gone less than ten minutes. And where was Katharine? All the tablecloths were on the tables, but she was nowhere to be seen. He shrugged. Perhaps she'd gone to the restroom.

He scanned the canoes again, which was getting harder, since they were about halfway across the lake now, but didn't spot Lindsey's blonde head anywhere. He stopped, forced himself to calm down and scanned the canoes again. His heart started pounding as he sprinted for the water's edge.

Something wasn't right.

****

Lindsey turned back to look at Jimmy Wayne and a strange feeling slid over the back of her neck. Like the time she thought someone was following her in the woods. Something wasn't right. She stuck her paddle into the water and pushed with all her might, trying to steer them back towards the rest of the group.

She looked over her shoulder again. There was something...odd...about the way Jimmy Wayne's face looked, like he was wearing a Halloween mask or something. Everything seemed frozen in place. "Jimmy Wayne, let's go back with everyone else. I don't like being over here all by ourselves."

He smiled, but Lindsey saw the smile only went as far as his teeth; his eyes still has the weird frozen look in them. One stroke from his paddle and they were further than ever from the rest of the canoes.

"We're having our own little adventure, Lindsey. Just the two of us."

"But I want to be with all my friends."

"I thought you wanted to be with me. This is a father-daughter day, isn't it?"

Lindsey heard his irritation and frowned. She looked over her shoulder again, worried at how far away everyone was by now. They probably wouldn't even be able to hear her if she screamed. The thought suddenly made her afraid. She looked back the other way. She couldn't see Danny and the picnic area, either. They were all alone in a little cove, well away from everyone else.

"Jimmy Wayne, let's go back. Please."

His eyes narrowed. "Aren't you having fun, Lindsey? I thought you like adventures and exploring new things and places."

She bit her lip. "I do, but...I just want to be with everyone else. Have an adventure with the whole group."

"Fine. We'll go back in a minute." He turned the

canoe around.

With the motion, water sloshed over Lindsey's tennis shoes and soaked her sock. "Ah!" she cried, lifting her feet out of the water. The sudden movement set the canoe to rocking.

"Don't move," Jimmy Wayne snapped. "You'll capsize us."

"Why is there water in here?" Lindsey gasped. She scanned the bottom of the canoe, panic climbing into her throat as she realized the water level was rising. Fast.

"I don't know." He tossed her a drinking cup. "Start baling. Quick."

Lindsey reached for the cup, trying to move quickly and carefully at the same time. She stretched across the seat as far as she could go, finally touching the cup. Once she had it, she started scooping water as fast as she could.

After a few minutes, she looked around, breathing hard. No matter how much she scooped, there seemed to be more water coming in. She looked towards the back to see Jimmy Wayne calmly watching her, canoe paddle resting across his lap. "Why aren't you helping me?"

He smiled his frozen smile again. "You're doing just fine, honey. Just fine."

"But there's still more water leaking in."

"I know."

"But-but what are we going to do?" Most lakes in Florida were very shallow; often no more than twenty feet at their deepest level. But Lindsey had been out on this lake many times and she knew there were several deep springs right in this area.

"Everything's going to be okay, Lindsey. Trust me." Jimmy Wayne scanned the area behind them and Lindsey followed his gaze. They were now hidden from not only the picnic area, but Lindsey couldn't see the other canoes either. And they were far enough from shore that Lindsey worried about being able to swim all the way back. Besides, she'd seen the size of the gators who sunned themselves along the banks in this area.

She just wanted to get back to Danny. He'd take care of her. Lindsey grabbed her oar and started paddling. "We've got to get back. I don't want to sink out here."

Paddle in, stroke, up. Paddle in, stroke, up.

Sweat beaded her brow and her breath came in shallow pants, but they still weren't getting anywhere. Finally, Lindsey looked over her shoulder and saw Jimmy Wayne with his paddle straight in the water, stopping their forward motion. He was making sure they didn't go anywhere.

Lindsey's heart started pounding like her friend's horse when it galloped across the pasture. Her eyes widened and she swallowed hard when she saw that frozen look in his eyes again. He slowly pulled his paddle up out of the water and said, "I'm sorry, Lindsey. I really am."

Then he suddenly raised the paddle and before she could raise her arm to block the blow, the paddle came at her. Pain exploded in her head.

Then everything went black.

****

Lindsey and Jimmy Wayne weren't with the others. The thought thundered in Danny's mind as he reached the water's edge. He looked from side to side. Where was the extra "emergency" canoe they'd purposely left on shore? He searched the shoreline, breath coming in a relieved whoosh when he spotted an ancient rowboat tied to a sapling about fifty yards away. He ran to it, untied the line and shoved it into the water, hopping in after it. He scooped up the oars and started rowing with all his might.

Lindsey and Jimmy Wayne might have just rounded the bend to have a look at a large spring

Sam had told him about, but every instinct and intuition he had was screaming a warning. Since the day his brother disappeared, his instinct had been right. He wasn't going to doubt it now. He had to find them, had to make sure Lindsey was okay. If something happened to her...he wouldn't finish the thought.

It probably only took him a few minutes to round the bend, but to Danny's mind it seemed like years passed before he spotted their canoe. Their capsized canoe. And bearing down on them with all her might, Katharine, paddling the emergency canoe.

Danny rowed harder, searching for Lindsey's shiny blonde head beside the canoe. All he could see was Jimmy Wayne's ball cap. Bile rose in his throat, but he swallowed it back

"Where's Lindsey?" he shouted.

Startled, Jimmy Wayne spun around, clutching the side of the canoe. "I don't know. I can't find her."

Katharine gasped as Danny pulled up along the other side. "Where'd you last see her?"

"This side of the canoe. She stood up too fast and we went in. I..." his voice broke. "I can't find her."

"Well keep looking!" Danny shouted. He met Katharine's terrified eyes across the hull. "You take that side; I'll take this one."

Then he dove into the water a few feet from the canoe and opened his eyes. The tannin in the water made it a murky brown, so visibility was almost nil, but he strained anyway, looking this way and that, trying to find Lindsey. He dove all the way to the bottom and then started moving in a small search pattern, sweeping his arms in front of him, hoping to run into her. He made several sweeps before his lungs forced him to the surface for more air. When he popped to the surface, gasping, Jimmy Wayne still clung to the side of the canoe. Danny couldn't believe what he was seeing. The other man's ball cap was dry, so he hadn't been underwater.

"Why the hell aren't you looking for her?"

"I figured I should stay here in case she surfaced."

If there'd been time, Danny would have knocked him out. He dove again, this time moving his search pattern out a little further. Still nothing. As he pushed off the bottom to surface again, a new horror occurred to him.

Chapter Twenty One

For a moment, Katharine sat in her canoe, paralyzed with fear. But when she saw Danny suck in a breath and disappear, her frozen limbs began to move. She didn't know how to dive, so she simply leaped over the edge of the canoe. Once she'd surfaced, she sucked in air as she'd seen Danny do, and dove under the water. She ignored the way her dress billowed around her, and the way her heavy shoes wanted to drag her under. Mostly she ignored the terrifying feeling of all that water above her head. None of it mattered. For Sam's sake—and Lindsey's own—she had to find her granddaughter.

When her lungs began screaming for air, she pushed back up to the surface, just in time to hear Danny shout at Jimmy Wayne and then dive under again. Katharine quickly did the same, straining through the soupy water for some glimpse of Lindsey. She fanned her hands out, praying all the while. "Help me find our girl. Please God, help me find our girl."

She was just about back to the surface again when an idea struck. She changed the angle of her ascent and popped up underneath the overturned canoe—which Jimmy Wayne seemed to be trying to right—and her hand brushed something as she went.

As soon as her head cleared the water and she'd sucked in a breath, she ducked under again, this time grabbing for whatever she'd felt.

Her hand connected with something solid and

she almost cried out when she realized it was an arm. With all her strength, she pulled Lindsey with her, swimming at a slight angle to get out from under the canoe and Jimmy Wayne's flailing feet.

When Katherine's head cleared the water, she pulled Lindsey's head up also. Her granddaughter didn't move, just floated, lifeless.

"Noooooo," Katharine screamed. She spun in a circle, spotting the rowboat right behind her. Frantic, she pulled Lindsey towards the boat, then shoved her over the side and into it. It took three more heaving tries before she heaved herself over the side, scraping her arms as she went. Chest heaving, heart pounding, Katharine rolled Lindsey over onto her stomach in the bottom of the rowboat and pushed on her back. It took several tries, but suddenly Lindsey expelled the water she'd swallowed and began coughing. "Oh, thank God," Katharine breathed.

****

Danny's panic was affecting his ability to think and he knew it. He deliberately tried to slow his racing heart as he made another sweep along the lake bottom. His girl had to be here somewhere and he wouldn't quit until he found her, but please God, don't let them be too late.

Out of necessity, he surfaced again, gasping for air. He turned, but didn't see the capsized canoe. Or Jimmy Wayne. He spun around just in time to see the other man climbing into Katharine's canoe. "Where's yours?"

Jimmy Wayne shrugged. "It sank while I was trying to right it."

Something wasn't right, but now wasn't the time. Danny drew breath to dive again. They were running out of time.

"I've got her, Danny," Katharine shouted.

Danny's heart leapt and his body shuddered in

231

relief. Oh, thank you, God. He turned and saw Katharine sitting in the rowboat, Lindsey clutched in her arms.

"Is she okay?" he asked, swimming toward them with all his might.

He could hear the smile in Katharine's voice. "Our little lamb is going to be just fine."

Danny hauled his tired body over the side and sat for a minute, running his eyes and hands over Lindsey from stem to stern, needing to reassure himself that she was indeed fine. His heart stuttered when he found the bloody gash on the back of her head. She would need a stitch or two.

"Lindsey, honey. How are you?"

She fluttered her eyes open. "Hi. What are you doing here?" she mumbled.

Danny checked her eyes and noticed the difference in pupil size. Clearly a concussion. He turned to Katharine. "Try to keep her talking while I get us to shore. We'll need to get her checked out."

"Do you think she hit her head when she went overboard?"

Danny scowled. "That's my guess."

He turned to where Jimmy Wayne sat in the other canoe. "How is she?" he called.

"She'll be fine."

"Whew. What a close call. Guess we'd better get her back to the dock."

Danny met Katharine's gaze over Lindsey's head and saw the same mix of anger and questions he had.

****

Sam finally tucked Lindsey into bed after eleven p.m., her limbs shaking from exhaustion. She eased Lindsey's bedroom door closed and stood for a moment in the hallway, back against the wall, arms folded across her chest. Her head lolled against the wall and her eyelids drooped. She'd been running on sheer willpower and adrenaline since Danny's calm-but-frantic cell phone call from the park. Sam had ignored every boating rule of the road she'd ever learned and raced back upriver at full throttle. She almost dumped her guests into the water, she hit the dock so hard, but she gathered enough control to escort them to the office and offer them a full refund and a genuine apology. Then she hopped into her Jeep and hightailed it to the hospital, her not-quite-healed shoulder protesting with every mile. Sam ignored it.

At the hospital, despite the nurses' assurances that Lindsey had merely suffered a mild concussion and would need a few stitches, Sam didn't draw a full breath until after the various medical tests confirmed there was no hidden, internal danger. And since—like everywhere—there were more people needing help than the hospital had staff, they didn't get home until after eight p.m. Most of the girls in the Brownie troop, along with their parents, had come to the hospital, and once she was over her fright, Lindsey lapped up all the attention and was chattering like a magpie by the time they pulled into the driveway at the fish camp. The only thing she couldn't recall with absolute clarity was how she ended up in the water.

Danny insisted on carrying Lindsey into the house, saying she needed a little extra pampering, but Sam suspected it had more to do with Danny's need to hold her close, even if just for a minute. Their eyes met over Lindsey's head and Sam felt the emotion like an arrow deep in her heart. He was Lindsey's father. No matter what else happened, Sam had no doubt he loved his daughter.

Once Katharine and Sam had gotten some food into Lindsey's system and answered what seemed like dozens of telephone inquiries about how Lindsey was doing, the little girl's eyelids finally began to droop. Sam helped her into her jammies—though usually Lindsey insisted she was much too old for that—and finally calmed her daughter enough so she fell asleep.

Now, Sam straightened away from the wall and headed for the porch. The kitchen was dark; Mama had already gone to bed. Even though her body was exhausted, Sam knew her brain was still too busy trying to process the day's events for sleep to be an option anytime soon. So she went out onto the porch and plopped into a rocker, surprised when she looked up to find Danny leaning one shoulder against a porch pillar, arms and ankles crossed.

She squinted at him through the dim glow of the security light by the parking area. "Thought you'd gone to bed."

He shook his head. "How's our girl?"

Sam's heart swelled with longing. Two simple words; such a wealth of meaning implied. *Our girl.* Family. Partnership. Love. All three the very deepest wishes of her heart; all three utterly impossible and unattainable. Still, her foolish heart continued to hope. "Exhausted. She's finally asleep."

Danny grinned the same lopsided grin which always stole Sam's breath. "She's had a big day."

Sam smiled back at the understatement. When their eyes met and held, time seemed to stretch and expand. Sam gasped at the longing she saw reflected in Danny's eyes. Who would have guessed his wanderer's heart ached for family and connection just as hers did?

When he stepped away from the pillar, the intense expression on his face and purpose in his step had Sam leaping out of the chair to put a bit of distance between them. His face now reflected a different kind of need, one she wasn't sure she could deal with. Not now, not with so many unanswered questions swirling around them as well as inside

Sam's own heart.

Danny took another step closer and Sam took another instinctive step back. When her back hit the clapboard siding, she stopped, cocked her chin and met his eyes. "Don't crowd me, Hastings."

Eyes on hers, his next step brought his chest within inches of hers. One deep breath and they'd touch. He reached out and brushed a stray tendril of hair behind her ear. "I need to hold you tonight."

Sam couldn't look away from him, couldn't deny the loneliness she saw in his blue gaze.

"I think you need me, too, Samantha."

She shook her head, trying to deny it, even as her heart raced and his words sent a shiver down her spine. She wanted what he was offering. One night in his arms. One more night to be cherished and wanted and pampered, just like that night so long ago. One night to remember.

Before she was alone again.

The thought hit her like ice water, stopping Sam's instinctive move closer to him. He wasn't staying. He had no plans for them to be a family. All he was offering was one night—nothing more.

Even as the denial formed on her lips, he leaned in for a kiss so tender and devastating all her protests were buried in the overload of sensation. His lips were soft, yet hard with want. His tongue slipped out to tease the seam of her lips, seeking entry. When she didn't respond, he pulled back, her face cupped in his hands. "Don't run from me, from this," he whispered. "I need you."

For a moment, Sam just looked into his fathomless blue eyes. Yes, there was passion there, and desire, but it was much more, too. Beyond the thundering beat of his heart and evidence of his arousal pressed against her middle, Sam saw caring and gentleness—and tenderness.

When she was with Danny, he made her feel

like the beautiful, desirable and deserving woman she always wanted to be. With him, she saw her greatest longings reflected back from the depths of his soul. If it were only simple desire, merely a need for physical release, Sam could have walked away. But it was the way he cared for her, even when she didn't want him to, the way he was with Lindsey, which sealed the deal.

He would walk away. That was as sure as the next Florida sunrise. But Sam would survive. And tonight, she would bask in his feelings for her. She would take the chance, for the first time ever, to express her love—yes, love—for Danny, in the only way she could, the only way he would understand.

For this one night, Sam would give them both what they needed, what they wanted. Tomorrow would have to wait. All the fears and unanswered questions would still be there when the sun rose. Tonight was their time.

Heart pounding, she swallowed the last of her misgivings and leaned closer. She opened her lips and touched her tongue to his. He opened his mouth wider, inviting her to join him, to taste and tease, to rub and feel. Within moments, Sam's head spun as the kiss went on and on—and on.

Danny pulled her closer, his big hands circling her waist and Sam pressed her breasts against his hard chest, wrapping her arms around his neck and burying her hands in the thick hair at his nape. Someone moaned, but she could not have said if the sound came from him or her.

He felt like home. Over and under, through the onslaught of sensations, the thought replayed in Sam's heart and mind. Danny was home. In his arms, she was sheltered and safe, protected and loved.

"Not here," he muttered and Sam leaned back and blinked several times, totally disoriented.

Dimly, she realized they were still standing on the front porch in full view of anyone who cared to look.

"Come with me," Danny said, taking her hand and half dragging, half running towards his cabin.

Halfway there, the litany of reasons this was a bad idea chimed in with another round of protests, but Sam ignored them and concentrated instead on the way Danny's hand in hers made her feel safe, the way his hair glinted in the glow of the security light, the way his broad shoulders offered her a safe haven.

And the way his butt looked in those worn jeans. Sam chuckled and he turned to smile at her, one eyebrow raised. "Care to share the joke?"

Sam bit the inside of her cheek, her nervousness suddenly gone, all her misgivings replaced by the playful side he seemed able to draw out of her so effortlessly. "I was admiring your, ah, assets."

"My assets, huh?" he asked, drawing her up onto the small porch of his cabin. "If you like these, just wait till you see what else I've got." He wriggled both brows suggestively and Sam laughed.

He stopped, an arrested expression on his face.

"What?" Sam's smile slid off her face.

Danny reached over and cupped her cheek. "No, don't stop smiling. I just hadn't heard you laugh since, well, since the weekend we spent together. I missed it. You have a beautiful smile, Samantha. I'd like to see it more often."

She wanted to say she hadn't had much reason to smile, but he seemed to understand, for he leaned in and nibbled her bottom lip. "I think you have great assets, too, by the way." He leaned back, cheeky grin in place. "I'll show you mine if you show me yours."

Sam laughed out loud then, the sound full and free, surprising even to her own ears. They giggled together like idiots for several minutes and then

Sam stepped closer and this time, she cupped his cheeks in her palms. "Thank you," she said simply, and kissed him.

She's intended it to be a small kiss, of appreciation, but it went from chaste to scorching in nothing flat. This time, Danny took command, turning his head for a better angle, cupping the back of her head with one hand, his other cupping her breast. Sam reached for his broad shoulders, tugging him closer, hanging on.

"We're still outside," he muttered, dragging his mouth from hers.

They stumbled into the small cabin, not wanting to let go even for a second. They bumped into walls and furniture in their haste to reach the bed and shed their clothing—both at the same time. They kissed, they giggled, they played like children, nibbling, tasting, laughing.

Suddenly, Sam found herself flat on her back under Danny on his too-short double bed, their hands clasped, his eyes blue flames as they locked with hers. Eyes wide open, he leaned down and kissed her, long and slow and deep.

Time stood still as they looked into each other's eyes, neither moving, their hearts beating as one. Sam had felt this oneness, this complete sense of connection only once before: the last time she'd been with Danny.

Her heart bursting with emotion, Sam nearly said the three words she knew he wouldn't want to hear. Instead, she whispered, "Welcome home."

Time hung suspended while they stared at each other, separate, but not. Sam saw a myriad emotions chase through his eyes before he offered her his heart-stopping grin.

"Come fly with me, Samantha."

He began to move and the world disappeared. There was only the two of them and this moment in time.

****

Danny woke several hours later, temporarily disoriented. It wasn't a new feeling, but it was one he hadn't had lately. His brain slowly lumbered down its mental tracks, facts and impressions gradually turning to awareness. He turned on his side and smiled at the sight of Samantha lying perfectly still beside him. She was on her back, hands folded across her stomach, looking for all the world like a body laid out for burial. The thought brought back yesterday's picnic and his good humor fled.

He had spent a fair bit of time with Porter at the park yesterday, talking about what happened. There was no proof, but Danny would bet his best skis Jimmy Wayne had deliberately tried to sink the canoe. Hadn't he insisted they take that one, even though Lindsey had wanted another? The question Danny couldn't answer was why? And had he just wanted to sink the canoe or had he wanted to drown Lindsey?

At the mere thought of anyone trying to harm his daughter, Danny's entire body clenched, from jaw to fists. Sam must have felt it, because her eyes popped open and she sat straight up. "What's wrong?"

He leaned in for a long, wet kiss. "You're beautiful."

She angled her head back to see his face. "And that makes you growl?"

"No. Knowing I need to get you back into the house before our precocious daughter finds you here makes me growl."

Sam consulted her watch and growled, too, tossing back the covers. She stepped from the bed and Danny's breath hitched in his throat. The woman was amazing. Soft in all the right places and with a heart the size of the Grand Canyon. He loved her.

The knowledge sent him into an emotional freefall, as though he'd lost his grip on his climbing rope and was plummeting to earth. He couldn't love her. Love meant commitment. Love meant staying in one place forever.

Love meant pain and loss.

No, he was confusing caring and passion with love, that's all. If he ignored it, it would go away, like the twenty-four hour stomach flu. It wasn't much fun, but at least it didn't last long.

He decided to keep things light. He flashed a grin at Sam, who was trying to scoop up her clothes and hide her nakedness, all at the same time. "Don't cover up on my account. I'm enjoying the view."

She blushed, from the roots of her hair to the tips of her toes and kept scooping clothes until she had what she needed and escaped into the teensy bathroom.

Moments later she emerged, dressed, but awkwardness in every line of her magnificent body. "I'd better get back."

Despite his own confused feelings, he knew she needed reassurance. He walked over and gathered her in his arms. "Thank you for a beautiful night with a beautiful lady." He kissed her with all the feelings in his heart and hoped she understood.

When he pulled back, her eyes were wide and wary. "I..." she shook her head. "Never mind, I have to go."

****

Sam spent the short walk from Danny's cabin to her own bedroom cursing her awkwardness. Did she say something light and sophisticated? Something to show the night had been nothing more than a casual encounter? No. Instead, she'd stood there tongue-tied, doing her best to bite back the words begging to be said. Ever fiber of her being longed to tell him she loved him. But caution, and truth be told, self-preservation, held her back. Yes, she loved him. And she was pretty sure he loved her, too. But she knew it would never be enough. She couldn't leave. He'd never stay.

Love didn't matter at all.

But Lindsey did.

Chapter Twenty Two

It didn't take Sam long to set up a meeting with the commissioners at city hall. It took a lot longer to wrap her brain around what she was about to do.

She took a deep breath. For Lindsey, she could do this.

Sam studied the faces around the table. Bill Farley and Rudy Emerson held a whispered conference behind their Styrofoam cups, while Porter leaned back in his chair and flipped through his little notebook. Jimmy Wayne's expression was carefully blank, while beside him, Danny studied her, questions in his eyes.

She glanced at the clock, then back at Farley and Emerson. "Any word from Tommy?"

"Nope. Which ain't like him at all, now that I think on it," Emerson said.

Sam wasn't sure she could do this if she had to reschedule. So she cleared her throat and gripped the edge of the table for support. Best just to say it straight out.

"I've decided to sell the fish camp to Castle Development."

The room erupted in sound. Porter's chair legs hit the linoleum and Danny's "What?" burst like gunfire.

Emerson's "Ye Haw" could be heard in the next county, while Farley's muttered, "It's about time," brought up the rear.

Sam waited until they wound down.

Porter broke the sudden silence. "Are you sure,

Sam? They're not forcing you into this, are they?" He hitched a thumb toward the two commissioners.

"No. This is my decision."

Danny stood and came around the table. He leaned close. "You don't have to do this. Not right now. Give it a little more time."

Sam reared back as though he'd slapped her. "I don't *have* more time, Hastings. I won't risk my daughter's life for a piece of property."

"Maybe you won't have to."

She studied his face. "What are you saying?"

"Just give me a bit more time."

Sam shook her head. "I can't. I'm all out of time. And options." She sighed. "Just do the paperwork, okay?"

Before Danny could respond, Porter's cell phone rang. "Porter." Even though they all pretended not to listen, all ears were tuned into his conversation.

"What day was this?" Luke had his notebook out and was scribbling as he listened.

"He said he was going where?" His sharp gaze pierced Danny.

"When was he supposed to be back?" More nodding, more scribbling.

"What time did she leave?" Pause. "Okay, thanks. Tell her I'll be there in a few minutes."

He tucked his cell phone back in his uniform shirt pocket and eyed the assembled group with a razor-sharp glance. "Mrs. Sooner just got back from her mother's place in Orlando and heard your message, Sam. Gladys thought it was odd you wanted to set up a meeting, since the last time she talked to Tommy, he said he was flying to California with Hastings, here.

"When was he supposed to be back?" Bill asked.

"Yesterday. Gladys tried his cell phone, but said he often forgets to turn it on. She got home a little while ago, but he wasn't back. When she heard your message, she started to worry." The look he sent Danny could have cut glass. "What do you know about this?"

Danny put both hands up, palms out. "Absolutely nothing. I wouldn't have scheduled a meeting with Sooner, because we had nothing new to discuss, certainly nothing we couldn't talk about here."

Porter tipped his hat to Sam. "I'll be in touch."

After he left, Sam slumped back in her chair, not sure what to think. The commissioners sent angry glares in Danny's direction; Jimmy Wayne's expression wasn't much warmer.

Farley and Emerson stood at the same time. "I'm going out to see Gladys," Bill announced.

Rudy was right on his heels. "I'm going with you."

Jimmy Wayne stood, too. "Keep me posted, will you? I have to get back to the store."

When only she and Danny were left, he turned to her. "I'll draw up the papers, but I'm still hoping we can find another solution."

Sam huffed out a breath. "Just get it done, okay? I need Lindsey safe and since that seems tied in to the fish camp, this is the smart thing to do. I won't risk her life."

He nodded, then helped her to her feet.

****

Luke left Gladys to the dubious care of Bill and Rudy and walked back out to his SUV. He got behind the wheel and sighed. From what he gathered from a frantic Gladys, it wasn't unusual for Tommy to take off on the spur of the moment. Being unreachable by cell wasn't generally cause for concern, either. But if he was going to be late getting back, he always called. Always. The fact he hadn't, coupled with the message from Sam, had set off warning bells in her head. Yeah, well, they were clanging in Luke's brain, too.

He slammed a fist against the steering wheel. What was going on in this town? Had everyone gone crazy? He couldn't believe one piece of property could cause so much trouble. Though of course, he knew greed was one of the prime motivators in all kinds of crime.

Luke cranked up the air conditioning and called Sanchez. "What have you got?"

"Hey, boss. I was just going to call you. Your hunch was right. A little digging in the Sooner finances and whaddaya know? Tommy lost a bundle on a land speculation deal and then suddenly, all the money is back in his accounts."

Sanchez named a figure that widened Luke's eyes. "So where'd it come from?"

"That's the sixty-four-hundred-dollar question. I'm still digging."

Luke could only think of one place the man could get that kind of money. "Go through the city commission records with a fine-toothed comb. Then call me." He slapped the phone shut and pulled out of the driveway. Okay, so if Sooner had light-fingered some commission funds—and this was mere speculation at this point—why would he disappear? Why now, when they were close to getting this deal finalized?

He decided to let the thought simmer for a while and tried a new tact. If Sooner had wanted or needed to get out of town, where would he go? And if he decided to lay low for a while locally, same question: where?

Luke drove around for about two hours, checking the local campgrounds, fish camps and a few hunting camps. Nothing. On his way back into town he remembered one more place and swung his SUV in a tight circle. Way out in the forest was the old Miller place, where the locals often went to hunt.

Nothing left on the property now but a falling-down old barn, but it was worth a look.

Luke turned into the dirt track that led off the two-lane county road, searching for signs of a car passing this way recently. With all the rain they'd had, there were no fresh tire tracks, but he noticed several of the low-hanging branches were broken or missing leaves along the bottom, as though they'd scraped the top of a car.

He pulled up beside the barn, told dispatch his location and then stepped out of the car, keeping the door between himself and the gaping hole where the barn door used to be. He flipped open his holster and kept his hand on his weapon.

"Sooner? You out here? It's Luke Porter."

He waited, but heard nothing. He tried again. "Tommy, if you're out here, let me know. Your wife is pretty worried about you."

Again, silence.

Luke scanned the surrounding trees, looking for any signs of movement. No birds flew out of the trees signaling someone's passing and the squirrels gradually resumed their chatter. The barn itself was silent as a tomb.

Eyes scanning the area, Luke stepped through the barn door and the stench almost knocked him flat. Luke put his back to the wall, making himself less of a target—just in case—and gave his eyes time to adjust. Once they did, he groaned. "Aw, geez. No."

At the other end of the barn, Tommy Sooner hung suspended from a rope that reached the old hayloft. A quick look said he was dead, had been for a while, but Luke stepped closer and made sure. He breathed through his mouth while he felt for a pulse. There was none.

Rather than go back to his SUV, Luke took out his cell phone and called it in. Then he turned in a circle, studying the scene, getting his preliminary impressions down on paper while he waited for backup to arrive.

He rammed a hand through his hair. Poor Gladys.

****

Sam was at the tiny desk in her bedroom, paying bills, when Mama arrived home. Sam headed for the kitchen and poured them both some iced tea.

"Come out on the porch, Mama. I need to talk to you a minute."

Mama cocked her head, but simply nodded and took a seat in one of the rockers.

Now that the moment had come, Sam wasn't sure what to say. Straight out, she reminded herself. Just straight out.

"I, ah, want to thank you for what you did yesterday." Her throat closed and she had to force the words past a knot of tears. "You saved Lindsey's life." Sam stood and walked over to her mother, then wrapped her arms around her. "Thank you, Mama. For risking your life for her. I'll never be able to thank you enough."

Mama patted her head, then pulled back so they were eye to eye. "There's no need for thanks, Samantha. It's what family does, we take care of each other."

Sam nodded. "I know. We do. That's the other thing I need to tell you. I just met with Danny and the commission. I'm selling the fish camp."

Katharine gasped. "Are you sure?"

"I'm sure. I don't know how or why, but everything seems tied to Lindsey and the property. I won't risk her life, Mama." Sam shivered despite the heat. "We came too close to losing her yesterday."

Katharine gathered her close again. "Oh, honey. I know this is so hard, but I think you're doing the right thing. I really do."

Sam swallowed hard. "Thanks, Mama. It means

a lot."

****

"So what are you going to do now?" Emma Jean asked later the same afternoon, leaning back in her rickety office chair.

Sam slumped in one of the uncomfortable visitor's chairs. "I have no idea. This has been my whole life; it's all I know."

Emma Jean snorted. "Let's not get too dramatic, Sam. You have a degree in biology. You know how to run a business, you have all manner of skills." She peered at Sam over the top of her half glasses. "The real problem here is not so much what you'll do in the future, but of letting go of the past."

Sam nodded sadly, failure settling on her shoulders like a lead weight. "Trying to make Pop happy is all I've ever done."

"And maybe this is God's way of setting you free."

Sam narrowed her eyes.

"Amos was a good man, Sam, but a mean drunk. Somewhere inside you, there's a little girl still listening to the garbage he fed you all those years. But even if you spend the rest of your life trying, you'll never earn his approval. It isn't his to give, Sam. It never was."

Tears welled in Sam's eyes. "I just wanted to make him happy. To be the son he wanted so badly."

Emma Jean reached across the desk and clasped her hands. "I know honey, but it was an impossible task from the beginning. Look at me."

It was hard, with Pop's voice shouting in her mind and the shame of failure weighing her down. *Bah, you're nothing but a girl. You'll never do it. A son could have saved the fish camp. You're nothing but a worthless girl, a failure.*

"Look at me," Emma Jean repeated. "God didn't make you a son, he made you a strong, beautiful daughter. Throw out the poison Amos spent a lifetime pouring into you. Instead, listen to your Heavenly Father. He made you, and He gave you Lindsey and maybe...Lindsey's father."

Sam swallowed. "How did you figure it out?"

"Easy. I looked at you, and him, and Lindsey. And then I looked at how you two look at each other."

"He's only here for the property. Now that he has it, he'll be gone."

Emma Jean cocked her head in that knowing way she had. "How do you know?"

Sam looked away. "I just do."

"Have you asked him to stay?"

Sam snorted, though her heart thundered at the very idea. She could never ask. Besides, it would be a waste of time. "Why would he want someone like me?"

"Because you're lovable and wonderful," Emma Jean replied, and Sam realized she'd spoken aloud. "Don't you realize yet how others see you, Sam? Libbey and the others here, they want to be like you. Your acceptance shows them God's acceptance."

Sam sat for several minutes, trying to absorb it all. Finally, she said, "What if I ask Danny to stay and he says no?"

Emma Jean let the silence lengthen before she spoke. "What if he says yes?"

Chapter Twenty Three

For the next few days, Emma Jean's words circled round and round in Sam's head. She went about her business, Lindsey always at her side now that school was out for the summer. But since Marco Juarez had been arrested for Castle's murder, there had been no more eerie phone calls. Maybe Porter had caught the right man.

If only she could convince her gut it was true.

As for the development, Danny had convinced her to wait one more week. Why, exactly, he wouldn't say, just asked her to trust him.

In the meantime, Sam tried to figure out how to plan a future which didn't include the fish camp. The thought was terrifying. And sometimes, frighteningly freeing. To walk away, to be free of her father's accusing voice. Could her friend be right? Was it possible this was God's way of giving her and Lindsey a fresh start?

No sooner did she have the thought, than the next one inevitably followed: what about Danny? Could she risk asking him to stay with her and Lindsey? To try to be a real family? The thought made her palms sweat and her heart beat like a runaway train. Maybe it was worth the risk.

Several days later, Sam walked her last cruise customers of the day to their vehicle, then sent Lindsey up to the house to help Mama with supper. Sam headed for the bait shop where Danny spent several hours every day, without pay, no matter how many times Sam had told him he didn't need to.

The screen slapped shut behind her.

"Hey, beautiful," he greeted.

Even though he said it every single day, Sam couldn't get used to it. It was so contrary to how she saw herself. "Hi, yourself. How'd it go this afternoon?"

Her eyes adjusted and she saw his teeth flash in his killer grin. "Good. Since this all started, people are making it a point to stop by and support you." He paused. "And give me an earful about how rotten I am."

"And so they should," Sam replied, sliding onto a stool. She wiped her palms on her shorts. "I, ah..."

He reached over and gently tilted her chin up. "I want to see those gorgeous green eyes when you talk to me."

When he wouldn't let her pull away, she closed her eyes. "I'm not sure I can."

"Try," he insisted.

Sam forced her eyes open and found his face inches from hers, his blue eyes intent. She nervously licked her lips. "I, ah, wanted to know if your offer to take me to dinner was still open." She finished the sentence in a rush, before she could change her mind.

His grin widened, and he reached out to cup her cheeks. "I thought you'd never ask. I'm free tonight."

Tonight? So soon?

"Come on, Sam, don't back out now. You've come this far."

She slid off the stool and locked her knees to keep them from wobbling. "Okay, tonight. I'll see if Mama can watch Lindsey."

"I'll pick you up at seven." She was halfway out the door before he added, "Wear something fancy."

She stopped. Turned. Wanting to act nonchalant, but unable to pull it off. Instead, her voice came out sounding small and uncertain.

"Fancy? You know I don't do fancy."

His grin was wide, full of confidence. "Not normally, no. But a little birdie told me you have 'this really pretty skirt that looks awesome.' I figured we could go somewhere nice so you could show it off."

Lindsey told him. "Ah, casual is good."

"It is, but tonight I'd like to spoil you a little, show you off."

"I'm not a prize bass, Hastings."

His smile was pure male. "No ma'am, you're not. Bass aren't nearly as good looking." Then he sobered. "All right. Don't dress up for me, then. Do it for yourself."

Before she could argue further, the old black phone on the wall rang.

"Collins Marina and River Cruises, what can I do for you?" Danny asked. When he realized she was still standing frozen in the doorway, he covered the mouthpiece, whispered, "See you at seven," and then winked before he turned his attention back to the caller.

****

Could you slow time just by wishing it? Sam wondered. Sitting at the dinner table keeping Mama and Lindsey company while they ate, time seemed to vanish in seconds.

"Why do you keep looking at the clock, Mommy? And why aren't you eating? Are you going somewhere?"

Might as well fess up. "Danny asked me to have dinner with him a little later."

Lindsey's face lit up like Christmas morning. "Really? Cool. Are you going to wear one of your new skirts? I like the greenish-blue one best."

Sam made her voice stern. "Speaking of skirts, what were you doing talking to Danny about them, young lady?"

Lindsey ducked her head. "I just told him you bought the skirts and you never have anywhere nice to wear them to."

"Lindsey June Collins, you had no business telling him any such thing."

Her daughter's eyes filled with tears. "Why not? It's true."

Sam locked eyes with her daughter. "It might be true, but you told him to try to manipulate him into doing what you wanted, and that's wrong."

"What's manipulate?"

"It means being sneaky to try to get someone to do what you want, instead of just coming out and saying it plain."

Lindsey's face fell. "Oh. I was just trying to help."

Sam almost laughed. The very last thing she needed was romantic help from her eleven-year-old. "Tell you what, Princess, from here on out, you let me worry about Mr. Hastings, okay?" She glanced at Lindsey's plate, where she was trying to hide her peas under the mashed potatoes. "You worry about eating your vegetables."

"Aw, Mom."

Sam stood and ruffled Lindsey's hair. "Yeah, I know. And now I'm off to get ready."

****

When Danny knocked on the front door at seven, Sam was still standing in her bathrobe in an agony of indecision. She had put on both skirts, three times, and had taken them off and replaced them with tan and green khakis, twice. Sam sighed and plopped down on her bed, arms crossed over her middle.

In her mind, she saw Pop, fists raised. *Don't you ever show your face dressed like that again, boy.*

And then she heard Emma Jean's words: *Amos spent a lifetime pouring his poison into you. It's time to pour it out, Sam. You are exactly who God made you to be.*

Sam heard Danny coming down the hall. The tread was too heavy for Lindsey, too confident for Mama.

"Samantha?" Danny called. "You ready, Beautiful?"

Sam cleared her throat. "Almost."

"Lindsey said you were having a bit of trouble deciding what to wear. Do you want to model the options and let me help you decide?"

Model the options? In front of him? "No, thanks. I'll be out in a minute."

"Okay. But in the meantime, I have something for you."

The doorknob turned and Sam leaped up in a panic. "Danny!"

"My eyes are closed and I'll just hand it through the crack."

Sure enough, the door opened the merest sliver and a gorgeous bouquet of red roses poked through the opening. "No redneck roses this time."

Sam took the flowers with unsteady hands and Danny immediately pulled the door closed. She stood there, inhaling their fragrance, admiring their beauty. No man except Danny had ever given her flowers of any kind.

Sam caught a glimpse of herself in the mirror and frowned. *Get a grip.* He probably gave every woman red roses. Weren't they the most popular kind? So, don't read too much into it. They weren't a promise of a future, and neither was dinner.

Irritated with her own paralysis, Sam spun around and scooped up the blue-green skirt and pulled it on, along with a simple white shirt she often wore to church. It wasn't elegant, not by a long shot, but it was the best she could do.

Lindsey slipped into the room. "Oh, Mommy,

you look beautiful!" She walked over to Sam and proudly presented a shiny pink lip gloss. "Put this on; it'll make your lips look really nice."

Sam wasn't sure she wanted her lips to look nice. She didn't want to think about lips at all, because if she did, she would think about Danny's lips, and well, she wasn't going there.

But she couldn't disappoint her daughter. So, a quick slick of the gloss over her lips, a quick hug for Lindsey and Sam burst out of the room. Danny straightened away from the wall and his eyes widened as they traveled from her glossy lips to the hem of her skirt. "Wow. You look gorgeous." He offered his arm. "Are you ready to go, m'lady?"

Behind them, Lindsey giggled and Sam gave up trying not to let his mood infect her. For tonight, she would enjoy herself. Amos could stay home.

****

Sam had never been in such a fancy restaurant in her life. The Wayfarer was perched on the shores of the Withlacoochee, but it bore no other resemblance to their marina. The sun was sinking low on the horizon as the hostess seated them at a table by a wall of windows. Outside, a great blue heron waded at the water's edge and Sam smiled. She was familiar with his world, it was the one inside the restaurant she wasn't sure how to deal with. Peach linen cloths draped the tables, while a bowl of peach roses and a flickering candle decorated the center. Sam was pretty sure she'd knock something over before the evening was over. Her nerves were shot as it was.

As they sat perusing the menu, Sam surreptitiously studied Danny over the top of hers, wondering if he felt any of her nervousness. He was dressed in an immaculately tailored charcoal suit, his shirt starched white, and elegant tie completing the urban look.

"See anything you like?" he asked lazily, eyes twinkling.

Sam didn't miss the double meaning. He was gorgeous, but he lived in a totally different world. "I'm still deciding," she responded.

His grin was all white teeth. "Take your time, darling. And while you're thinking," he leaned forward and took one of her hands, "let me tell you how breathtaking you look tonight."

Sam snorted and pulled her hand back. "Save it for someone who'll believe it."

Danny cocked his head. "It was a statement of plain fact, Samantha. Those green eyes of yours take my breath away."

The waitress appeared and saved Sam from answering. When she asked whether they wanted cocktails, Danny sent Sam a questioning look, but Sam shook her head, no. After life with Pop, she wasn't sure she'd ever be comfortable with a drink.

"Two iced teas," he told the girl.

Once they'd placed their orders for fresh seafood, Danny turned back to her. "I got the feeling from Lindsey you haven't worn a skirt in a very long time. I have to tell you, it's a shame, because it makes you look even more beautiful. Feminine."

Sam looked away. Could she tell him? Should she?

"Samantha?" he prompted.

She glanced at Danny, then grabbed her napkin and twisted it in her hands. "I had a brother, Robert, who died when I was seven."

Danny's eyes widened. "I didn't know. I'm sorry. That must have been hard on your parents."

"It was. Pop...he...he never got over it. He wanted a son to pass on all this skills to, someone who would keep the fish camp going. It's what the men in the family did: they worked the fish camp and then passed it to their sons. Only, Robert died."

"But he had a beautiful girl. Bet you looked a lot like Lindsey."

Sam grimaced. "Not really. I was gangly and awkward." Here's where it got tough. "Pop needed a son, so I tried to become one. In every way."

Danny nodded. "Hunting, fishing, gator trapping." He paused. "Dressing like a boy."

"Right. He didn't like being reminded I was a girl."

Sam watched Danny process what she hadn't said. When he spoke, his voice was quiet, gentle. "And when he was? What did he do?"

Sam swallowed hard. She could do this. "Once, in third grade, I found a dress in Mama's room. Someone at church had given it to her, for me. I tried it on and it was so pretty. It made me feel pretty, too, the way it swirled around my legs. I ran out to the kitchen to show Mama and she hugged me and told me to go take it off, quick." Sam stopped and took a deep breath. "Only I wasn't quick enough. Pop stumbled in from the living room and saw me." She paused, remembering the ugly words, the fists. "Let's just say I didn't wear a dress again until Annie and Jimmy Wayne's wedding."

Danny leaned forward, his eyes full of equal parts fury and compassion for the girl she'd been. "If Amos was still alive, he'd been hearing from me." He reached for her hands, gently pulled them up from her lap to link with his. "But he's gone, Sam, and he was wrong. You're exactly the beautiful lady you're supposed to be. Celebrate it, don't hide it."

"A lifetime's habits are hard to change."

He met her eyes, his look intense. "I won't argue with you. But you took a risk tonight, wearing a skirt, telling me. Thank you for trusting me that much."

He looked so sincere, Sam's eyes filled. She'd never felt so cherished, so loved, as she did right now.

"Will you stay, after this is all over? Will you be a part of our lives?" she blurted.

Danny froze, his expression trapped, mouth opening and closing like a landed fish. He stared at her as if he couldn't quite understand what she had just said, as though she'd spoken Chinese.

And just that fast, Sam's heart shredded all over again. He wouldn't stay. Why should he? He was a rich California developer. She was nothing but a poor single mother.

"I—I—"

She waved a hand as he stammered and searched for a reply. "Never mind. It was a dumb thing to say. You have your own life."

The waitress appeared with their food. It looked delicious, but the smell suddenly turned Sam's stomach.

Danny waited until their waitress disappeared. Sam watched him struggle for words and part of her was glad. Why should this be easy for him, when she felt like she was bleeding all over the linen tablecloth?

"Samantha, honey, you caught me by surprise. I hadn't really thought about it. I know I want to be a part of Lindsey's life, but I can't stay here." He tried to smile. "I'm a wanderer, always moving from place to place. You need a guy who's going to be there, year in and year out, and I'm just not cut out for that." He tried to smile, but it fell flat.

Well, what had she expected? A pledge of undying love? Sam nodded and pushed her food around on her plate. "It's okay. I understand."

They finished the meal in silence and didn't say a word the whole drive back to the fish camp. The evening which had started with such promise was now as unappealing as day-old fish.

When he pulled up in front of the house, Sam

reached for the door handle. "Thank you."

He put a hand on her arm. "Sam, wait."

She did, but he said nothing. She glanced at him, saw him swallow once, twice.

"I'm sorry," he finally said, his eyes on hers.

Heartbroken, but determined to keep him from seeing it, she nodded and got out.

Once inside, she tore off the skirt, tossed it to the back of the closet and changed back into her shorts. She should have left it there to begin with. Amos was right. She was worthless.

Sam sat on the edge of her bed, arms wrapped around her middle and cried like she hadn't cried in twelve years.

Chapter Twenty Four

Danny woke the next morning as restless and agitated as a trapped panther pacing his cage. There was a hurricane brewing and it wasn't just the storm swirling in the Gulf of Mexico. Sam's words had echoed in his head, but it was the shattered expression in her eyes when he said he'd be leaving that kept him up all night. He was a heel, without question. This was why he'd never gotten seriously involved with anyone after Marla. As long as he kept things casual and friendly, he could walk away and no one got hurt.

But Sam wasn't a casual kind of girl. Woman, he amended. He'd known it from the first time he laid eyes on her. And then there was Lindsey. His daughter. He still couldn't quite wrap his brain around that idea, either.

What he'd told her last night was the truth, though it was obviously not what she wanted to hear. He did want to be part of Lindsey's life. He wanted to be part of Sam's, too. The idea of never seeing her again filled him with a loneliness he hadn't experienced since he walked away from her all those years ago.

But to stay? Here? He looked around the tiny porch of his cottage and scanned the property. It was beautiful, no doubt. And surprisingly, the quiet was growing on him. He found he liked working the bait shop, chewing the fat with the locals, discussing the weather and the day's catch. But could he do it long term? Did he want to?

Danny knew exactly what Sam hadn't said last night. Being part of their lives meant marriage, the whole kit and caboodle. Commitment, till death do us part, amen.

He ran a finger around the collar of his T-shirt, which suddenly felt too small. He couldn't do it, couldn't tie himself down forever. It was too risky.

His cell phone rang, ending his unexpected bout of introspection. "Hastings."

"Hey, boss. I think I may have found what you were looking for," his office manager said.

"Talk to me," Danny responded, heading inside for pen and paper.

"I found another possible property just about two hours north of there that might work. I made arrangements with the owner for you to see it this morning."

Danny glanced out the window toward the Collins' house. In his gut he knew things were coming to a head and he didn't want to be gone for any length of time. But maybe a few hours away would give both him and Sam time to think things through. She and Katharine would keep an eye on Lindsey while he was gone.

"I'll be there." But first, he walked over to the bait shop for a word with Katharine.

Ten minutes later, he was headed north.

****

Sam felt the Mustang's growl right down to her toes. Danny was leaving. Even though he'd said he would stay until this was resolved, he was disappearing, the same way he had the last time. Again, she'd thrown her foolish heart to him and he'd turned his back and walked away. When would she learn?

But before the dust from his passing settled, a mini-van of seniors pulled up for their river cruise.

Back to work. Sam spent the rest of the morning trying to keep a smile in place and reassuring them the expected hurricane wasn't due until the next day. They were in no danger on the river today.

Once they were gone, Sam began the lengthy and exhausting process of tying down anything and everything in and around the marina that could fly around like a missile. Danny had said he would help put plywood on the windows, but she supposed she'd do it herself. She and Mama had done it for many years now.

She was securing several canoes when she heard Mama calling her name. "Sam! Sam!"

Sam raced down the dock, trying not to panic at the fear she heard in Mama's voice.

"What's wrong?" she demanded, grasping Mama by the shoulders.

"Luke just called. Tommy Sooner is dead. Looks like suicide."

Sam's belly knotted. "Looks like?"

Mama nodded shortly. "That's what he said. He said he's not sure yet, but he wanted me to tell you and Danny."

"Danny's gone," Sam said shortly.

"He'll be back. He just had some errands."

Sam didn't believe it for a minute, but it wasn't the issue right now.

Sam looked around, fear wrapping her in its sticky grasp. "Where's Lindsey?"

Mama's eyes widened. "Why, I—I thought she was with you."

Sam spun away and pounded towards the house. "Lindsey! Where are you?"

Mama was right behind her. "She's not in the bait shop. I've been there all morning."

Sam swallowed her fear as she entered the house. When she called again her voice was quieter. "Lindsey? Princess? Where are you?"

Nothing. For good measure, they checked under all the beds and in all the closets. Lindsey wasn't in the house.

Sam's heart pounded and her hands shook as they went back outside. "We need to find her."

****

When Luke Porter finally got back to his office, it was late afternoon. He was hot, tired, and grumpy. Murder wasn't the kind of thing that happened in his town, and now it was happening too often. Sooner's death didn't make any sense. None whatsoever. He'd bet his badge Sooner had been helped to his death. The trick would be in proving it. Hopefully, the ME would be able to help.

He poured a cup of what looked like sludge out of the bottom of the coffeepot and then slumped into his chair. He was missing something here, something big, but he just didn't know what.

"Sheriff? You got a minute?"

He looked up to see the always-immaculate Jimmy Wayne Drake standing in the doorway. He waved him to a chair. "What can I do for you, Jimmy Wayne?"

"I just heard about Tommy Sooner. Tragic. Really tragic."

Luke harrumphed. "You know anything about it?"

Drake started as if he'd been poked in the butt. "What? Me? What would I know?"

Luke shrugged as though it didn't matter. "You were both on the city commission. We've been checking Sooner's finances. He had a sudden loss, then just as suddenly the money was back as if by magic." He leaned forward in his chair. "You wouldn't happen to know anything about it, would you?"

Drake laughed. "Come on, Sheriff. You know I've never been close to those three. Why not ask Bill and

Rudy?"

"I have. They don't know anything. Figured maybe you did."

He looked contrite. "Sorry, Sheriff. I wish I could help." He paused. "But maybe I can. That's why I'm here."

Luke motioned for him to continue.

"The night the Castle guy disappeared, I ran out to the convenience store for a candy bar." His lips quirked up in a smile. "I have a real weakness for chocolate and peanuts. Anyway, on my way back home, I passed the old trailer where the Darby's live. I saw Jeff outside, hosing off what looked like a pair of boots."

Luke's eyes narrowed. "Why didn't you tell me this right after it happened?"

Another careless shrug. "I'd forgotten, I guess. But hearing about Tommy today made me think about Castle and, well, here I am."

Luke's internal lie detector beeped loud and clear. He had known Jimmy Wayne Drake since he was a boy. He'd been a liar as a kid, and he was lying now.

"Well, thanks for stopping by, Jimmy Wayne. I appreciate it."

The other man stood. "Glad I could help."

Luke watched him go. Had Jimmy Wayne seen something that night? Maybe. But Drake wasn't coming forward with his story now out of a sense of civic duty. He had another motive up his sleeve. And Luke intended to find out what it was.

****

The man sat in his favorite chair and tried to relax. But it wasn't easy. Everything was starting to unravel. Porter wasn't stupid. He'd eventually figure it out, given enough time. Well, he couldn't let that happen. If he acted quickly, he could still turn everything around and come out smelling like a rose, just like always. Sam would finally understand what he'd done for her, and appreciate his love. He picked up the picture of the two of them and kissed her gently on the lips. "Soon, we'll be together as we should have been all along."

But first, there were a few more loose ends to tie up. Sam's daughter had proven surprisingly hard to kill. And Hastings was underfoot all the time.

He got up, opened the hall closet and pulled out what looked like an ordinary toolbox. Then he set it on the bed and started assembling what he'd need.

****

Sam stopped running and braced her hands on her knees while she tried to catch her breath. She had to slow down or she wouldn't be able to keep going. Fear for Lindsey kept her moving; but she had to be able to think clearly, too. If Lindsey was afraid, where would she go?

From nearby, she heard Mama calling for Lindsey. Sam shaded her eyes with her hand and sent a worried glance up to the sky. They were in the deceptive calm before the storm. Except for the wind, you'd never know a severe storm was barreling their way.

"Lindsey, honey? Where are you?"

Sam raced down to the dock and checked the other pontoon boat. Because this one was old and dilapidated, they didn't use it for paying guests. Lindsey had been known to curl up on one of the seats with a good book and be lost to the world. But not today. Since the night Castle disappeared, Lindsey had avoided getting anywhere near the river. "Lindsey?"

Sam checked the lean-to where she'd been securing the canoes, then the small shed where they kept the boating and fishing supplies. After that, she searched every nook and cranny of the bait shop and lunch counter. No sign of her.

The purr of Danny's Mustang stopped Sam in her tracks. He'd come back. He hadn't abandoned them. He may not be staying forever, but he was here now, and that's what mattered. Sam ran towards him.

When he saw her coming, he met her halfway. "What's wrong?"

"Porter called," Sam panted. "Tommy Sooner is dead, apparent suicide."

"Apparent suicide?"

"That's what he said. He also said to watch Linds like a hawk." Sam gripped his arms, trying to keep the panic from her voice. "We can't find her."

He yanked her into his arms for a quick, strong hug. Then released her and looked into her eyes. "We'll find her, Sam. Tell me where you've already looked."

Within moments, Danny joined the search and they combed the grounds, calling Lindsey's name.

An hour later, discouraged and filled with rising panic, Sam saw Danny making his way down the row of empty cabins, key in hand, opening the padlock securing each door. Sam was peering behind a stack of old firewood when Danny shouted her name. "Sam! Over here!"

Sam was racing in his direction when Danny emerged from the last cabin with Lindsey cradled in his arms. Sam saw her daughter's head lolling against his chest and her breath lodged in her throat. She sped up and flew towards them, barely slowing down in time to keep from knocking them over. "What's wrong? What's happened?"

"Shhh, easy. She's asleep." Danny sat down on the top step, cuddling Lindsey close.

As her terror melted away, another, much more confusing and difficult to describe emotion took his place. A lump formed in Sam's throat. There was something so natural, so right, about Danny cradling their daughter.

Danny's eyes met hers and a dozen things Sam couldn't say passed between them. A wish that things were different, a longing for family. The crazy need to start over with him, to be the family they should have been all along. But Sam couldn't find the words and she knew he didn't want to hear them anyway. Not after last night. Danny's eyes, too, were filled with regret and longing—and something else Sam couldn't name.

Maybe someday they could talk about this, but not today. Land, storms, everything was secondary to the need to protect their daughter. As much as she might like to claim Lindsey as wholly hers, Lindsey needed Danny in her life. And she suspected Danny needed their daughter just as much.

Sam leaned forward and brushed a lock of hair off her daughter's cheek. "What was she doing in there?"

"She was curled up in a little ball, sound asleep."

"I thought all the cabins were locked. I just checked them the other day."

"This one wasn't. Maybe she took the key."

Sam looked closer and saw the tracks tears had made down Lindsey's soft cheeks. "My baby's been crying."

Danny's mouth kicked up on one side. "Seems to be lots of that going around today."

Sam merely raised a brow and leaned forward as if to take Lindsey from him.

Danny simply tightened his grip and stood. "I've got her. Why don't you lock up the cabin and we'll get her to bed."

Sam didn't like being given orders, but in this case, it made no sense to argue with the same plan she would have proposed. So she frowned in his direction and turned to go.

"Get down!" Danny shouted.

Chapter Twenty Five

Before she could figure out what he meant,
something whistled past her head and Danny
yanked her arm hard enough to tumble her flat on
her back. "Stay down and crawl into the cabin. Go!"

"Lindsey!"

He dropped down on the porch beside her and
gave her a shove. "Move! I've got her."

Above their heads, wood splintered.

Lindsey woke with a start and cried out.

"Shh, baby, I've got you," Danny crooned. "Keep
moving, Sam. We need to get inside."

Using her elbows, Sam crawled across the
sagging porch, while shots rang out mere inches
above their heads. She slithered into the little cabin
and Danny ducked in right behind her, Lindsey still
safely tucked in his arms.

They scooted across the floor and huddled in the
corner, both adults instinctively shielding Lindsey
from the direction of the shots.

"Mama!"

Sam made a grab for Lindsey, but her daughter
surprised her by keeping one arm firmly around
Danny's neck, too. Lindsey pulled her closer, so she
was sandwiched securely between the two adults.
They crooned and stroked her while she clung to
them and shivered. Outside, the sound of gunshots
faded away.

"Lindsey, honey, I need to sit back a minute,"
Danny said. Lindsey released her death grip on his
neck, but still held onto his hand. Danny eased

backward and plopped down on the floor, his foot braced against one of the metal bed frames. He moved carefully as though he didn't want his back to make contact with the wall.

Sam looked at him and saw a grimace cross his face. "Danny?"

His eyes flashed a warning. "Everything's fine."

Everything was obviously not fine. Sam sent him a questioning look. He tilted his eyes back over his shoulder.

Casually, so as not to alarm their daughter, Sam leaned back far enough to look behind him and stifled a gasp. The back of his shirt was red with blood. *Oh, God, he'd been shot.*

Sam tried to calm her thundering heart. She needed to get him back to the house where she kept an extensive first aid kit. Living and running a business way out here, both she and Mama had extensive first aid training. But if there was a crazy outside with a gun, going to the house wasn't an option.

Another thought struck. Where was Mama?

She and Danny exchanged a look. "I'm sure she'll be fine," he whispered, his thoughts obviously on the same frequency as hers.

He grimaced and Sam turned to her daughter, ignoring Danny's silent warning. "Lindsey, honey, I need you to let go of Danny for a minute. I think he hurt himself a little bit, and Mommy needs to see how bad it is. Okay?"

Lindsey jumped up, terror in her eyes. "Is he okay? What happened? I'm sorry, it's all my fault. I didn't mean it."

Danny instantly snatched her hand and pulled her back down. "Whoa, Linds. Easy now, girl. This is not your fault and I'm fine. Really." He smiled reassuringly and Sam hoped Lindsey was too young to read it for the lie it was.

Sam's breath wheezed in and out of her lungs as she lifted the hem of his T-shirt. She forced everything to the back of her mind but the task at hand. From what she could see in the cabin's dim light, the bullet had merely grazed his side. It didn't look like it went through, but the wound was bleeding too much for her comfort. Sam looked around for something to use as a bandage.

He met her eyes. "I'll lean forward and you pull my shirt off. You can use it to wrap my side."

His ability to read her mind pierced Sam's heart all over again. What would it be like to connect like this all the time, to feel she was never alone, that there was someone else in the world who shared her heart?

He leaned over and placed a gentle kiss on her forehead. "One thing at a time, Samantha, okay?"

By the time Sam wrapped his shirt around the wound and he caught his breath, there was silence outside the cabin. Then they heard Mama's voice. "Sam? Lindsey? Danny? Are you all right?"

Lindsey started to leap up, but again, Danny stopped her.

Sam inched her way to the door and eased it open a crack. Mama stood by a small opening in the outer door of the bait shop. "We're fine, Mama. You?" The shooter already knew their location, so speaking wouldn't alert him, but Sam didn't want to broadcast Danny's condition.

"I'm okay," Mama called back. "Just a little shook up, is all. Luke is on his way. He's sending the medics, too, just in case. The maniac is gone, I think. I heard a car drive away."

Sam didn't miss Mama's use of the sheriff's given name, but she found it didn't bother her. Wasn't Mama allowed to be happy, too? Hadn't she done enough penance, just like Sam? Maybe it was time for both of them to come out of the storm.

Speaking of storms...Sam snapped her thoughts back to the present. Above her, the wind continued to pick up speed, swaying through the live oaks. She eyed the thick canopy, wishing she'd been able to have the trees trimmed. It was a yearly dilemma. Having them thinned out was expensive, but it lessened the chances the wind would knock one of the huge trees down. Cleaning up a downed tree cost more than trimming all of them did. She sighed. Nothing she could do about it at the moment.

Danny shifted and stifled a moan. Sam closed the door and dropped down beside them. "Did you hear? Medics are on their way."

He nodded. "I'll be fine. It's just a scratch."

Sam met his eyes and he dared her to refute him in front of Lindsey. Instead, she leaned over and placed a kiss on his forehead, much as he'd done to her earlier. "Hang in there."

He gripped her hand and brought it to his lips, placing a gentle kiss there. "We are all going to be fine, Sam. Trust me, okay?"

Sam nodded, then stood as the sound of approaching sirens drifted towards them.

****

It was very late when an unusually silent Mike Sanchez dropped Sam and Danny off at the fish camp. Sam was so exhausted she would have slid onto the ground in a boneless heap if not for Danny's supporting arm around her waist. She sent him a grateful smile, laying a hand against his cheek. Tears threatened. She could easily have lost him today. But the paramedics had pronounced Danny "very lucky" at the scene; the ER doc had echoed their sentiments as he put several neat stitches in Danny's side.

When the two stepped out of Sanchez's SUV, Porter and Mama rose from their porch rockers. After questioning everyone, Luke Porter had personally driven Mama and Lindsey back to the fish camp. He had promised to wait with them until the docs released Sam and Danny.

Mama gathered Sam in a careful hug, and for once, Sam didn't have the urge to pull away. "You're sure you're okay?" Mama asked, seeking confirmation from Danny as well.

"We're both fine. Truly," Sam said, giving Mama another hug.

A little while later, Porter nodded to Mike, who'd been awkwardly hovering on the sidelines, scowling and sullen. "Thanks, Sanchez. Go on home and get some rest. Between this mess and the incoming storm, it might be your last chance for a while."

Sanchez nodded curtly. "Sure, Sheriff. Nite, Sam. Take care, Hastings."

After he left, Danny turned to Porter. "Is it me, or he one unhappy man?"

Porter nodded once. "He's a good guy; just going through a tough time."

Sam had more important things to worry about. She walked over and sat beside Mama. "Lindsey asleep?"

"She fell asleep in the car and didn't wake up, even when we carried her into the house."

"You holding up okay?" Sam was worried about the grayish cast to her mother's features, visible even in the porch light.

Mama's eyes filled as she met Sam's. "I thought if we sold the property, it would stop. That you and Lindsey would be safe. But it's only gotten worse."

Porter stepped up behind Mama and gently put his arm around her. She leaned back and closed her eyes, seeming to absorb his strength. This time, the sight didn't bother Sam. She understood the need to feel safe and protected, and it seemed Porter—albeit years late, in Sam's opinion—was providing it for

Mama.

"It's never been that simple, Katharine," Porter said, softly stroking Mama's arm, "but we'll get to the bottom of it. In the meantime," he glanced at Danny, "I'm thinking if you're up to it, you and I will take turns keeping watch over the place tonight."

Danny gave a curt nod of agreement and something passed between them, a commitment to keeping the women safe, no matter the cost. Sam shivered. She didn't like to think it might come to that.

"I'll take a turn, too," she said, daring either man to argue. Neither one did.

****

Sam's shift had ended at four a.m. and she'd managed to fall asleep immediately. The smell of coffee woke her about eight a.m. When she flipped on the television in the living room, hurricane coverage had now preempted all regular programming in the area. Lindsey wandered in from her room and curled up beside Sam, her eyes haunted, even though she'd slept through the night.

In the kitchen, Sam could hear Mama bustling about and soon the smell of biscuits and gravy mingled with fresh coffee.

She brushed Lindsey's hair back from her face. "You ready for some grub, Princess?"

Lindsey burrowed closer. "I'm scared, Mommy."

Sam tightened her grip. "Listen, Princess, I don't want you to worry, okay? Between Sheriff Porter and Deputy Sanchez and Danny and me, we'll figure this all out, okay? Besides, God is right here with us, looking out for us. Let's not forget that." A gust of wind rattled one of the shutters. "After breakfast, you and me need to board up some windows, so we'd better get cracking."

Just as they entered the kitchen, Luke came through the back door, which meant Danny was taking his turn keeping watch. "Smells great, Katharine."

"Help yourself, Sher—I mean, Luke."

Once they were all seated with steaming plates, Porter said, "I need to get back to town and make some calls, get this sorted out. Danny says he's feeling better this morning. I'll send Sanchez to stop by periodically, but this storm means we're going to have our hands full." He glanced at Lindsey, then at Sam and Mama. "Be careful."

When he glanced at Sam, she nodded and patted the gun tucked in her waistband.

As soon as he was finished, he thanked Mama and left, stopping to chat with Danny before he disappeared down the drive.

Sam walked over to Danny. "Mama has breakfast ready. Go on in and eat."

"I'm okay."

He looked like road kill. His hair stood on end, dark circles ringed his eyes. "Right. But go eat anyway." She narrowed her eyes. "Did you sleep at all?"

He shrugged. "Not much. But I'm fine."

Sam planted her hands on her fists, ready to argue with him, but he forestalled her by heading up the porch steps. "I won't be long."

"Stubborn man," she mumbled, a small smile playing around her lips.

While he was gone, Sam studied her surroundings, but the normal chatter and chirp of the woods convinced her there was no one out there right now. But she wouldn't make assumptions, so she kept her ears open while she made a mental list of tasks which needed handling before the storm hit later today. Yesterday's commotion had set them far behind schedule. The bait shop and cottages needed boarding up; they needed canned goods and extra batteries. The house still had the original wooden shutters, which Sam would hold off closing for last. The feeling was oppressive when they were shut.

When Danny reappeared, Sam said, "I need to make a run to town for more hurricane supplies. With everything else going on, I forgot to restock. Mama and Lindsey will start filling water bottles. Can you keep an eye on things here?"

He looked like he wanted to argue, but all he said was, "Sure. But be careful, okay?"

"You bet."

Sam took off, her sense of foreboding growing with every mile. It wasn't just the usual unease of an incoming storm, but something deeper. She couldn't shake the bone-deep knowledge that things were going to get a whole lot worse. And soon. She pounded the steering wheel in frustration. Who was behind this? And how could they stop him before he tried again? They had to find out. Had to.

****

When Sam got to Jimmy Wayne's hardware store, she was surprised to find his part-time helper behind the counter, especially since the place was crowded with people just like her, grabbing last-minute supplies.

"Hi Zach. Where's Jimmy Wayne?"

Zach licked his lips and scanned the room to make sure no one could overhear, then lowered his voice. "He seemed kind of upset this morning, distracted, like something was bothering him. He told me to cover for him and left. Said he was going home for a while."

That wasn't like Jimmy Wayne. Nothing bothered him. He was generally the calm voice of reason when others were flailing about. Sam paid for her batteries, duct tape, bottled water and extra tarp, and headed back to the Jeep. If the storm turned out to be as bad as predicted, they would be better prepared and equipped than most. While they didn't have a generator—it was on Sam's wish list of things to buy—they had a gas stove and could haul buckets of water from the river to flush toilets, since the well pump was electric. Mama's extensive canning would also serve them well, but Lindsey was a sucker for tuna and canned spaghetti.

Still troubled over Zach's words, Sam decided to stop off and make sure Jimmy Wayne was okay. His house was on the way out of town anyway, so it wouldn't take long.

She walked up to the neat brick ranch house and marveled again at the meticulously-arranged flower beds and weed-free lawn. Jimmy Wayne was a stickler for neatness, she'd give him that. But his obsession with tidiness was becoming a bit...unsettling. She was surprised when no one answered her knock.

She waited a minute and knocked again. "Jimmy Wayne?" When no one stirred, she walked around to the back of the tidy lot to the detached two-car garage, half of which he'd converted into a workshop. The garage door was closed and a peek in the window showed his car missing. A sliver of light shone from under the door to the workshop side, though, so Sam walked around the building to try to see in the window on the other side.

Oddly enough, the window was covered in some sort of black paper, almost like it was being used as a darkroom. Sam knocked on the window. "Jimmy Wayne? Are you in there? Are you all right?"

She knew since Annie's death, he sometimes struggled with bouts of loneliness and depression. And with Annie's birthday coming up...

Annie. The key.

Of course.

With everything going on, Sam's worry kicked up a notch. What if he was hurt in there?

She ran back to the front of the house and

stepped into the flower bed, praying he hadn't removed the spare keys from under the fake rock. She flipped the rock over, opened the bottom, and breathed a sigh of relief as two keys fell into her hand.

Sam sped back to the garage and let herself in through the side door. "Jimmy Wayne? Are you in here?"

Still no answer. Her heart was racing as she knocked on the door to the workshop and then inserted the key into the lock. When it turned, she shoved her way into the room and stopped short, stunned.

Every available surface was covered in photos.

Of her.

Chapter Twenty Six

Bile backed up in her throat as Sam stood frozen in place, her heart racing as she stepped further into the room. What was going on? She turned and looked behind her, the pattern suddenly clear.

Chronologically arranged, the photos began to the left of the door, from when the two of them were children. Jimmy Wayne's father had been big into photography and taken lots of photos at church picnics and school events, Sam remembered. Apparently, Jimmy Wayne had saved them all.

She followed her own chronological progression from skinny kid to gangly teen and remembered how Jimmy Wayne had gotten obsessed with photography in high school. But she'd thought it had just been a passing fad. Apparently not.

Sam turned around, her eyes going to the most recent photos. *Oh, dear God.*

There were several shots of her, stripping down for a quick dive to her cave. How dare he spy on her this way!

Wanting to marry her was one thing, but this...this was some kind of sick obsession.

She scanned the photos again, freezing when she came to the wedding pictures. There was the same picture of her and Annie which Sam kept tucked into her bedroom mirror. And here was the one of her and Danny Sam had never been able to bring herself to throw away.

Sam wrapped her arms around her middle as chills shook her body. Except this wasn't the same picture. Jimmy Wayne had pasted his face over Danny's.

Sam leaned closer. Oh, God. It wasn't the only one. In their wedding photo, Jimmy Wayne had pasted her face over Annie's.

Her knees gave out and Sam slid to the ground, her back against the door frame. What was going on? But she knew, in some small corner of her heart, she knew.

Sam closed her eyes, then reopened them as sick certainty seeped into her bones.

Straight ahead was proof. On the desk directly across from her sat a small easel with photos arranged in a seeming random pattern. Jeremy Castle, the developer who'd disappeared last year, Annie, her father, Tommy Sooner, Danny and...

Lindsey.

All the faces had a big red "X" drawn through them.

Including Danny and Lindsey's.

It took a moment for it to sink in, but the second it did, Sam was on her feet.

Somehow, Jimmy Wayne, her childhood friend and champion, had become a killer.

And Danny and Lindsey were next on his list. She had to warn them, had to call Porter.

A whisper of motion behind her was her only warning before pain exploded in her head and everything went black.

****

Out at the marina, Danny, Katharine and Lindsey raced against the incoming storm. Hurricane Bella was scheduled to make landfall late in the afternoon. Before she left, Sam had given him a quick rundown on all that needed to be done beforehand. A native Californian, Danny understood earthquakes; but hurricanes were a mystery. Today he was getting a crash course.

He found Katharine in the kitchen, filling gallon jugs with water and lining them up along the perimeter of the room. "Where's Lindsey?"

"Filling the bathtub."

"For?"

"Water to wash dishes. Once the electricity goes out, the well pump stops, so we have no water."

"Got it. Drinking water in jugs; dishwater in the tub."

"What about perishables?"

"Sam will get ice for the cooler, and we'll transfer things we'll need in the next few days into the cooler. As long as we keep the fridge and freezer closed, they'll keep for several days.

"I saw some lanterns in one of the sheds. Do we have kerosene?"

"Should be in the shed, too." She nodded towards a cabinet out on the back porch's lean-to, beside the washing machine. "There should be more oil and lamps there, too. Could you bring them in?"

They worked steadily all morning, the lingering pain in his side nothing compared to the growing worry about Sam. She should have been back long ago.

He went outside and pulled out his cell phone. No need to add to Katharine's worry.

"Drake's Hardware, Zach speaking. How can I help you?"

"Hi. May I speak to Jimmy Wayne?"

"Sorry. He's not here this morning."

That was odd. Sam said the store would be packed today. "Has Sam Collins been there?"

"Sure, she was here a while ago, picking up supplies." The young man paused, then added, "She was asking about Jimmy Wayne, too. Is something wrong?"

Unease slithered down Danny's side. "Nothing to worry about," Danny said, though he wasn't so sure. "Can you tell me what time Sam left there?"

"Um, about ten, I think. But it's hard to remember exactly. We've been swamped all morning. Why people wait until the last second when they know—"

"Thanks, Zach. Gotta go."

Danny stood in the yard, trying to decide what to do. Every instinct he possessed said Sam was in trouble and it had something to do with Jimmy Wayne. If it did, he needed to find her, pronto.

He turned to go, stopped. But he couldn't just leave Lindsey and Katharine out here all alone. What if he was wrong, and this had nothing to do with Jimmy Wayne. Then the two of them would be sitting ducks for whoever was hunting people.

He tried Porter's cell, but the line was busy. He called Sanchez next. "Hey Mike, Danny Hastings. When are you scheduled to come by the marina again?"

"Actually, I'm about a mile away. Why? What's up?"

Danny hesitated, not sure how much to say. Porter seemed to think his deputy was on the up-and-up, but...there was too much at stake to make any mistakes. "Sam is late getting back from town and I wanted to be sure she didn't have car trouble or anything. But I don't want to leave Katharine and Lindsey alone."

"I didn't see any sign of her Jeep on the way out, but I'll stick around while you check...as long as I don't get another call, you understand."

"Of course."

By the time Sanchez pulled into the parking lot, Danny was on his way to town.

****

Sam woke to the sound of someone moaning, her cheek resting on cold concrete, her whole body aching and sore. It took a minute to realize the pitiful groans came from her own throat. She tried to roll over and sit up, but her hands were tied. So were her feet.

She waited for her eyes to adjust to the dark room and looked around. She was still in Jimmy Wayne's workshop.

Her earlier discovery came flooding back. Jimmy Wayne was a killer. He'd killed Jeremy Castle. And Annie. And her father.

Her stomach heaved and she turned her head and threw up. The man she'd loved like a brother since childhood was a killer.

And her daughter and Danny were next on his list.

She spared a moment's thought for why he hadn't killed her when he had the chance, but it didn't matter. She had to get out of here. Save them.

Think, Samantha. Think.

It took several precious minutes, but she maneuvered herself to a sitting position with her hands behind her. Biting her lip against the pain, she forced her wrists under her body and up under her knees. She had to stop and catch her breath, then she inched her legs through and finally got her hands up in front of her.

Her hunting knife and gun were gone; Jimmy Wayne must have taken them. What he didn't know was how she always kept a spare pocket knife inside a hidden pocket of her cargo shorts. The little knife could cut the ropes, given time and patience. Which she didn't have.

Twice she had to fish the knife off the floor where she dropped it in her haste. But eventually, panting from exertion, she freed her hands. In moments, she had her feet free, too.

The temptation to barrel through the doorway almost overwhelmed her, but her training kicked in. She was hunting a predator and the first rule was not to give herself away.

So she stood silently and inched her way to the door, listening for several agonizing minutes.

Once she determined Jimmy Wayne was long gone, she eased the door open and slipped out. She approached her Jeep with caution, keeping the vehicle between her and the house, expecting a hail of bullets at any time. Although it didn't seem to be Jimmy Wayne's style. All the other deaths had looked like an accident.

Accident?

She dropped to her knees and looked under the car, not sure if she'd recognize a bomb if she saw one. But nothing seemed out of place or looked like it had been recently added, so she climbed in. He'd taken her keys, of course, but hotwiring the Jeep was something she'd been doing for years.

In moments, she was racing towards home.

Please God, protect Lindsey, Danny, and Mama.

****

Danny's heart pounded and his hands gripped the steering wheel as he pushed the Mustang to its limit. Adrenaline pumped through his system, terror heightening all his senses, but this time the high wasn't euphoric. Before, the more dangerous, the better he liked it. He never worried much about dying, because he figured it would happen on God's timetable, not his.

Now everything was different. Would he be too late? Instead of protecting the people he finally realized he loved, he had been wasting time thinking about running away. Coward.

He whipped the car around a sharp curve and had to stand on the brakes to keep from running smack into the "road closed" sign. Up ahead, some poor guy from the county was filling potholes all by himself. From the looks of things, he wouldn't be finished anytime soon.

A little orange sign read "detour" and pointed to a dirt road veering off to the left. He considered stopping for more detailed directions, but decided it'd be quicker just to follow the signs around the problem.

He thumped and bumped down the dirt track, wincing when his head hit the ceiling after a particularly nasty pothole. He kept his eyes peeled for more "detour" signs, but didn't see any. A quick glance at his watch said he'd been driving for ten minutes. Surely it couldn't take that long to get around one little road problem.

He flipped on his cell phone to call Katharine for directions. No signal.

Of course.

He tossed the phone on the seat and squinted through the trees. Since he left the fish camp, the weather had deteriorated at an alarming pace. The wind had whipped around him, as the sky opened up and rain began pounding the car. Suddenly, the warnings the weathermen had been spouting for days made a sick kind of sense. This wasn't just a bad thunderstorm, He suddenly understood the kind of force a hurricane packed. This was a monster and it was barreling down on them. He had to take shelter.

But Sam was somewhere out in this.

Every nagging doubt he'd ever had about Jimmy Wayne Drake rolled over in his mind, sending his nerve endings into hyper-drive. Jimmy Wayne was around for every single killing.

Danny huffed out a breath. Course, so were about fifty other locals, too.

He stomped on the brakes as the dirt road suddenly hooked right and ended at an abandoned little shack.

Now what?

He banged the steering wheel, spun the car in a

circle and headed back the way he'd come—faster this time.

****

Sam squinted at the darkening sky. The hurricane was moving in, the wind bringing the first rain bands with it. The road was slick so she forced her speed down to sixty, riding the knife edge between getting there fast and getting there alive.

She rounded a curve in the road and slid to a stop. Up ahead, a utility crewman was just clearing away the last of the detour signs. Thank goodness, she wouldn't have to go traipsing through the woods.

"Come on, come on," she murmured, tapping the steering wheel as the drenched worker scurried out of the pickup to scoop the next barricade into the back. His hood was pulled down over his face, and his shoulders hunched — the poor man looked miserable.

The minute he cleared enough space for Sam to squeeze through, she eased the Jeep past him. She raised her hand in acknowledgement, but he didn't even glance her way.

With the wheel gripped in her sweaty palms, Sam covered the last few miles with her heart thundering in time to the wheels on the rain-slick pavement. *Hurry, hurry, hurry.*

The sky was dark as night when she raced down the marina's gravel drive, oblivious to the way her tires spit rocks into the trees. She skidded to a stop in front of the house and raced up the porch steps and into the kitchen.

"Mama! Lindsey!" she shouted, but even as she raced from room to room, she knew they weren't there. Despite the storm bearing down on them, the house was quiet as a tomb.

She didn't want to, but she forced herself to slow down, to read the signs just as she would if she was out hunting. Nothing out of place, no sign of a struggle, thank God.

Still, she knew he was here, knew with sinking certainty that if he'd left her alive before, it was because it was part of his plan. Somehow, Lindsey was part of his plan, too. Sam wasn't sure how or why, she just knew she had to get to Lindsey and keep her safe. A terrifying domino effect had been set in motion the night of Castle's death and it was up to Sam to keep her whole world from falling.

Sam paused and braced her hands on her knees, trying to catch her breath. She kept her head down and took one slow, deep breath, then another. And another. *Please God, help me stay calm and clear-headed.*

She stood up and glanced at the outbuildings. Where would Jimmy Wayne take them? Did he even have them? Or had Mama managed to grab Lindsey and hide in the woods?

She had no way of knowing, but she didn't want to get caught again, either. If he had them, Sam's best hope was to offer herself in exchange. She ran to her room and pulled the lock box off the top shelf of her closet where she kept her spare gun. Quickly, she loaded it and stuffed more ammunition in her pockets. A quick check confirmed Jimmy Wayne had cut the phone lines. He'd taken her cell phone earlier.

Sam leaped up and the room spun crazily. She steadied herself and blinked, waiting for the spots to disappear. She felt the back of her head, gingerly probing the lump. Maybe a slight concussion. She could only pray if she had to act, her body would do what she wanted.

Slowly, carefully, Sam slipped out the back door, down the steps and slipped into the woods, making her way slowly to the bait shop. On the way, she checked the supply shed, relieved to find it empty.

Rain pounded down and the wind howled, which

was both good and bad. It masked the sounds of her passing, but kept her from hearing anyone else moving, either.

She flattened her body against the side of the bait shop and eased closer until she could peek through the back window.

One glance and she ducked down, heart pounding.

Dear God, no.

Chapter Twenty Seven

By the time Danny finally found the main road again, he was frustrated and frantic. The wipers were going full blast and he still couldn't see beyond the hood of the car. The utility worker had mysteriously disappeared, but he didn't have time to worry about where he could have gone so fast.

All he knew was that he had to get to Jimmy Wayne's, pronto. He hadn't been there in a long time, but two wrong turns later, he found it.

No sign of Sam or her Jeep. He ran to the front door. "Jimmy Wayne!" he shouted, pounding on the wood.

No answer.

All the verticals were pulled shut and there were no lights on inside, so he ran to the back of the property and checked the garage. No sign of Drake's car either, but there was a light on inside the adjoining workshop.

He ran around the building and found the back door ajar.

When he stepped inside, his heart stopped as he looked around.

Oh. My. God.

Sam. Lindsey. Katharine.

He turned and ran. His hands shook as he fumbled for his cell phone, and he started shouting the minute Porter picked up. "Get to the Collins's place. Drake's the killer."

"What? Who is this?"

"It's Hastings. You need to get to Sam's with as

many men as you can. Drake is the killer." He was soaked and his hands slid on the steering wheel as he swung the car in a tight u-turn.

Porter's response was succinct. "I know. I've been trying to call you. I'm heading there now. Where are you?"

"Drake's place. Wait. You know?"

"I'll explain later. Sanchez and I should be at Sam's in five minutes. Here's—"

"Why isn't Sanchez there? He was when I left." Danny's tires squealed as he rounded the corner and raced through a yellow light.

"He got another call. Turned out to be a false alarm. I can't raise anyone at the fish camp."

Dread settled in the pit of Danny's stomach and he stomped on the accelerator. "Not a false alarm, then."

It sounded like Porter banged a fist on the steering wheel. "Probably not. How far out are you?"

"About five minutes."

"I'll scope things out when I get there. You wait for my signal, hear?"

Danny had no intention of waiting, so he simply ended the call. He tossed his phone onto the passenger seat, then rubbed his hands on his damp jeans to get a better grip on the steering wheel.

God, please. Protect them.
****

Luke Porter raced towards the fish camp from the opposite direction, similar prayers on his lips. Katharine and Sam had been through more in their lives than anyone should, and he had failed them too many times. It wasn't going to happen again. He'd go to his grave wishing he'd done something about Amos, despite Katharine's pleading to the contrary. He'd loved the woman since high school. He should have protected her from the monster she married. But he'd taken the coward's way out. Told himself he was following the law, trying not to make things worse. Horse feathers. He was a yellow-bellied coward.

Not this time. He would do whatever it took to protect them.

When he reached the gravel drive to the fish camp, he killed his lights. With the storm howling, no one would hear him approach. He didn't want Drake to see him, either.

After the call from the lab about the DNA match between Drake's glass from the diner and the strand of hair found in Castle's rental car, the rest of the puzzle pieces had locked into place with frightening precision. Annie's mysterious death. The other missing developer. Possibly even Sam's father, years ago. Fury burned in Porter's gut to think he'd sat in church beside a cold-blooded killer and hadn't known, hadn't suspected. Sure, he'd never liked the man, but until recently, he hadn't thought him capable of murder.

Maybe it was time to hang up his badge. Let someone younger and quicker take over.

Today, though, he had a murderer to apprehend. Luke pulled his SUV off the drive and tucked it into the woods, facing towards town in case he needed to make a quick getaway. He clicked his mic.

"Dispatch, this is Porter. I'm at the Collins place. What's Sanchez's ETA?"

Sanchez answered. "Almost there, Boss. What's up?"

"Was Jimmy Wayne Drake here when you left?"

There was a pause. "He arrived just as I was heading out, said he'd keep an eye on things until I got back."

Porter pinched the bridge above his nose. "Drake killed Castle."

Alice gasped.

"Holy—" Sanchez swallowed the rest. "I'll be

right there. Sam and Katharine okay?"

Porter squinted through the driving rain. "Don't know yet. Just got here. I'm going to scope out the house and bait shop. Hastings is en route. Corral him before he goes charging into trouble."

"Got it boss."

"Be careful, Sheriff...over," Alice in dispatch added.

"Thanks, Alice. Over."

Porter checked his gun before he got out of the car. He was instantly soaked to the skin, but his Stetson kept most of the rain out of his eyes.

He kept to the trees and made his way to the back door of the house.

****

Sam leaned against the outside wall of the bait shop, chest heaving, gun gripped in both hands, trying to gather her scattered thoughts. There was blood on the floor, fresh blood from the looks of it. What she didn't know was who it belonged to.

She forced a slow, deep breath into her lungs. She had to think smart. The wind would cover any sounds, but she needed to keep quiet more for her mental state. She wouldn't do Mama or Lindsey any good if she reacted in panic. She needed a clear head.

Sam moved to the next window and tried to get a better view into the shop. She saw more blood, leading out the back door, but that was it. There was no sign of anyone inside, no sound of them, either.

In a low crouch, Sam ran around the side of the building to the back door. The blood trailed in little drips across the porch and down the wooden steps. Sam forced her mind to process them as clues, not a sign of injury. The trail ended on the bottom step where the rain washed all other evidence away.

Where had Jimmy Wayne taken them? From where she hid by the steps, she checked the dock.

Both pontoons tugged at their ropes, bobbing in the churning water. They hadn't left the marina by boat.

Her mind wanted to shut down to think her childhood friend, her protector, had killed her father, and Castle, maybe even Annie. It was too much. If she didn't block it out of her mind, she wouldn't be able to function. She had to keep the goal in mind: get Lindsey and Mama away from him.

Did Jimmy Wayne have Danny, too? She hadn't seen his car when she pulled in. Sanchez either, and she knew they were planning to take turns. Had Danny come looking for her when she was late getting back? She wished she knew, wished there was a way to find out.

But there wasn't. She just had to do her best and pray God gave her the strength to do whatever she needed to protect her loved ones.

She peered through the driving rain and scanned the cottages, seeking some sign of where Jimmy Wayne had taken them. Slowly, slowly, she looked from one to the next, looking for something, anything...

Wait. There. In Hastings' cottage. Had the curtain twitched? Sam focused all her energy on one spot. Yes. There is was again.

Sam looked around. A straight line was the fastest route, but he'd see her. It would take longer to slip into the woods and approach from the other side. Every maternal instinct in her body screamed at her to storm the citadel and race straight for Lindsey, but common sense prevailed.

She left the shelter of the overhang and eased into the nearby woods, just far enough so she couldn't be seen. Then she made her way around the perimeter of the property and came up behind Danny's cottage.

Flat against the wall, she inched over to the back window and peeked into the bedroom. The door into the small hallway stood open, giving her a view straight through the cottage and into the tiny living room at the front.

Bingo. Jimmy Wayne stood calmly at the front window as though he was waiting for dinner guests, never mind the gun clasped loosely in his hand. Sam strained to see more, but couldn't.

Sam slipped back down, trying to decide her next move. Another peek and the decision was taken from her. Jimmy Wayne had his arm around Lindsey, pointing her towards the front door.

"Sam!" he shouted, easing the front door open several inches. "I know you're out there. I've got Lindsey with me. If you want her to live out the afternoon, you'd better show yourself."

Sam's mouth went dry and she almost leaped forward when Jimmy Wayne moved his arm up around Lindsey's throat. Even from here she could feel her daughter's fear, the thrumming of her heart.

"Stop playing games, Sam. Get out here, NOW!"

Lindsey whimpered as the arm around her neck tightened.

Sam slipped around the side of the building. There really was only one plan she could live with. Offer herself in exchange for Lindsey and hope it was enough.

God, please. It was all she could manage.

She stepped out from between the cottages, gun raised and ready to shoot if she had the opportunity. "Let her go, Jimmy Wayne. She has nothing to do with this."

"Oh, but she does. Did you think I wouldn't figure out who her father was? Did you think it wouldn't matter?" His voice rose, and for the first time, Sam saw the madness which had always been hidden behind his calm exterior. Chills raced down Sam's back as she realized the man she'd loved like a brother her whole life was someone else, a monster.

Sam used every bit of self control she possessed to keep her voice steady. Firm. "Let her go, Jimmy Wayne. Set her free and you can do anything you want with me."

"No, Mama," Lindsey protested, but the sound ended in a squeak as Jimmy Wayne tightened his hold. Lindsey clawed at his hands, desperate eyes fixed on Sam.

Beyond one quick, reassuring glance, Sam refused to look at Lindsey. She couldn't. She had to stay focused on Jimmy Wayne. She'd always been able to look into his eyes and see what he was thinking. She prayed she could still do it today, when it mattered most.

She locked eyes with him, taking in the madness, yes, but beyond it pain, and a horror he couldn't conceal. He flicked his gaze around the room, to the windows, back and forth. He was getting edgy. Panicking.

Did he hate what he'd become? Could she use it to save her daughter's life?

Sam lowered her voice so he'd focus on her. "Jimmy Wayne, I've loved you since we were kids. You've always been my friend. If you're angry with me, then we need to talk, just you and me."

He studied her, head cocked to one side. "Do you know how many years I've protected you?"

Sam swallowed, pushing back the images she'd seen in his workshop. "You've looked out for me since we were both just little kids. Remember when you fixed my first pair of glasses? Pop smashed them, but you fixed them for me." His look turned dark, angry, and Sam wished she hadn't brought up Amos. But she needed to keep him talking, keep his attention away from Lindsey. And please, God, let Danny and Porter be on their way.

"Amos paid for that," he said darkly, and Sam

decided not to ask what he meant.

"You've always protected me, Jimmy Wayne, that's why I need you to do it again. I need you to—"

"I *am* protecting you, don't you see?" he shouted, his frustration evident.

Sam kept her gun level, her eyes on his, despite the trickle of sweat running down her temple. She chose her words with care. "You can't protect me while you're scaring my daughter, Jimmy Wayne."

"She should have been mine. Mine."

"You've always been like a father to her, Jimmy Wayne. She loves you." Sam flicked a quick glance toward Lindsey, begging her not to argue.

He shifted his grip and Lindsey whimpered. "She wants Danny." He spat the other man's name. "The Interloper. He has no place here. It's time he learns it."

Sam shuddered inwardly. Danny was next on Jimmy Wayne's list.

Outside, the wind howled through the trees, branches slapping the cottage's tin roof. Rain beat on the windows, obscuring the outside world. It was as though nothing existed but the three of them.

Sam's arm was getting tired from holding the gun, but she ignored it. No time for weakness; there was too much at stake. Jimmy Wayne's movements were getting more frantic, panicked. His eyes darted around the room before finally meeting hers squarely. "Make your choice, Sam."

Sam kept her voice calm, rational. "What are you talking about…Jimmy Wayne? What choice?"

He shook his head as though he couldn't believe she didn't understand such a simple question. "Which one will die first, Samantha? You or Lindsey?"

While he spoke, his eyes had gone flat and hard. Sam realized with chilling clarity that there was no conscience screaming in Jimmy Wayne's mind. He didn't have one. Certainly not anymore, if he ever had. Appealing to something he didn't possess wouldn't help. What now?

Before Sam had time to come up with another response, Jimmy Wayne raised his gun and cocked the trigger.

Lindsey screamed.

****

Danny careened around corners and fishtailed on the slippery road. Even a dedicated limit-pusher knew when he was spinning out of control. He eased his pressure on the accelerator a fraction, just enough to regain control. But it was the hardest thing he'd ever done, because every cell in his body screamed, hurry, hurry, hurry.

When he whipped onto the gravel drive to the fish camp, he flipped off his headlights.

He squinted through the trees, looking for either the sheriff or Sanchez's SUV. There was no way he would sit and wait for them, but he didn't want to get shot by mistake, either. As he bumped down the drive, he caught a glimpse of something. He eased closer, stopped.

Porter's SUV. Danny twisted in his seat and looked all around, but there was no sign of the man.

He squinted through the rain looking for Sanchez, but he didn't see him, either. Just before the fish camp came into view, Danny spun his car around and backed it into the trees, nose to the main road, like Porter's.

For a moment he stopped, realizing he had no weapon. Nothing. He checked the almost-empty glove box, but knew there wasn't anything there. He'd have to rely on his wits and speed.

With a quick prayer for guidance, he plunged into the rain.

****

Luke Porter was not only scared, he was mad.

Furious. At himself, more than anything. How could he have missed recognizing Drake for what he was? He'd always considered himself a sound judge of character, but not after today.

He eased up the back porch steps, gun ready, and cleared his mind of everything but the task at hand. He wouldn't fail Katharine and her family again.

Porter flattened himself against the wall beside the door, then slipped through it, gun sweeping the kitchen. He stopped, listened. The house was empty.

But he had to be sure. With a silent tread, he moved through the house, checking each room, gun first. There was no sign of them.

No signs of a struggle, either.

He couldn't decide if that was good news or bad.

Oblivious to the pounding rain, Luke ran to the bait shop and peered through the door. Same as before, he went through the doorway gun first, sweeping the area. His instincts twitched and he froze. There was someone here.

The hair on his nape stood on end as he moved through the small shop, back to the wall. He heard a slight thump and cocked his head, listening. There it was again.

He eased around the counter and noticed the door to the storage room was slightly ajar.

Thump. Thump.

He followed the sound and tried to push the door open. It wouldn't budge, as though there was something wedged behind it. He pushed again. *Thump. Thump.*

Luke crouched down and used his shoulder to push the door open just far enough to slip through. He took in the small room at a glance, then dropped to his knees.

Katharine lay on the dirty wooden floor, trussed up like a steer, hands and feet bound behind her, a bandana over her mouth.

But she was alive, thank God. And from the looks of it, terrified. Understandably so.

"I've got you, Katharine. Give me just a minute to cut you loose."

He used his utility knife and sliced through the rope in record time. As soon as her hands were free, she yanked at the gag. "He's got them, Luke. Jimmy Wayne has them. You've got to help them."

Porter cut the ropes at her feet then lifted her up and into his arms, wrapping her so tight neither of them could breathe. "I've got you, Katharine, and I'm not letting go. Ever." For precious moments, he simply held her and rocked her, lending her his strength, absorbing the smell and feel of her. "I love you, Katharine. I always have."

Katharine squirmed until he eased his grip enough so she could lean back and see his face. "I love you, too, Luke, but it doesn't matter now. Please. Go help Sam and Lindsey."

Luke shook his head, appalled that he could get so sidetracked. He set Katharine carefully on her feet. "I'm on my way." He ran a hand down her cheek and handed her his utility knife. "Do you know which way they went?"

"To Danny's cottage."

"I need you to stay here, in the storage room. Keep the door cracked so you can hear anyone coming."

Katharine's chin came up. "I want to go with you."

Atta girl, he thought. "I know you do, honey. But I need you here. We don't want to give him any more hostages, okay? I'll be better able to do my job if I know you're safely out of harm's way."

"But—"

"Please, Katharine. Don't divide my attention." He leaned forward, kissed her forehead, and then gave her a gentle nudge further into the storeroom. "I'll be back as soon as I can. Pray."

She met his gaze without flinching. "I'll be here."

He nodded and then headed back into the storm, praying he wasn't too late.

****

Danny didn't stop to check the house or bait shop. Something told him Jimmy Wayne would have taken them to his cottage. His presence had become a threat to the man. Near as he could figure, Jimmy Wayne had decided to become Sam's protector years ago and had been doing it ever since. A chill raced down his spine. The man was clearly insane.

He was also a murderer, one who'd killed Danny's friend. He had to be stopped before he tried to kill Sam and Lindsey, too.

Danny eased up to the back window of his cottage, panic and fury churning in his gut. He wiped the rain from his eyes and peered through the sheers. He froze.

Jimmy Wayne stood by the front window, his arm around Lindsey's neck, a gun in his other hand. Sam stood opposite him, her gun also raised.

Stalemate. With Lindsey in the middle.

No way was he letting his daughter get caught in the crossfire.

Without stopping to think about it, Danny ran around to the front of the cottage, took the porch steps in one leap, and burst through the door.

For just a moment, Jimmy Wayne was off balance, gun moving between Sam and him, back and forth. Out of the corner of his eye, Danny saw Sam searching for an opening, trying to gauge the moment to take her shot—without hitting Lindsey by mistake.

It was just the sort of diversion he'd been hoping to create. *Come on, Sam. Do it.*

Jimmy Wayne must have seen the look that

299

passed between them, for a slow grin spread across his lips before he casually raised his gun to Lindsey's temple. "It'll take more than an interloper like you to distract me from the real goal, Hastings," he purred.

Danny saw the silent scream in Lindsey's eyes and wanted to tear Drake limb from limb.

In that moment, a curtain parted in his mind and Danny saw clearly. All his life, he'd kept his heart guarded, kept people away, tried to play it safe, emotionally. The risk had always been too great.

Yet at this moment, he realized the risk wasn't really a risk at all. Lindsey was his daughter, flesh of his flesh and blood of his blood. She deserved a future, filled with love and laughter and all good things.

He flicked his gaze to Sam. His beloved Samantha. The one woman he'd never forgotten, the one he had been too cowardly to love. What idiocy. He'd loved her for years; not telling her didn't change a thing. He wanted for her the same things he wanted for his daughter: love, laughter and happiness.

He wished for the chance to give them those things. To share them. He wanted to spend his life with his family.

But it looked like his first and last act as a family man would be one of sacrifice. It was fitting, in its way. The man who'd never given anything, would now give his life to save theirs. They deserved that and more.

Danny looked into Lindsey's frightened eyes and smiled reassuringly. "It's going to be okay, honey. I love you."

He turned to Sam, all the love in his heart in his smile. *I love you, Samantha. I wish I could tell you.* But he couldn't, didn't want to risk Jimmy Wayne shifting his wrath to them. He needed to keep the other man's attention on him.

He met Jimmy Wayne's eyes. "It's me you want, Drake. Not them. I'm the developer, the one trying to take Sam's fish camp away. This is between you and me."

"Danny?" Sam's voice was wary, filled with suspicion.

Danny ignored her. "You don't want to hurt this little girl, Jimmy Wayne. That won't protect Sam. But getting rid of me, will."

As he spoke, Danny kept inching closer and closer, until he could reach out and touch Lindsey.

"That's far enough, Hastings."

Danny took another half step. "Let her go."

Jimmy Wayne shoved the gun harder against Lindsey's temple. "And let your spawn live? I don't think so."

Danny hid his shock. How did the man know?

Jimmy Wayne's lips cursed in a mocking smile. "I'm not stupid, Hastings. She's got your hair, your eyes." He paused and his expression hardened, his fingers gripping the gun. "You took what was mine, took Sam from me. Now you'll both pay."

Danny leaped forward, shouting, "Duck" while he shoved Lindsey to the floor behind him.

Jimmy Wayne fired.

At the same time Danny heard the shot, he felt like someone punched him in the chest. Hard.

He landed on his back on the floor, Lindsey under him. He tried to prop himself on his elbows so he wouldn't crush her, but he couldn't let her go, either.

He heard another shot and the world went black.

****

"Danny!" Sam shouted.

"Mama!" Lindsey whimpered.

The cottage door banged open and Sheriff Porter

burst through the door, gun raised. Sanchez came in from the bedroom, also in a shooter's stance.

"Everyone okay?" Porter asked, gun aimed at Jimmy Wayne's still form.

Sam dropped down and eased Danny aside enough so Lindsey could wiggle out from under him. Lindsey leaped into her arms, legs wrapped around her waist, sobbing and shaking.

Sam made soothing sounds, but her eyes were on Danny and the spreading red stain on his chest.

Under Porter's steady gun, Sanchez checked Jimmy Wayne for a pulse and shook his head.

Porter holstered his weapon and crouched beside Danny. "Pulse is there, but thready." He looked up.

"EMT's are on their way, storm or no storm, but it'll take 'em a while to get here, boss."

"Lindsey, honey, let mama go, so I can help Danny, okay?"

Lindsey clutched her tighter, but then nodded and slowly loosened her grasp. Porter had already cut Danny's shirt open to check the wound. Sam leaped for the bathroom and grabbed several towels. It would take the EMTs a while to get here; in the meantime, they had to stop the bleeding.

Sam leaned over and placed several folded towels over the wound, applying pressure. Her head snapped up. "Wait. Where's Mama?"

"She's fine. She's hiding in the bait shop." Sam wanted to ask more questions, but Porter shook his head. Later.

The sheriff turned to Sanchez. "Why don't you take Lindsey over to the bait shop to wait with Katharine?"

Sanchez stood, held out a hand to Lindsey. "Let's go see Grandma, Lindsey."

"I want to stay here, with Mama and Danny."

Sam smiled at her daughter. "I know, Princess,

but this way you can tell Memaw we're okay and tell the EMTs where we are, okay? I need your help."

Lindsey's eyes went from Sam to Danny and back again. A big tear rolled down her cheek. "Make him better, Mommy?"

Sam's eyes filled. "We're doing the very best we can, Linds."

As soon as the door closed behind them, Porter looked at her. "Katharine is fine. I found her tied up in the storage room."

Sam nodded, but her thoughts were on Danny. The wound wouldn't stop bleeding. She couldn't tell if the bullet had hit any vital organs. She knew first aid, but Danny needed someone with far more extensive knowledge than she had.

"Take it easy, Sam. He's holding his own and help is coming. Don't quit on me now."

Sam met his eyes. There was sorrow, and understanding in them. "You did what you had to do to save your family, Sam."

Tears rolled down Sam's cheeks as she glanced at Jimmy Wayne. She would always love the boy he'd been and hate the monster he'd become. "He was my very first friend, my champion."

Porter nodded. "Try to remember the good things, Sam."

"He killed Pop."

"I know."

"His workshop..." Sam swallowed. "He had pictures."

Porter cocked his head, listening. "EMT's are here. Let's focus on the living, Sam, not the dead."

He stood and opened the door for the ambulance crew.

****

"You're an idiot, you know that?"

Danny smiled without opening his eyes. Had there ever been a sweeter sound than Sam's voice growling in his ear? "Yeah, but it worked, didn't it?"

"Open your eyes, Hastings. I want to see your face when I yell at you."

His forced his lids open. "Yes, ma'am." All around, machines beeped and hummed, so he knew he was in the hospital, not heaven. Surely Sam wouldn't be scolding in heaven, would she?

Danny looked into her gorgeous green eyes. "They tell me you saved my sorry hide, Beautiful. Thank you."

Those eyes sparkled with tears. "Don't you ever scare me like that again. Or do anything so stupid. You walked right into his gun, Danny."

Danny shifted and pain shot through him like fire. "It was the only way I could think of to get Lindsey away from him."

Sam planted her fists on her hips. "I was waiting for the right shot."

"We were out of time and you know it."

"You could have died."

Danny's grin was lopsided. "That was the plan, Beautiful."

"You...you..."

Danny held up a hand, surprised at how much effort it required. "Come here."

Sam moved up beside him, her hand strong and warm in his. "I didn't want to die, Samantha, but it was the only way I knew to protect my family." He paused and raised her hand to his lips. "But since you saved my life, how about us becoming an official family?" He paused. "Marry me, Samantha?"

****

Out in the waiting room, Luke Porter paced, eyeing Katharine over his coffee cup and trying to find the right words. Lindsey slept on the plastic couch beside her, while Katharine calmly kept knitting.

"You're going to wear a hole in the linoleum if

you keep pacing, Luke," she chided.

"Well, I'm trying to figure out what to say," he snapped, annoyed with his own waffling.

Katharine peered at him through her half glasses. "Straight out is usually the best way."

Porter nodded and tossed the Styrofoam cup in the trash. "All right then." He walked over to Katharine and gently took her knitting from her hands. Then he bent on one knee and took her hands in his. "I love you, Katharine. Will you do me the honor of becoming my wife?"

Katharine just stared for a moment, and then a smile lit up her whole face. "It would be my pleasure."

Lindsey chose that moment to wake up. She took one look at the adults kissing beside her and said, "Oh, gross." But she was smiling as she said it.

Epilogue

Sam stepped out onto the front porch and grinned as the first fireflies lit up the evening sky. The breeze swirled her skirt around her calves and blew her hair into her face. She pushed the loose strands behind her ear and leaned against the porch railing, content to savor the moment.

Lindsey's birthday party had turned out to be the event of the year in Riverlake. She and Lindsey had issued a few invitations, but half the town had taken it upon themselves to show up, casserole dishes and birthday gifts in hand. After so many years on the sidelines, Sam still couldn't quite get used to the outpouring of love and acceptance.

Country music blared from the speakers and Sam watched Libbey pull several of the other girls from Haven House onto the impromptu dance floor on the lawn. Libbey spun around, saw Sam and waved. She and the other girls had been so excited about the party, hanging balloons, streamers and twinkling lights everywhere.

Swarms of squealing, laughing children chased each other around the yard with the water guns Danny had brought, sneaking shots at the adults every chance they got.

When a stream of water hit an unsuspecting Emma Jean right in the backside, she spun around. "Careful, now," she chided, wagging a finger in their direction. She caught Sam's eye and winked.

Sam's heart expanded as she looked around. Here and there, the townsfolk gathered in clusters to sip tea, exchange gossip and find their bearings once again. Sam could almost see everyone breathe a collective sigh of relief, glad the worst was over, glad they could stop eyeing each other with suspicion and distrust.

A small commotion drew Sam's eye as Gladys Sooner arrived, flanked by Rudy Emerson and Bill Farley. Sam started Gladys' way, then stopped as the townsfolk wrapped her in hugs and support. She'd catch her a bit later. Nobody in town held the news of Tommy's embezzlement of commission funds against her, as evidenced by the standing-room-only crowd which had turned out for Tommy's funeral. It had provided a stark contrast to the handful of people who reluctantly stopped by to pay their respects to Jimmy Wayne.

Sam swallowed hard. It would take some time to deal with her conflicting feelings about Jimmy Wayne. For tonight, it was enough he couldn't hurt anyone else.

Behind her, the screen door opened and Danny stepped out. He wrapped his arms around her waist, and rested his chin on her head. "You holding up okay, Beautiful?"

Sam leaned back into his embrace and nodded, her heart full. So many emotions filled her, she wasn't sure where to start sorting them out. But over, around, and through every feeling was an overriding sense of peace. Everything was going to be okay.

"Katharine looks happy," Danny commented.

Sam followed his gaze to where Mama presided over the groaning tables of food, her radiant smile and confident air a sight Sam never expected she'd see. Beside her, Luke grinned like an idiot, one hand on her shoulder as though he never wanted her out of his reach again. Sam blinked back sudden tears. Helping Mama start moving her things into the house she and Luke had bought had been bittersweet. She was glad they were getting married, but part of her was afraid to lose the closeness they'd finally found as mother and daughter.

As if she'd heard her thoughts, Mama turned and looked right at Sam. "I love you," she mouthed.

Sam said the words right back. "Love you too, Mama."

The four of them were getting married in a double ceremony in two weeks, with an exuberant Lindsey as junior bridesmaid for both Sam and Katharine.

Lindsey was adjusting to the idea of not living at the fish camp anymore, but she was thrilled with the house Sam and Danny had bought just a few miles further down the Withlacoochee. Sam would continue to offer river cruises and Danny planned to work out of a small office in one of the outbuildings. Together, he and Sam would finalize plans for the fish camp's development, preserving as much as possible.

Sam looked around and sighed. Yes, the old fish camp would be gone, but with it, so would lots of bad memories. Besides, Emma Jean was beside herself with joy at the new place Danny had purchased for Haven House. More room, less upkeep; it was the perfect solution.

It was time to let the past go.

Lindsey suddenly broke free of a group of children and pounded up the porch steps and straight into Sam's arms. The nightmares had ended and she was again a boundless mass of energy. "I love you, Mama. Thanks for my party. It's the best ever."

Sam pulled back so she could look into her sparkling blue eyes, exact replicas of Danny's. "You're so very welcome, Princess. I'm glad you're having fun."

Lindsey studied her a moment, then sent a speculative glance Danny's way. "Daddy, did you tell Mama how pretty she looks in her skirt?"

Danny laughed and ruffled her curls. "Of course, I did, you little schemer. How could I not? She's gorgeous."

Lindsey flung herself into his arms and hugged him tight. "I love you, Daddy."

Above her head, Sam met Danny's eyes, her own filling at the tears shimmering in his.

"I love you, too, Princess. Always and forever."

Lindsey pulled back. "Can we do the piñata now?"

Danny looked over to where the children gathered under the alligator-shaped creature the girls from Haven House had strung in a live oak. "You bet."

He held out his hand to Sam, tucked Lindsey's into his other one, and the three of them headed down the steps.

Sam rested her head on his shoulder. As long as they were together, they would always be home.

A word about the author...

Connie Mann lives in Central Florida where she writes romance and suspense with a touch of Southern style. Beyond the glitz of Miami, Disney World and the beaches lies Old Florida--the sleepy little towns that infuse Connie's "Stories You Can Sink Your Teeth Into." She lives with her husband, two teenagers and two rambunctious dogs by a lake that's home to several shy alligators. She is a member of Romance Writers of America, Volusia County Romance Writers, Central Florida Romance Writers and Faith, Hope and Love, RWA's inspirational chapter. When she's not spinning tales of love and happily-ever-after, Connie pilots a boat at Silver Springs, Nature's Theme Park. A U.S.C.G.-licensed boat captain, she says the guests inspire her love of this unique part of the world.

Visit Connie at www.conniemann.com

Thank you for purchasing
this Wild Rose Press publication.
For other wonderful stories of romance,
please visit our on-line bookstore at
www.thewildrosepress.com.

For questions or more information,
contact us at info@thewildrosepress.com.

The Wild Rose Press
www.TheWildRosePress.com

Printed in the United States
147351LV00001B/1/P

9 781601 544551